A Mind for Mischief

Philip Why

OPTION 3

This edition published in 2022 by Option 3.

Printed and distributed by Amazon.

Cover and interior design and
typesetting by Ideas Included

ISBN 9 798 41589 356 0

For John Molloy

A man is not dead while his name is still spoken.

PROLOGUE

Lorraine Plaza – Midnight.

The rain pattered onto her hair. She knew the feel of the cold vertical slot of the zat gun barrel pressed against her forehead would be one of her last thoughts. Soon, the hot knife of the zat bolt would cut her brain in half and that would be it. But she was prepared. She didn't get to be a leader in the Alliance by being unrealistic. She knew this ending was a valid possibility. All was lost.

And yet . . .

. . . glancing at her husband, knelt beside her in the mud, she could see him looking up at something. He smiled.

He was gazing at the face of the officer who was pressing the gun to her head.

She looked too, into the cold grey eyes like two surf polished rocks on a bleak windy beach. Something in those eyes. He was trying to keep them level and angry, but there was something else there. Resignation.

The thing he was most angry about was he knew they saw it.

Oh my gods. They were afraid of losing The War.

They were losing.

So, there it was, killing her and her husband was a desperate act. They hoped that personally executing the leaders of the Alliance would cut the head off the beast.

But they weren't really the leaders. They were only human. And now they were dead.

She'd do it again. For their daughter, for One Mind,

for Sol III . . . for love.

A hot flash and lightning boom, the light fading to a violet darkness and rest. In the distance further away each second a burst of nervous laughter.

The darkness folded in on itself again and again, spreading out to infinity until it was nothing and more than nothing. A serene flat nothingness and a so very absolute silence.

Her consciousness, that thing she fought so hard for was still there, but it was changed. It had taken another form, such a form that describing it was impossible with ordinary words. Only one ordinary word came close, but even that lacked enough dimensions.

Peace.

CHAPTER 1

I'll be honest with you. I don't know if this story is going to be comprehensible to anyone but me. It's complicated, a story that traverses multiple universes and multiple timelines, but I promise in the end you will see there are common threads running through it.

It may be the only common thread running through any of it is my perception, my viewpoint, my ideas. That's a distinct possibility. It could also be that my viewpoint is totally subjective and wide of the mark. You'll have to take a risk, like I did. But if at any point you feel you are lost and don't know where the path is leading, don't worry. I've been there before you and I'm just as clueless and shaky on the truth as you are, for reasons that will become obvious over time.

Who am I? I'll let you figure that out, but don't sweat it, it's really not that important.

You'll see why.

It's customary at times like this, when relating the events of a story, to start with "It all began . . ." This is not that kind of story.

In real life the clockwork parts of any story never truly begin in one place or with one thing, there's no sharply defined beginning. This is what makes true stories so hard to tell.

Nobody ever said "once upon a time there were a handful of random people who didn't know each other and never met, and their actions never really came together neatly and tidily, but somehow it all made sense at the time." That's reality. It's messy. What you want of course with a story is for all the events in it to mean something, and come together in an exquisite and unique way to bring about an impossibly tidy and satisfying conclusion.

No.

Only made up stories have structure. They have pace, they have arcs, they have meaningful interactions between people and those meetings change them and move the story forwards.

This is not that kind of story.

Well, sometimes it is. It depends who you ask.

All stories are true, even if they are not real . . . but wait, I'm getting ahead of myself, let me try to focus; I don't want to tell this story by describing what it is not.

Let me see if I can make a meaningful start.

Something wonderful and strange is about to happen and the person it's about to strangely happen to has no idea it's coming towards them. The person was clueless about the train tracks they were standing on and the whistle and rushing air of the locomotive charging towards them. Don't worry. It's not a real train, it's a metaphor for destiny. Perhaps that's too strong a word for it. Life. They were unaware of their life. That's at least a realistic beginning.

Dirk P. Kinder was not his real name. It was the name he was known by. Dirk was a writer. He still is a writer, but we are talking about him as he was then at this specific moment in his world.

I want you to picture him. He is almost universally described as having a kind face. Although in his mid forties, or perhaps even early fifties, hard to tell, he was lucky to still have most of his hair, although his forehead in truth was getting higher. His hair was thick and dark brown, cut neatly at the neck, as he detested ponytails, and swept smoothly over the crown of his head. He occasionally pushed this sweep of hair over his head with thumb and little finger while concentrating on something. His beard was dark and neatly trimmed, but not often. He despised men who were too well groomed. Either side of the impressive, sculptural nose were two dark, glossy brown eyes like bitter chocolate candies, under straight but unmanicured brows. Fine lines at the corners of the eyes lent a cheekiness to his gaze, which smiled at you even when he wasn't.

He sat at his desk, a Slate computer on the top, his hands in his lap, his eyes closed and covered by an eye mask. He could hear the giant Nemesis butterflies thrumming about in the garden, but coming from a hidden speaker in the room was a repetitive hypnotic beat.

The tall terrace windows were open with fresh, sweet air wafting through from a grassy valley beyond, a little too picture postcard perfect and beautiful.

The wooden frames of the windows were untreated but clean. A woven rustic rug covered a red tile floor. On the walls of the study were family portraits and photos of Dirk when he was young and handsome. He thought they were his better years that were behind him. He was often told that was untrue. Although it was quiet in the room and he wasn't moving, he was working.

His writing process was a ritual. He liked to keep it sacred. That's an odd word to use, but perhaps an appropriate one. Not sacred then, but protected, preserved. The ritual was a large part of that protection.

The first part was the desire for an idea. If you wanted an idea you'd have to sit and wait for it. Not in a passive way. It's not like waiting for a land bus when you're not sure if they're running today. No, it's more like waiting for a baby to be born. You sowed the seed, so to speak, and the baby grows and is born on automatic pilot. It's a usually inevitable and predictable process.

Obviously following this analogy, also sometimes babies aren't born. Medical matters intervene. Through luck or chance or genetics, the process is . . . interrupted. Sometimes instead of birth you get death. It's sad and sorry and unfortunate, but it happens.

It's precisely the same with ideas. You sow the seed, then you sit in quiet non judgemental patience until at that point in time, which is acceptable to the idea, when gestation is finished and it is born.

Why the lack of "judgement"? Well, when a baby is still inside its mother, you don't know who it is, what it wants to be. Your first thought is that you hope the child is healthy, viable, able to grow and become a person. But the destiny is unknown, who it is, who it wants to be, is undefined. You don't prejudge that, you patiently wait and see.

So it is with ideas. If you pass judgement on an idea before it's born (what kind of idea it is, what its purpose is, what other ideas it might hang out with, where its ultimate destination lies etc.), you are trying to steer its birth. You are not allowing it to be what it is. Instead you are trying to brute force it into a mould.

This is not good for the development of babies and it's most *definitely* not good for the development of ideas.

So the first part of Dirk P. Kinder's ritual was a form of meditation.

Over the years he developed a lot of techniques for perfect meditation. He did a lot of courses, read lots of books, and watched trillions of videos on The Feed. He tried many ways to do it. All it really boiled down to in the end was closing your eyes for an hour and not falling asleep.

His takeaway from studying all the different disciplines was that no single discipline worked for everyone; Transcendental Meditation, Yogic, Buddhist, Technophagic, Elemental, Quantum, all of these things were varying shades of the same colour.

For Dirk P. Kinder what worked was a quiet, comfortable space, an eye shade for complete darkness, and a repetitive sound, preferably binaural beats. He found the sound tuned his brain out really quickly and the lack of light gave his brain the mistaken idea that it was night-time. Using this method he could even do just 20 minutes and have a meaningful experience.

He loved the pulse of the beats. The gentle frequency was instantly relaxing to him, but perhaps this was because he had trained his mind to respond to that particular stimulus.

In this environment of peace and low level brainwaves, he found his mind to be at its most facile, the most productive and creative. It'd taken a little bit of practice to get to this point, but now he was here, ideas could be sown and harvested at will.

The second part of the ritual was sticking ideas together. Once you have an idea, you must sit and wait for another idea that goes with the first. This is where the magic happens. Another round of non judgemental idea holding, and this time he would turn the first idea over in his mind and meditate on it.

It's like looking at a single Lego brick or jigsaw puzzle piece. It has almost infinite potential but, he reasoned, you must not force it together with just any other random piece. You must let it find its own friends and join with them willingly and authentically. That's the most common bit people get wrong.

It's like the baby analogy again. Cells divide and organise themselves according to a plan, the DNA. They multiply and divide and proliferate in ever increasing numbers according to a built in design. But with ideas there is no map, no DNA, no design or at least no explicit one. They know where they belong. You need to let them find it.

So he sits and turns the ideas over in his mind until he gets another idea and it fits with the first. The little nubblies on the top of the Lego go into the little holes underneath the other and they fit together in a pleasing way.

Snap!

Repeat until you have enough ideas so that they have enough weight.

It had been a protracted and soggy winter, but finally Spring sunshine was glinting off the glass dew drops hanging by threads in the windows. Outside he could see the tortoise in his little house was emerging, stretching his neck.

On the desk his Slate was resting on its little wooden wedge, which lifted the glass surface to a perfect typing angle. As thoughts occurred to him, he tapped them in.

His teacup, beside the Slate, had a picture of a biplane on it and the tea in it was Asian. He added milk to the tea even though he knew most purists would take it without. "I take it with milk", he'd say to himself every time he made it. Another ritual.

He learned a long time ago that doing things the "best" way was an unhealthy obsession which could easily take over a person's actual taste. How would you ever know what your true taste is unless you abandon all the "right" ways and find your own way? Well you just wouldn't. You'd be pleasing someone else and never yourself.

Pleasing yourself is very important, he thought. It's a kind of mindfulness exercise.

Mindfulness was a much misused term in all the airy-fairy, wool-hatted, alt-lifestyle fringes on The Feed. It was a term misapplied to any and every activity, but in his experience it only applied to one. Your own consciousness.

It's quite scary how dangerous it is to forget to mind

your state of consciousness. Everyone thinks everyone is aware, "they just are", but in fact few people had an authentic grip on their own consciousness. In this age and era, with the omnipotent Feed shining out day and night through every Slate, Desky and AI, it was easy to lose yourself. You forgot you were a unique and complex individual consciousness, and slowly over time became a passive consumer and conduit for the whims of The Feed.

Dirk knew all about the perils of indiscriminate sucking on the Feed. So many people he once knew and liked were now lost to it, lost to him now too. Sometimes you have to make painful choices. Cut off the lost souls to protect your own mind. Cut the rope to prevent them pulling you off the mountain. He was okay with that.

As the level and quality of your input arises, the level and quality of your output reduces. The more ideas you ingest from others, the more distracting content you consume, the less you create and produce. You have no room in your brain for ideas to form and to flourish. The ideas you do have, such as they are, are just pale imitations of the trash from The Feed. No original thought, just plastic, fun-house mirror reflections. The only way to be free is to cut yourself free.

Obviously the Feed has its uses. No Man is an island. You can't live in a shack in the woods forever, appalling as that sometimes may seem. You just have to consume it wisely. Live in the woods but maintain the road back to town in case you need milk.

Wise consumption is a transferable skill. Alcohol is like that, cigarettes too.

With that thought Dirk drew and lit a cigarette from a box on the table. He blew the smoke into the air in the room where it hung over the table like a cloud. The tobacco was Ottoman, sweet and delicious. He allowed himself two a day, if he wanted them. This was the first. Wise consumption.

When he used to be a full time smoker, he would smoke indiscriminately. If was bored or stressed, which was often, he would light a cigarette. Many times he drew a cigarette from the packet only to find he couldn't light it, because he already had a lit cigarette in his other hand.

So he evolved his new rituals after discovering his addiction to The Feed. To create, you must destroy.

You must ruthlessly cut off sources of input which contribute nothing positive to your consciousness.

Protect your output.

There is a phase in the first part of the ritual, regarding input. When feeling an idea hovering out of sight, you must immerse yourself in objects, sounds, sights, places and smells which stimulate the kinds of thoughts you find which bring the idea closer.

A desire for an idea comes as an unformed feeling, an image in the mind that you can't quite see, but you know that it means something. All creative thought begins this way, he thought. Whether you're writing a novel, painting a picture, carving a sculpture, or inventing a new entertaining gadget to distract others from their own consciousness, the idea starts with an unformed thought. It's an orphan, a mutant thought form that doesn't fit with any of the complete, better worked out thoughts and ideas in the mind.

Sitting with an object or song or anything that makes the thought brighter and clearer and not dimmer and more quiet was all he needed. Once he learned the ritual, he repeated it, over and over, and it bore fruit. Much fruit.

He put out the cigarette and picked up the lighter. Its steel surface was buffed to a high shine, but it was pitted with tiny holes and lines so small that you could only see them when the sunlight glanced across it. It looked like spider webs in the grass.

He put the lighter on top of the box of cigarettes and returned his hands to hover over the keyboard on the screen of the Slate. In the distance through his window, he could see an airship and faintly hear the whine of its engines as it banked gently into a turn. He got a lot of those blue and white painted ships over the house as there were a few airports nearby.

He watched it turn lazily past the nearby Tesla Tower, which tirelessly radiated the carriers for The Feed and wireless power for his Slate and Desky, his heating, oven and his lights. The tower was quiet at this distance, but he remembered the sound. They made a gentle crackling hum that you felt more than you heard. They were so high frequency that you could touch the emitters with a naked hand without fear of harm, but once done you would not do it again. It was not an entirely pleasant sensation.

Outages were rare, but they did happen. He took comfort from the fact of the bank of accumulator cells in the wall of the garage where he parked his land car. No interruption of the entirely free provision of The Feed. "The Feed must flow" was the slogan on all the Visor adverts.

Even in daylight there was a faint purple glow around the top of the Tesla Tower. The tall tower was made of straight beams, which due to the cross over construction looked curved from a distance, flaring out towards the ground and the head. The emitter was a huge doughnut of tiny gold spheres.

Dirk made himself a coffee with the Beantec globe and poured it reverently into the small chunky white cup. The coffee was Icelandic, produced in one of the hundreds of glass factories that dotted the dark volcanic landscape. The coffee was smoky with a hint of grass.

He switched on a large round audio speaker, went back to his Slate and chose a music selection to be played through it. A little metal jazz to lift his energy. Johnny and the Straights came on and he paused to listen to them. The track was called "Hell to my Leather". It was an Oldie back from the days of The War, back "when men and women fought, side by side, on some damn fool idealistic crusade" according to the lyrics. Dirk didn't remember The War too clearly, but was old enough to recall the song very fondly.

The song featured Billy Jesus on vocals, long since gone, but remembered by all as the voice of his generation. When the song ended, he sat back down in front of his Slate, the dark glass waiting to be activated by his fingerprints anywhere on the surface. He touched it and a soft bong sounded from somewhere inside.

He was writing fluently at the moment. The words were tumbling out of him, fully formed. This was the main benefit of thinking a lot before you write. If you think enough, the rest is just typing. You hold the mood, keep it in the cinema inside your mind and just type what you see.

That's another part of the ritual. Flexing that muscle, the invisible hand that keeps a thought in your mind until it comes alive and becomes its own thing. Balancing an idea in front of your mind, holding it *just so*, so that you're barely touching it yet keeping it *right there*, holding it.

You're not holding it back. You're just stopping it from flying free. You're making it believe it wants to stay.

The book he was writing was his fifth. His third was a success while he was writing his fourth, which although wonderful really disturbed his ritual. Fame does that to an art, makes it mean something it shouldn't. It did not turn out so good, but that didn't seem to matter. Everyone liked book three so much they accepted book four much more warmly and with much more widely open arms than they should have. They then read or reread books one and two and re-evaluated them and judged them to be masterpieces, and he took the fame and the money even though he knew that to be totally untrue.

Then all people could talk about was book five. That

was four years ago. It's not that he had writer's block. He didn't believe in writer's block. Not starting work on the fifth book was a conscious decision. The ritual was everything and the ritual was ruined by all this fame-and-fortune-and-expectations nonsense. He knew he needed to take some time and think about what he wanted to do. Number five needed to be authentic. It needed to be real.

He needed it to be good.

Finally now it was in progress. Finally he had a story he wanted to tell and things he wanted to say. It felt real. Finally he was free of interruptions to his ritual.

At first the tapping noise was inaudible to him. He was hearing it but his brain was not processing it and telling him about it. Then he heard it and realised retrospectively how long it had been going on for before it registered. He scrambled up and went to find out where it was coming from.

When he opened the front door, a woman was standing there. Shoulder length dark hair, brown almond eyes and quite short, wearing a waxed cotton jacket with a rather heavy looking brown leather bag, the strap cutting diagonally across her chest. She wore a mask over her nose and mouth, not a medical mask but a rather fashionable fabric print. He couldn't figure out why she would be masked. There was no pollution here.

Her expression was hard to read, but from her eyes it looked like the face of someone about to deliver bad news. She also looked like she was afraid he might attack her. Her right hand gripped the bag strap where it crossed her chest and her fingers were clenching and working the leather as she spoke. Her voice was clear and hypnotically beautiful in some way, full of emotion. Her appearance and expression made it very hard for him to speak, but his look of surprise and confusion was very eloquent.

"Sorry to bother you," she said, "I know this is going to

sound insane, but I think I might be from an alternate universe. You have no reason to trust me, but can I please come inside. I just need to get my bearings and figure out what to do. Can you help me please."

He didn't speak for an uncomfortably long amount of time. Most questions you answer at the threshold of your home have a list of obvious and carefully rehearsed responses.

"No thanks. Not Today. I gave at the office. Let me stop you there," etc.

None of these seemed appropriate. For a further few moments he opened and closed his mouth. Then in a burst of recklessness, he heard himself saying, "Oh, of course, sorry. Come in".

They sat in silence for quite a long time. She was looking at another airship passing by, clearly fascinated. Then she looked at the Tesla tower as if she didn't know what she was looking at. Then she spent a bit of time looking at the Visor in the corner with a quizzical eyebrow raised. She pointed.

"Is that a TV?" She said

"A what? What's a TV?" he was genuinely puzzled by the term.

"Television. It looks a bit like a TV." She pulled her mask away from her face as she spoke in case he was having difficulty understanding her.

"Oh, I don't know what that means. That's a Visor. It shows performances and news events."

"Why isn't it plugged into anything?" She pointed at the wall.

He was confused. What was she talking about? "What would it be plugged into?"

"The wall, for power." Her eyes smiled a little.

"Again, not sure what you mean, but it has its own power. It's powered by the Feed?"

She paused and put her hands back in her lap. She twirled one of the rings on her finger.

He coughed a little and she flinched. "I'm sorry," he said slowly, "would it be possible to take off your mask? There's no pollution here."

She blanched a little. "It's not for pollution, it's for the virus."

"What virus?"

"The children of covid. The Raven. The pandemics."

"I don't know what that means either. There hasn't been a pandemic for over a century. You're safe here. You can take off your mask. I'm not sick."

Her eyes were wide. She thought for a second and gingerly removed the mask as if it was physically difficult. Underneath it she revealed an adorable button nose, and when she spoke her mouth was mobile and had large, slightly skewed but very white teeth.

"I don't know what's happening. Everything is different. One minute I'm at home leaving the house to go to shop. The next I'm in a field by one of those towers and purple energy is crackling around it. I see airships, butterflies the size of dinner plates and now you've never heard of the viruses. *Where am I?*" Her lip trembled.

He tried to be calming, "Ok let's not worry about how and why for now. Let's concentrate on what I can *actually* do for you. Let's . . . let's start with your name. My name is Dirk. What's yours?"

"My name is. It's. Oh. It's. I mean . . ."

Her mind was completely blank.

CHAPTER 2

Robert Watson Banks put down his bag in the changing room and began to remove his clothes.

He hated this part and at the same time he knew how absolutely essential it was.

As he undressed and put his clothes carefully in his locker, he thought through what he was going to say in the chamber. It was going to be a tough sell, he smiled to himself, and this was why he got paid the big coin. He was good, damn good, but was he good enough?

He removed his underwear and stowed it in the locker and turned reluctantly to view himself in a full length mirror. He was a little overweight, but not too bad. Some people who did this job looked ugly naked. Sometimes it looked like someone had punctured a chamois leather balloon and were waiting for all the air to finally come out of it. He hated people seeing his round stomach and small penis. It was inevitable so that was that. He'd learned to live with it.

He read through his speech one more time. He knew it upside down and back to front by now, of course he did. His nerves made him go over it anyway.

His speech today was fairly routine. He was fully committed to the contents and hoped others would be too. The inevitable debate that followed the speech might drag out, so he was trying to keep it quite short. No sense in having the cameras on him for longer than was absolutely necessary.

Around him other males preparing for the chamber were also divesting themselves. Very little eye contact happened here, although some hardened nudists were a little too comfortable with their bodies and had personal spaces measured in inches, or worse, centimetres.

A couple of the older members were so comfortable with the daily divestment that they drove here naked. That was admirable commitment to the craft, perversion or laziness. He couldn't fully decide which. Either way this had been a tradition for so long now, few could conceive of the job being done without it.

A delicate bell from somewhere in the corridor was all that was needed to summon them to the chamber. They filed out of the locker room along the warm floor of the tunnel and into the spacious wood lined chamber. It was comfortably heated to about 24 degrees and the rows of pews facing each other across the debating floor were padded with soft, expensive and of course washable cushions.

Wood panelling inscribed with the tenets of the new order surrounded the room, and the flags of the various regions of the continent hung appropriately limply.

Around the chamber the members, both male and female, took their places, exchanged curt small talk and began to take their seats for the morning session. Banks was the deputy head of The Life Party, a party whose central values were social responsibility, environmental concerns and long-term economic stability. The body of the assembly were the Unity Party, whose goals were old-fashioned notions of family and the promotion of business needs, and The Moderate Tendency, a middle road party mostly composed of people who couldn't make definite decisions. The ruling party at present was Unity with a slim number advantage over the Life Party. The Moderates were a minority party, the largest of the niche parties. There were a number of niche parties represented in the chamber, but few had more than one elected member.

The leader of Unity was named Nicholas Chalice and as

leader of the ruling party, he was the chairman of the government. He was not the leader of the government, but he was its highest official. He was tall, fresh faced and fit for his 45 years. Banks hated him. He hated standing opposite him in the chamber. Chalice's penis was quietly impressive and he knew it. Oh, Banks knew that the government didn't officially run a penis contest and there was more that mattered in life, but it still rankled with him on a personal level.

He'd left his notes in the locker room, he didn't need them. He just wished he could have something in his hands to tinker with. He knew the idea of naked government, but he knew in practice it was just as divisive and ego-driven as clothed politics.

The reasons for it were simple, the promotion of honesty. It is hard to spin out a lie or be egotistical when, if you don't hold your listeners' attention intently, their eyes will drift naturally to your balls. For centuries, politicians had evolved from public servants into self serving businesses and at a certain point everything came crashing down. When something is broken, it must be fixed or replaced. In this case, politics needed to return to basics.

Take out all the power dynamics, but most of all do everything possible to reinforce honesty and a robust commitment to the craft of public service. That's the notion of naked politics. What more potent symbol of having nothing to hide was there than utter nakedness. What better way to marshal our cute little monkey brain's tendency to preen and pose than remove all the added finery and present to the world the raw person, all your flaws and folds revealed?

It was easy, the architects of the new politics reasoned, when wearing fine suits and dresses of the best cloth to start believing the cloth was your skin. Over time, this spread prudery and ego, it bolstered a kind of cognitive bubble, within which you could fool yourself about your own worth in society, your own physical superiority. It's harder to be taken seriously when penis or breasts are swinging in the breeze.

If you want to convince anyone of anything in those circumstances, you really have to mean it. Nudity enhances both honesty and conviction and both of these are traits that people who are in charge, or at least responsible for others, need to possess.

With your expensive suit on, you can pretend to be many things that you are not. So much of life was driven by people who thought their suit was their skin, that nudity was bad, breastfeeding, even swimming should be banned. It was feared that nudity would inflame passions that it was impossible to control. Of course this was nonsense. If nudity is disgusting, then you've got mental health problems, not nudity problems.

So it was decided that for the sake of humanity's future mental stability and sexual health, that being naked needed reformation in the public consciousness. The so-called Pink and Brown Act, as it was jocularly known, was passed in the 23rd year of The Empress and politics and all sensitive negotiations were performed naked.

Banks was chatting with his boss, the leader of The Life Party, Margaret Trusscomb, a white haired brown skinned lesbian who was very comfortable with her nakedness. Her curves were the source of much media Chit Chat, most of which was respectful given her brutal stance on sexual harassment, positive body consciousness and LGBT∞ rights and wrongs. She'd broken the nose of a drunken journalist once and the rest of them hadn't forgotten it. Margaret sat back and had her arms folded comfortably under her globe like breasts and her calf was resting on top of her knee. She had a small tattoo on her ankle of a single snowflake around which was delicately inscribed in a circle, "Beware of the avalanche."

"Chalice is toughing it out, but he knows nobody is buying his Article 25 bullshit," Margaret was whispering, "he also knows it's doomed, but I'll bet you 100 coin, he'll style it out like that was the game plan all along. Old School politics, but then he always was a traditionalist."

Banks laughed and whispered back. "He's a good politician, but a lousy liar. Personal charm and a big knob gets you a long way in this business, but at some point there has to be substance behind it. You'll always be found out and he will be. I'll still take the bet though."

Margaret Trusscomb chuckled and took this as her cue and drew herself up to her full height, such as it was, and spoke in a clear voice heard by the whole chamber. "Thank you madam chair, I now call my friend and colleague Mr. Robert Watson Banks who will put The Life Party's case against the proposed Article 25."

She sat down with the hand gesture of rolling an invisible marble off her palm into his lap. Banks rose and began with the traditional litany.

"Ladies and gentlemen. I am a liar and a cheat. I'm probably in this job for myself to line my pockets so you cannot trust anything I say, but I urge you to first listen to what I say and judge my words on their merit. I ask you this with honesty you cannot rely on and humility you would be ill advised to believe."

There was a short but heartfelt ripple of applause and murmurs of assent. "Okay. Good afternoon and with the formalities out of the way, I would like to begin on our reaction to Article 25 . . ."

He began to outline the article and picked it apart with erudite and exquisite precision. The listeners, the other 649 Pink and Browns in the room listened politely, some taking notes into recording devices.

The litany, though it was full of intentionally self deprecating language, was designed to be spoken and not recited. It was not a piece of inconsequential boilerplate to be ignored like an airship security briefing or a licence declaration on The Feed. It was meant to be spoken with feeling and all present knew the meaning of the words and took them seriously.

Since The War, nobody was in government for personal gain. There was no point. The penalty for using political positions for gain, or UPPG for short, was brutal and swift and nobody ever forgot that. There were mistakes of course, and these were dealt with fairly. The lesser charge of error of judgement, or EOJ, carried a stiff sentence, but the charge for UPPG was the stiffest, if proven.

Death.

One or two miscarriages of justice, discovered too late, had produced the lesser charge. EOJ had been making it easier for public servants to survive their mistakes. The EOJ cases highlighted ways in which people could lapse in their honesty, through mental health and stress issues. But like murder it was decided that before you could put someone to death for a crime, you had to establish the motivation, the intent, behind it.

If the reason for breaking the very serious UPPG laws was a momentary impulse based on depression or loss or loneliness, then the person was guilty of nothing more sinister than being human, and their charge was reduced to EOJ, a lengthy prison sentence and counselling. If however any proof of premeditation of UPPG with no mitigating circumstances, well, the methods of death were numerous and delivered at the dark whimsy of the prosecutors. They were dedicated and humourless purveyors of public disappointment.

But as with all capital punishment, some treated it as a challenge or game. The high stakes tapped into the lingering traces of sociopathy still sleeping in the cute little monkey brains of the public servants.

So it was with many cases who faced the prosecutors'

blades, needles and work tables. For some the high stakes game was totally worth the risk, but the penalty for getting away with UPPG for a long time was so much worse. Torture. Medieval grade torture. Not to reform. Not as an example to those who may sin in the future. It was basic and honest revenge. "This is what we do to people who betray us", said the punishment, through the hands of the prosecutors, "this is what we do to monsters like you."

Occasionally if genuine psychopathy was discovered, those people with the gift of blankness or empathy blindness, were channelled into the execution corps. There they had a chance to pay off their debt to society through honest service. Here they could plough their hatred of humanity into a good cause, salvation through pain. In this the modified message of the punishment was "this is what we do to monsters like you. We place you into the hands of monsters like you."

Banks completed his speech and it was greeted with warmth and gentle applause. There was too much scope in Article 25 to undermine the teeth of the UPPG laws. It was an ill prepared and seemingly pointless risk to allow such subtle subversion of the chamber's long traditions of honesty and service. His thoughts on the matter were well received and it was agreed quite quickly afterwards that Article 25 should be dropped for a rewrite or eliminated altogether.

Although Nicholas Chalice was known to be one of the authors of Article 25, he praised Banks for his eloquent rebuttal and humbly sought the chamber's forgiveness, while skilfully avoiding any implication he was wrong to bring it to life in the first place.

During Chalice's speech a note was passed to Banks from the Ministry of Truth. On reading it, he had to quickly control a few emotions from taking over his face. He leaned a little closer to Trusscomb's ear and whispered "enclave" and handed her the note. The emotions which flitted across her face were very clear: surprise, sadness and rage.

Enclave was the name for an important unscheduled meeting of the heads of the elected parties, meeting in secret in a panelled room at the far corner of the building. All the heads were present with one notable exception.

"Is it true?" said Ashley Tate, leader at the Environmental Faction. Trusscomb nodded gravely. She indicated to Banks who put a small metal cylinder in the middle of the table and activated it. Several documents appeared in the air like genies fleeing a bottle. They hung in the air and Trusscomb leant forwards and sifted through them with her finger.

"There's no doubt?" said a grim faced bald gentleman with a long grey beard.

There was no doubt. The investigation had been going on for a year. The tracks had been buried well, the money had been sifted through literally hundreds of accounts making the task of uncovering the corruption an expensive and labour intensive task. Unluckily for the culprit weeding out corruption at this level had deep pockets. Whatever it costs, however long it takes, you will be found out and you will be punished.

Trusscomb quickly read out the charges to the assembled heads, and the vote was clear . . . rubber stamp the arrest warrant and pass it back to the Ministry of Truth with no further delay. They left quickly before anyone noticed they had met.

Nicholas Chalice sipped on a Tequila sunrise. The Tequila was very expensive, the orange juice freshly squeezed. He sat on a plump cushion in the centre of his lawn. Two of his regular concubines were splashing in the pool. His wife was watching him out of the bedroom window of their massive home. She was absent mindedly putting earrings in while waiting for her escort to pick her up for the evening. Her face was sour.

She stopped when she noticed a dark figure at the edge of the grounds. The figure moved swiftly and silently. It was wearing a dark hoodie jacket or short robe, a skull like mask and she saw with rising horror in his hand was a pole with a loop of wire at the end.

Mrs Chalice walked quickly to the front door. She was planning to go anyway. She'd have to advance her timetable and get out tonight. Now.

The doorbell chimed. Thank the gods, perfect timing. She grabbed her go-bag from the hall closet and opened the big front door.

Chalice watched the two naked girls cavorting and squealing in the pool through half closed eyes. He sighed contentedly. This was what he deserved. This thought occurred to him every day.

If you're golden, then golden things come to you. If you're base metal, then you deserve poverty, misery, and death. I am golden. I always knew I was. My mother told me I was her golden boy and I knew that was true. Those people out there needed leaders like me. Those people, the tranks, the job sores, the mentals, the devos, the "preverts" (nasty slang word for those heading for trouble), the seething masses of hateful, dumb, stupid bovines. I am superior. I am almost the ultimate being.

Out of the corner of his eye he saw a dark hooded figure and for a moment his mouth gaped open. He was caught. No! His mind was unable to process a failure of this magnitude, and after a short tingly ride down through his stomach and scrotum his mind rose quickly back up into his perfect head.

Wait! He smiled, slowly at first and then he beamed. Oh yes, I'm going to beat this, he thrilled, no stupid UPPG for the golden boy. Not even EOJ. They don't know it yet, but after this they're going to love me even more.

He drained his drink and set the glass down on the close cropped lawn. "Come on then," he said languidly, "I'm ready."

"But are you though?" said a shockingly close voice, filtered through a mask. Chalice flicked his eyes around just in time to see a second hooded figure swing a long wooden club with a glossy lobe the size of an orange. The blow was not meant to kill and it succeeded in that aim. It merely knocked him off the cushion and his body fell to the grass like a bag of plumbing tools.

Chalice was trying to object. Golden, he said, Golden, except all that came out was "go, go, go."

Through red mist he saw the girls being herded out of the pool, their wet skin and hair, shivering now.

His wife came out of the house, face white, she was manacled and two more hooded and masked figures were leading her. One carried her go-bag. He sat her down on one of the pool chairs and walked around the pool, lowering the hood and removing the pale mask. Chalice knew the face. Everybody knew the face.

"Good day, Mr Chalice. We've never met socially, but I am Arthur Smiles. In my capacity as head of the Ministry of Truth I arrest you under the UPPG laws, you will be taken from here to an MoT facility where you will be held, oh so briefly, until our investigations conclude."

Smiles bared his small teeth. His head was shaved and his face was slim and brown and handsome. For a man who must be in his early fifties he looked fit and hard.

"I have an intuition that they will not find any mitigation in this case, and so then it will be my pleasure to terminate you with prejudice as an expression of society's rage at your crimes."

The calm grinning face bent close. "I shall derive much personal satisfaction and professional joy from executing this duty. You, I'm afraid, will get no joy whatsoever from the transaction, but then you have had quite enough joy at society's expense, wouldn't you agree?"

The sterile off white room at the MoT contained a bed, a toilet, and a wash basin. Chalice lay staring at the white ceiling. Unmoving.

In the control room Arthur Smiles watched the monitor over his steepled fingers. "Paralysed. That is most unsatisfactory. He feels nothing below the shoulders?"

"No, sir."

"Hmm. Well, okay. There are more than enough nerve endings in the face, mouth, jaw and neck anyway, so let's limit our ministrations to that area for now. Start slow, my friend, as I have it on good authority that the public appetite for revenge is very keen with this one.

"Soften him up for a bit. I'll be there directly."

As the junior executioner left the control room, Arthur Smiles was deep in thought. He looked troubled. Something was bothering him. He appeared to reach a difficult decision. He touched the intercom.

"Petra, can I change my order to chicken? Thank you." Ah, that was better. Now that was off his mind. He could fully relax and enjoy the show.

CHAPTER 3

That morning two stories landed on the news desk of Bleeb - The Social Memwork. The first was the scandal about Nicholas Chalice and his UPPG nest-feathering activities and capture. The second involved award winning writer, Dirk P. Kinder, and his bizarre assertion that he had been visited by a woman from an alternate universe.

Both the stories had a heft that could not easily be ignored. The public had a right to be informed, but the thoughts in the mind of the lead news blogger, Belle Patience, were not what had to be said, but how best to say it.

Before The War it was depressingly easy. Back then in the "good old days" as long as it sold newspapers, you could slant the news any way you wished and even, gods forbid, make stuff up for kicks and for clicks. The excuse was always "because who could really know the truth?" Back then the truth was just a plaything for the elite. That died in The War.

In the postwar reformation there was a new legal and moral objective to news, to not just drive clicks, sensationalise or speculate or manipulate, but to strive to enlighten. This task, while a privilege, was also a burden. It was a burden that Belle Patience took very seriously.

If you asked anyone what she looked like the first thing they would say was that she had the reddest hair of anyone they knew. Her face, while pleasant, was quite forgettable. Jewel-like, deep set blue eyes in a white, freckled face with a thin, considerate mouth. But you'd never forget the hair. It was good to be nondescript as a reporter so she sometimes wished she was less memorable in that one respect. As she got older she was okay that her personality, according to others, was entirely invested in that alarming red fire on her head.

So, she mused, what are the stories here? Was Chalice an unwitting dupe? Doubtful. Nobody is going to buy that. Was he an addict or suffering from some kind of disease of the brain? Arguably true. Should he have been convicted of a lesser charge? No. That prick deserved everything he was going to get. She made a mental note to not say any of that out loud.

All these thoughts, the variables of the story, finding it and telling it, were her own. Nobody was telling her what to say. There was a time before The War when writers and editors had preset agendas. The agendas were usually driven by the needs of politics or business. Journalism, the job of the press, was not to inform or educate or edify the population. It was to steer it.

But Belle Patience was brought up by an old fashioned news man. Her grandfather, Witham Patience, was old when she was born. He took early retirement because although The War was won, he'd spent every ounce of energy and personal power and consciousness he had keeping that flare of truth alive.

The pursuit of truth as an aim in journalism had been perverted for decades. In the end, it merely became a tool for the powerful to influence the powerless, a way of scientifically farming their emotions to feed agendas. The bait was sensational drama. Everything. Was. Dramatic. That's the thing about sensationalism, there is no real story. There is no truth to speak. There's no right or wrong, just a long protracted gasp of idiot surprise.

Real news means there are facts to be uncovered, perpetrators to be identified and consequences to be predicted and described. This is not the kind of news politics or business could allow. Politics and business were the perpetrators, and they feared facing those consequences. The War changed all that. Her parents changed all that, them and millions of others like them.

Belle remembered The War, but more as a feeling than a fact. Her parents fought in the battles, returning to the cardboard cities of light after each conflict, covered with filth, but glowing with hope. She remembered their faces. How she loved their faces.

Anyway. Where was she? She shifted some prints around on her desk. Most people worked with Slate screens, but it was her opinion that something wasn't real unless it was spoken out loud or seen as words on a sheet of paper. Somehow printed-out or written-on sheets of paper helped her collate her thoughts. Either way it was more viscerally satisfying.

Ok, then there was the matter of popular author Dirk P. Kinder. According to the report, he had had some kind of psychotic break and was telling friends and family that he'd been visited by a dark haired woman from the fourth dimension. Well, an alternative reality anyway. This was fascinating. Kinder was apparently a slightly reclusive figure, rarely giving out much in terms of interviews. It was a golden opportunity to do a piece on him, if he was feeling talkative.

Besides, privately she knew all she wanted to know about the Nicholas Chalice case. It had been a bit of a secret side project of hers for months. Now it was breaking and she'd lost interest. She'd get one of her freelances to dot the i's and cross the t's on that one. The guy was in custody, open and shut.

She was more interested in the writer. What the heck was going on there? She knew she'd have to go and speak to him personally. She Feed tapped *his people*. Not only was he interested in talking, he could do so today. She ordered a land car, bought a Maglev ticket and ran out of the office.

The Maglevs were enormous. A blunt nosed bullet train hovering over a single flat rail. Belle sat in a roomy green armchair and watched the blurry 200 miles an hour landscape. It was very soothing. After the cardiovascular rush to get to the station she felt very relaxed, and sank into the seat and dozed.

Before The War, air travel was the most popular mode of transport. It was fast and kind of fancy. Everybody did it. Ultimately the environmental impact was too great and something had to be done about curbing it. Belle was secretly delighted at the death of planes as she went on a plane once when she was very little and it terrified the crap out of her. Over land the planes were replaced by the Maglev trains and the hybrid electric land buses. Intercontinental trips, travel over water, were made by the fast moving grey airships.

The grey Prussian made Sturm class airships were enormous helium filled torpedoes with an hourglass shaped venturi tube down the centre. Ponderous grey ship sized gondolas underneath carried hundreds of people. The smaller, more colourful Drang class airships were local and much slower. There were also boats, but boats were not as fast or as comfortable as the Sturm airships. Nothing was as fast as the venturi airships.

That said Belle eschewed the airship for the train most of the time. It was slower, sure, but it was on the ground and to her mind she could not fall any further.

The train cruised dreamily on its Maglev track skimming the steel without touching it, and the magfield elegantly self-adjusted in real time to prevent cavitation or wobbling. Inside the cabin the landscape sped smoothly and silently by. The chair was very comfortable and she tried to read, but soon the overwhelming hypnotic motion of it all finally got to her and she slept.

She dreamed of the woman, dark hair and bright shining eyes, an additional pinpoint of light in the middle of her forehead. Her right hand showed the open palm, a similar purple light at its centre, and the left rested in her lap as she sat. The light on her forehead grew brighter and her skin took on a bluish hue. A sound, a kind of electronic shriek started to fill her ears and the girl's mouth opened. The light was in there too, and it poured out of her mouth, obscuring her sight.

Belle woke with a start to the distant shrilling of the train's air brakes. It was pulling into the Rural Mile station.

Dirk P. Kinder lived in a house quite far outside of Rural Mile. It was cut into the side of the valley looking down on a beautiful view, miles of green, dotted by Tesla towers and water farms with their distinctive beehive moisture collectors.

The land car took her to the end of the paved roads. She happily walked the half mile to the house along a mostly dirt track edged by fields and patches of unusual yellow bulb shaped flowers and blue grasses. It was overcast but warm.

Dirk P. Kinder was expecting her. When the house first came into view he was sitting on his porch smoking. At first she assumed it was an electric cigarette like everyone has, but on closer inspection it was real actual tobacco burning in a paper tube. She was impressed and disgusted. Those things are quite expensive and wow so bad for you.

As she approached the porch an enormous butterfly, the size of a dinner plate, flew between them startling her. She was born in the city and the bushes in the wilds being full of animals still freaked her out a little bit. He saw her frozen facial expression and hands and laughed.

"Excuse the Purple Nemesis butterflies. They are huge, but totally harmless. There are lots of them around here and *unlucky for you* it's mating season so they are everywhere and quite frisky." He stepped forward. "Good to met you, I'm Dirk Kinder, you must be Miss Patience."

"Yes." She took his offered hand firmly. "Call me Belle."

"What a euphonious appellation." He smiled oddly at some kind of private joke.

Belle didn't get it. She followed him up the sturdy wooden steps into the house.

The living room (he called it the drawing room) looked more like it was inside a log cabin. The walls were burnished planks of wood with occasional photographs and paintings hung tastefully here and there and the odd non pictorial knick-knack. There were shelves filled with ornaments and artefacts from his travels. A coffee machine composed of two glass globes bubbled away as she examined a row of small, very worn stone figures on an eye level shelf.

"They're around about 500 years old," he said, "I bought them on a trip to Calamarta with my ex wife. The native Cala people of that region worship women, goddesses. Women are the creators of life, so it stands to reason they revere the source of life. That one is Soma."

The figure was curvy and its small breasts pointed out slightly at right angles. The tummy was round and had a stone in the navel and she rubbed it unconsciously with her finger. There was a dust ring on the shelf. One was missing.

"Sorry," she said nervously, "am I allowed to touch it?"

Kinder laughed. "Of course, everyone does. I encourage it. It's not a pregnant belly by the way, as you might assume. She's just, uh, *comfortable in her skin*."

Belle was surprised it even needed saying. Before The War it was compulsory for women to try to conform to impossible physical standards. When those unhealthy mental aberrations were outlawed in the new order, a generation of women had grown up loving and nurturing themselves. She thought about questioning him hard on his attitude to women, but she thought perhaps a softer ball to start.

"Looking around, you have a lot of religious artefacts. Do you believe in the gods?" She replaced the figure and shimmied it around next to the goddess shaped hole in the delicate coating of dust on the shelf.

"At various times yes, but I wasn't brought up with the gods. I am fascinated by faith. A lot of my stories are thinly veiled explorations of religious experience."

"Even the one where at one point the guy turns into a giant tortoise?"

Kinder chuckled, "*especially* that one."

Belle smiled. This was going well.

He indicated a sofa. "Okay, I don't mean to rush you but should we get started?"

She agreed that they should begin.

The sun room off the drawing room was a spacious timber and glass wedge along one side of the house, containing a handful of plump sofas. Here and there were beautifully decorated ceramic topped side tables, and all along the wall were bookshelves creaking with books you could just dip into on a sunny Saturday, or even a rainy Tuesday. The view down the Green Valley was best from here and the Tesla towers like bookends at either end of the valley glowed enigmatically in the mist.

In the countryside, if you spent enough time there, all weather was good weather.

Belle set her Slate down on one of the side tables and seated herself on one of the firmer sofas. Kinder seated himself heavily on the other sofa, which met the first in a corner. She touched the surface of the Slate a few times and popped an earpiece like a pink plastic bean into her ear. She pressed an invisible button on the earbean and the Slate beeped. In her ear she could hear the sound of the room and the two of them breathing.

"So, Mr Kinder . . ."

"Mr Kinder is my father, call me Dirk."

"Of course, Dirk. Surely Kinder is not your real name."

"No, it's not. Dirk P. Kinder is the name I'm known by."

"Of course. I'm sorry if that offended you."

"You apologise a lot, Miss Patience . . . Belle."

"Oh yes, I suppose I do. It's an effort to put people at their ease."

"Well, then your work here is done. I'm completely at ease. What did you want to know?"

"You've said that you had a visitor . . ." She let the end of the sentence dangle, the dangling end inviting an answer. She knew it was an interview technique she overused, but by now it was more of an annoying intractable habit than a conscious choice.

"I have many visitors, but I suspect you are referring to the most unusual one I had recently."

"Yes." Again, she was resisting direct questioning, hoping the truth would come out in his own words.

"It's true. I was visited by a woman from an alternate reality. There was nothing obviously mystical or strange about the experience. She just knocked at my front door.

"She seemed terrified and confused and so I let her in. We talked. We talked for a really long time. I made her tea. She sat over there by the window. She was fascinated by the Tesla towers. She expressed surprise that none of my devices were plugged in. I asked her what that means. Apparently in her version of the present day, people power their devices and appliances by plugging in a wire to a socket on the wall. Apparently the plug links with embedded wires in the wall and the power is all transmitted by wire." He finished the sentence and sipped his coffee. "You think I'm making it up?"

"No, Mr, erm, Dirk. It's my job to listen to what people say and report it accurately."

"There's a very large chasm between listening and believing."

"I tend to agree," she allowed herself a little smile, "but I can't really decide if I believe or not until I'm fully in receipt of the facts."

"Fair enough."

Silence fell for a moment and Belle let it fall fully and settle into its own shape in the hollows in the room. She felt if she prodded too much, he'd either stop talking freely or modify what he was saying to please her. She looked at her hands folded in her lap and concentrated on not moving for as long as possible.

Eventually he spoke. "She seemed very upset, so I tried to help. I assumed, as you probably would, that she was some kind of mental health case. I have some experience in these matters. She didn't seem dangerous, just scared, so I did what anyone would do in those circumstances. I talked to her and tried to find some way I could help.

"I started out by asking if there was anyone I could contact for her, any relatives. She said she tried calling her friends and family, but she couldn't get a 'signal', whatever that means. She took out this device. It looked a little bit like a miniature Slate, but it had buttons on the side. It looked like it had an earpiece built in because she tried to use it, tapping numbers on the screen and holding one end to her ear. She turned it off saying she was saving power and asked me if I had a charger. I told her I didn't know what that was. Then she got very flustered and shut up for a while.

"Eventually she asked me if she could have one of my cigarettes. I was a bit put out because as you know they're very expensive. I don't normally share them, but I figured what the hell and let her have one. I helped her light it because for some reason she didn't know how to operate my lighter. It was then I started to wonder quite seriously if she was telling me the truth or if this was some sort of scam."

"Was she telling the truth? Or was she just in it for the cigarettes?"

Kinder laughed. "I have absolutely no idea. She seemed very credible and lots of the things we talked about were really, really elaborate. How anyone could make up such a complex world . . . well, I suppose I do that all the time. The thing is if this was an elaborate fabrication, she was not the one who made it up. This world she was talking about was made by someone or something outside of her. There were lots of things she mentioned but she couldn't explain how they worked. If you made it all up you'd think of that."

"And why would anyone want to deceive you?"

"More to the point, yes. Making me look foolish might be to many people's taste, but I can't see much of a point to it. Destroying my credibility would make more sense if my credibility was important to anyone. I'm a writer, Belle, not a politician or a doctor, thank the gods. The only thing that matters to me is my ideas. The only thing that matters to anyone else is whether I keep writing books or not. It's mystifying. The only interpretation that makes sense is the simple obvious one."

"She's mad?"

"She's from another world."

Belle let that hang in the air for a beat. "So what else did she say?"

"So many things. We talked for about four or five hours off and on. She slept for a short while and I went around the house dealing with things I would have taken care of before, had I known I was due interdimensional visitors. You know, washing up, picking up laundry off the floor, etc. When I came back, she was awake. She apologised, a woman after your own heart, Belle, and we resumed talking.

"The Earth, as she called her version of the world, was being destroyed by disease, pollution, corruption, greed, ignorance and hatred. It seems to me it was like Sol III was before The War, but much more well advanced. Advanced is the wrong word, more decayed, progressed in the sense of a disease can be said to be progressing.

"Their people were slaves to technology, to ignorance and a bizarre, almost medieval absence of consciousness. Nobody seemed to know who they are or what they wanted. They reacted to everything around them either in a totally face value way, or this bizarre devil's advocacy way, arguing a point on the behalf of someone they don't know.

"It's the height of insanity running your life solely in the service of what someone else might want. What about defining your life's purpose, meaningful connection and things of a higher nature? No. For the 'Earth' people, what's more important is telling off people online, taking ever more flattering but fake photos of yourself and arguing about politics as if it was some kind of low stakes game show. Seriously on alt-Earth, the president of the United States used to be an actual game show host. Apparently he nearly started a war because someone said he was fat in his selfies."

"But the President of the United States is a Native American woman."

"Yes, of course she is. I mentioned this fact to my visitor, and she looked really pleased for a moment. I asked why and she said it was thrilling to hear a Native American was in such a high office. I told her this was not surprising as the current president was the fifth Native American and third consecutive woman."

"Yes, Bravebird. Then Alberty. Then I think

41

Swiftwater, Cornfield of course, and now Branham Cloud."

Kinder was impressed.

Belle shrugged. "I could do quizzes on American presidents. So wow, she genuinely had no idea?"

"Her responses seemed very genuine. She could be a fantastic actor, but it seemed real to me."

"What about the British Republic?"

"Well she called it the United Kingdom and she said it has a Queen, Elizabeth The Second. The prime minister is the head of the government and although there are many parties only the two of them are ever in absolute power. Corruption is rife and big business owns the parties one way and another. Oh, and you'll love this. The press is run by big business too. It deals in sensationalism and hatred."

Belle sat with her mouth open "Are there no penalties for lies and hidden agendas. No UPPG?"

"In reality, yes, but in practice, nobody ever suffers for their lies. It's like a self interest free for all. Dog eat dog."

They sat again in silence. This time it weighed heavily on them both. Belle watched the giant butterflies puttering about outside in their search for a mate. It sounded as if this "Earth" was still steeped in the barbarism and greed so prevalent here before The War. The thought of any people returning to those times made her feel ill.

"So it's all about money. That's all that drives people, acquisition of funds?" She was openly disgusted.

"Except those that don't have any money. They get driven into madness, through lack of conscious connection to their fellow men. Oh!" he sat forward. "I forgot the weirdest part. She wore a mask. She told me they had a pandemic, a really bad one, which killed about 10 million people worldwide in the end. I told her no such thing had happened here, not for a century or so. She was still very reluctant to take the mask off. Like I say it was all a very elaborate story if it's a lie. A flu-like, lung killing virus spreading worldwide, mask mandates, vaccination, the whole dystopian nine yards. It's all very detailed and scary."

Belle sighed. She was having trouble digesting all of this. "So, after all these revelations, what happened next? When did she leave? Where did she go?"

Kinder grinned. "I wondered how long it would take you to ask me that. She didn't leave." He leaned back in his chair. "She popped out of existence like a soap bubble right in front of my eyes."

CHAPTER 4

It was an indescribable sensation the feeling of being "not there" and then without warning "being there". Her stomach felt like it had been stretched and there was an odd scary yawning sensation in the back of her throat which made it hard to breathe. The centre of her brain felt hot and her breath was incredibly dry.

She sat still. She took a little time to calm herself and looked around. She seemed to be sitting in her own house, in the front room. The TV was on, the book she was reading at the moment was open, pages down, on the coffee table. A cup of tea was also there and when she could reach out, she felt that it was lukewarm.

How long had she been "gone"? How long had she been "back"?

Words were still hanging in the air, a conversation interrupted. The memory of a sound rather than the sound itself. It was the absence of a recent sound. The sound is gone and all that's left is the millions of tiny, holographic reverberations, clinging like static dust to the hard surfaces of the room.

She was back, although she wasn't sure what back meant. Back from where?

On the TV the prime minister was defending the current austerity measures. Then a reporter in a heavy coat with red London buses passing behind him, tried to paint the PM's words as cowardly and evasive. The reporter tried really hard to make every nuance, no matter how neutral, sound negative.

A copy of a newspaper was on the coffee table under the book, the folded headline barked ENERGY CO

BOSSES SLAMMED FOR PAY HIKE OUTRAGE.

The phone was ringing. She slid it out of her pocket and looked at the screen. A friend. Wrong friend. This was not the friend to share stories of interdimensional travel with. She cancelled the call and chose another friend.

The right friend was at home and picked up on the third ring.

"Hi, it's . . . me," she said, stumbling on her name as it hadn't yet come back to her.

"Hey, hello, you. Funny, I was thinking about you today. I had the strongest feeling you were not feeling good. What are you doing today? You up to a visit?"

"Yeah, that would be really good." She sounded too eager. Too late, it was out.

"Oh. Sounds ominous. Okay, look I'm coming over right now. Be there in about an hour. Put the kettle on."

That's how you know it's the right friend. They know how you're feeling without asking, they listen and especially today, she hoped, they also listen without judgement and believe everything you say.

She went into the kitchen and washed up. Then she cleaned the kitchen floor. That burned about 30 minutes. She had a shower and got dressed in fresh clothes. 45 minutes. Why was time moving so slowly? In the end she just sat on the sofa, twiddling an ornament in her fingers and watching the hands of the clock go round.

Time is so flexible. Why is it not a constant like all the textbooks say? There was a joke among musicians that an hour with an English accordion could seem like a day, the joke being they were covered in buttons which were easily mistyped. Time passes slowly when you're making a lot of mistakes. She felt like a lot of life could be described that way.

Eventually the doorbell went and her friend was at the door. She had a smiley v-shaped mouth, gorgeous brown eyes glossy with mirth, and a massive pile of untidy curly hair. In the kitchen they made small talk about the weather. Tea was made. Then they sat in the front room. The words "drawing room" floated into her mind. Her friend could clearly sense that moment when the conversation would turn and you could tell she was almost engineering a break in the flow of words. She pounced.

"So yeah, I'm not stupid so what's bothering you, love?" she said simply.

"I've had an uh experience."

"What kind of experience?"

She looked at her friend's big receptive eyes and began. "I want to say out of body, but I was in my body the whole time. What I was out of was . . . here. The Earth. Sorry. I know that sounds bonkers, but please believe me this is real."

Her friend sat for a moment, searching her face and eyes.

"Okay," she said, and it sounded like a decision. "Cough it up. Tell me."

She spoke about how she found herself in a field in a valley with purple glowing towers and massive butterflies and how huge grey airships cruised overhead. She told her about stumbling across the road and how the silent cars avoided her so fast they must have been self driving. She told her about buildings in the distance which seemed to turn to face the sun and the massive ceramic teepees distilling water from the air.

She talked about the towers with the purple glowing heads. She talked about the sweet smell of the air, like no other air she'd ever breathed. Then she talked about the writer. His lovely house in the valley. His conservatory filled with light and his kind, dark eyes. She talked about the tea. Saying it all out loud it all sounded stupid.

Her friend took this all in. As she listened, she seemed

to be picturing it in her mind. She picked fluff off the couch and herself as she listened and puffed her electronic cigarette, filling the room with cinnamon and clove smelling vapour.

Eventually she stopped talking and her friend just sat there looking at her. She was smiling but not speaking, nodding slightly. *Surely she should have something to say about all this.* She waited looking at her friend and her eyes must have been pleading now because eventually her friend spoke.

"It's a lot to take in, I won't lie. This is not a normal everyday thing, obviously, it's um well a lot to process. Okay, phew, okay. I'm not going to ask you to prove this is real because self-evidently it's very real to you. I'm also not going to ask you what it means because my guess is as good as yours. I'm going to ask you something though . . . how does this experience make you feel?"

She was surprised by her friend's question. How *did* she feel? She felt surprised and afraid to be propelled into an alternate universe by forces unknown against her will. She felt a sense of wonder at the alternative Earth she had witnessed. She felt somewhat complex feelings about the writer. She had strong emotions concerning him that she couldn't fully put into words. It wasn't a romantic feeling. It wasn't love. What was it? It was a connection, a very different, definite and important connection. It was unlike any personal relationship she'd ever had before. Even besides the whole alt-Earth thing, it was a strange and powerful something.

She tried to explain this. It was like trying to find your way towards a tall building you can see in the distance but can't find your way to through the streets in an unfamiliar city.

Finally, she felt she had got as close as she could. She had to stop, she was starting to repeat herself. There was something more important. "Now I have a question for you." She took her friend's hand and she knew she must be looking fearful and pleading from her friend's expression. "When I went to this other place, I realised I'd forgotten my name. It wasn't like I'd forgotten it. It was like I'd never known it, like it was erased. It's still gone. So, please tell me. What's my name?"

Her friend smiled sympathetically and opened her mouth to say the name but then stopped with a frown and closed it again. "Wow. That's weird. I'm, I'm just, um, I'm blanking on your name. Of course. I, I know it. I just, wow."

"What's happening?"

"I don't know. I don't know, but we'll figure this out together. We'll figure it out." Her friend looked scared now.

"Oh", she said, "oh". Her friend hugged her tightly. The "oh" coming out of her mouth was an odd sound. It sounded like pain and fear, but also like an animal sound, the call of a scared creature in a trap. Why had her friend also forgotten her name? Perhaps it was something to do with her being taken out of this reality for a while. Maybe it broke her identity here? Maybe the ripples of her shift in space were radiating out from her and were affecting this reality now. She didn't exist here for a while. Perhaps reality had fixed the problem. Perhaps it would take a while for her to be here again?

They were both crying, not loud sobs or wails of pain, but just silent water flowing from their eyes as they gripped each other tightly. Her friend said, "this is crazy" a few times and she said "oh" some more, so much so that she began to be afraid that that would be her only syllable from now on. She couldn't stop.

"This is crazy."

"Oh."

"This is *crazy*."

"*Oh*."

She could see a vision of a man lying on his side, on grass, with blood leaking out of his head. All he could say was "go, go, go". She felt like him, his brain was damaged and he couldn't move or speak. All thoughts of the girls and his wife are gone and all that was left was "go, go, go".

A spike of fear ran through her and she jumped out of her friend's embrace, struggled out of her arms and stood in the middle of the room shaking her hands like she was trying to dry them. "Oh," she said, "Oh".

Her friend was really alarmed now. She grabbed her by the elbows and shouted, "you're going to be okay. Come on, stay with me, Jane . . ."

And there it was. Her name popped back into being.

They stood with their mouths open for a few seconds and then laughed and cried and hugged.

Jane's friend held her face. "See, I told you it would come back to me. You silly sausage. Now come on, pop quiz: What's my name?"

Jane thought for a second. "Don't overthink it, what's my name? Just say it now! Say it, what's my name?" She stared into Jane's eyes.

"Terry."

Terry hugged her. "That's right, Love, fricking Terry. God. You scared me. You're going to be okay. You're going to be okay."

They stood that way for a long time.

Eventually they noticed they were hungry, so Terry ordered some takeaway Chinese food. They were eating and Jane looked in her kitchen and discovered she had a bottle of wine. She poured herself a glass and one for Terry. She kept testing herself on the memories of Terry. Where did they meet? Sixth Form College. What was their common interest? Fringe science, boys, all kinds of kook literature, boys. And bad films, so many bad films. And boys. What was Terry's mother called? Grace. Who was Terry's boyfriend? Frank. He was a Milkman. What was her favourite colour? Purple. In the days before Frank they used to go out on the pull. Who was the pretty one? Jury's still out on that one. Leave it.

They ate and talked about anything else, but there was this massive grey elephant in the room. It was behind them, and so dusty and big and so grey and its patient brown eyes were boring into the back of their skulls. Eventually she named the elephant, and it looked grateful. She said out loud, "What am I going to do, Terry?"

"About what?" Terry had a mouthful of noodles, some dangling comically from the side of her mouth.

"About being a traveller between worlds. I've had an experience. It's real. What should I do about it?"

Terry pondered this for a second. She took off the elastic doughnut holding her huge hair in its fat ponytail. She joked it was more of a horse tail. She scraped her hair back expertly and secured it with a deft figure of eight twist motion of the elastic ring.

"The way I see it, you have two choices," she said.

"Including a lifetime of therapy and screaming."

"Okay, three including that. Firstly, you keep it to yourself and explore it and try to learn something from it. Second, you share your experience, um, very selectively, so that others can learn from it."

"Or get myself sectioned so I can represent no threat to myself and others."

Terry ignored the comment. "Bugger that, listen, experiences are personal. People believe some wacky shit. At least your experience has a basis in some kind of accepted scientific fact. Alternate worlds is a school of thought in physics, albeit a slightly divisive one."

"That doesn't answer my question. I want to know what I'm going to do."

"All I can tell you is what you *can* do. These

conversations are better answered by a priest."

"Do you know any priests?"

"Not any that are allowed to practice any more. I only know defrocked priests and fringe scientists and some people who are both. Fupping Weirdos." She stopped. "Hmm. Well, actually you know what, thinking about it, perhaps they are exactly the kinds of people you should be talking to."

"I don't know, Terry. I'm not 100% sure I should share this with anyone."

"Wait. Hear me out. Even if it's not reality. Even, no, wait, let me finish, even if it's not what the general consensus would call reality, I think it really needs to be explored."

Jane clamped her mouth shut. Terry had a point, even if she didn't share her experience fully, at least she was doing it the honour of taking it seriously. She thought about her talk with Dirk P. Kinder, how he took her seriously even though from his perspective, she must've sounded batshit crazy. Maybe she should extend the same courtesy to the experience itself, non judgemental consideration and yes, exploration.

She turned the ornament over in her hand again. Terry saw her turning it over and stilled her hands, "That's lovely. What is it?"

"It's a goddess from Calamarta. They worshipped women as the source of life." She didn't even look down, but she could feel the bulbous breasts under her fingertips.

"It's lovely. I don't know where Calamarta is, but that's not surprising. Listen, I'm sorry love, but I have to go. It's a work thing. I'm just going to go in, show my face and come right back. Your need is greater than theirs."

"Oh, there's no need to . . ."

"Yes. There is a need and it's your need. I'm going to bring someone back with me, an expert in all kinds of woo. Trust me. He's a great guy."

"Sure, whatever you want."

"You're tired, you've gone all day-dreamy. Have a lie down. I'll take the spare key and let myself back in."

Terry kissed her firmly on the face and let herself out.

Jane blinked and it was dark. A weird long blink and now it was dark and her mouth was dry. Also she was lying down. She'd woken up because the goddess ornament had fallen out of her hand with a bang and roll on the polished floorboards. Oh.

Terry was there earlier, but she had left. Jane felt all dreamy, soft focus and slow motion. She must've slept.

Terry was such a good friend. What was Terry Short for? Theresa? No wait, was it French? Thierry? No that's a boy's name. God, why did she find it so hard to think? Anyway she was a friend. There's friends and friends, and she was the latter.

Friends do things for you. They go the extra mile, but more than that they were with you for all the previous miles. Some friends are with you for the second and fifth, and miles seven and eight, and then only 12 and 21 but you knew they were with you in spirit for the whole journey. When they finally rejoin you, as they will, you know they are friends because you can't wait to tell them what they missed.

Of course there's the awful friends that are with you for every mile, but you wish they weren't. The ones where you wonder why they make the effort. They object to the miles they travel with you. They let you know that their feet hurt and they wouldn't be walking these miles with you if it was their choice and they hope you appreciate it. After all, they say, I've walked these miles with you and you still haven't said thank you. In fact, you've been quite rude to me, but I'm such a good friend, I'll ignore your rudeness and walk the miles with you, even though you never thanked me. I mean I carry your bags. I paid for you and gave you advice about where you should be walking to, which you didn't take, by the way.

They help you in a hundred ways you don't want to be helped and then they shout YOU'RE WELCOME in your face.

Why do those people try so hard to be and stay your friend? What's in it for them? They need you more than you need them.

What's the litmus test for friends? You can't have only perfect friends or you'd have none. You can't know a random collection of fellow humans without suffering the quirks, the eccentricities, the coping strategies, the OCD's, the weird upbringings, the hidden agendas, the needy lies. So how do any of us hang onto any worthwhile friends? How do we stop our own damage alienating worthwhile friends?

If a friend makes you be the best that you can be then that is a good friend. If a friend knows when to be around and when to be absent. If a friend sends you a message about a book or a piece of music or a film and you love it. If a friend says, I saw this and thought of you and you know that they did, and if you know their taste as well as they know yours. And if you've been apart for years and yet when you talk, it was like it was only yesterday. Or you look at them arguing a point angrily to some nobhead and marvel at how bright and beautiful and funny they are and how your life would be pale and shabby and pointless without them.

Even those times when they annoy you, or bore the piss out of you, or stay too long, you cut them some slack. Or let them off this time. Or tell them they crossed a line and you can't be around them right now.

Even those times, that's when you know, not having

them in your life at all would kill you.

The litmus test, the pH value of friendship is, can you put up with them? Is your anger with them momentary and your love for them eternal? Who do you tell the most stories about to other friends?

True friends live in our anecdotes about them, the stories we tell about them or the tales we tell about the adventures shared. True friends are co-conspirators. True friends are the first people you tell your best and worst news to. They are the person you turn to when hope is lost or joy is found.

True friends don't eat your time. They fill it up. They don't do favours. Favours must be returned. Friends do things for you that never have to be repaid. Never.

True friends, when you tell them you think you travelled to an alternate reality and saw giant butterflies and airships, help you remember your name, sit with you until you do and nearly get fired in the process. True friends come back with an ex boyfriend who is a renowned expert on alternative worlds, a psychotherapist, a former Tibetan monk and possibly the only person on your version of Earth who could explain this experience and help you survive it.

That's what friends do.

CHAPTER 5

Dirk P. Kinder wasn't his real name. He was born John Philip Denkert, to Joseph and Mary Denkert, and they lived in a quiet suburb of Rochwell city where Joe worked shifts in a factory and Mary was a hairdresser.

His mother worked at a local salon and also received neighbourhood women in her kitchen, which had enormous mirrors all down one side. Kinder grew up with the aromas of setting lotion and hairspray heated by hair-dryers. He saw all the local mothers and daughters and sons with wet hair and no make-up, which gave him a very healthy appreciation of women in all their diverse forms. It also meant he was always treated fairly by boys at school so he didn't spill the beans.

Instead of being full of cutlery, the drawers were stacked with hair grips, rollers, and bottles of chemicals. He'd sit and draw and listen to the small talk about life, love, death, marriage, gender, courage in adversity and joy. He was drenched from head to toe in ideas about human experience, so no wonder he became a writer. His books were science fiction ostensibly, but what they were really about was philosophy. The imponderables of human life.

When he was young, he wrote hundreds of short stories about robots in love, astronauts who found themselves reliving the same day and children whose parents had been replaced by aliens.

He became a professional writer but not fiction. He worked most of his adult life writing about electronics. After 20 years of magazine work, he got replaced by some kid who could work for half the price. But then he was getting stale and repetitive. It was time for a change. He ditched magazines for art, doing graphic design. He hadn't mentioned it to Belle Patience during the interview, but in a former life he had even been a junior on the team that designed the original Bleeb logo, all lower case letters and a reversed B at the end to make it symmetrical. Most people thought it read bleed, but in that sense it was controversial therefore a success.

Both his parents were agnostic and came from a long line of unionists and humanists, so of course his teenage rebellion came in the form of faith. He was a "born again" follower of the old gods for a time, a believer in an Asian fish god for a while and a mystic with the Nordic Ancients for a shorter time. All gods lead to the same place, he concluded. If you're serious about spirituality, he discovered, they all lead back to the self, the consciousness within, the body temple, the inner point of contact with the divine.

As a consequence of his religious experience, he became a staunch opponent of fundamentalism and dogma and extremism in religion.

Soon after returning from a retreat in Asia, he started work on this first novel. He'd written the first chapter in his head on the airship back from the mountains. So when he came to write it, it was just typing, getting the ideas down fast enough.

The book was called "The Opportunist Thief" and it told the story of a dystopian future where cinema was a religion and it was kept alive by a small group of adherents who built makeshift cinemas, refurbished projectors, and restored the ever dwindling supply of films. The central pillars of the religion were the life lessons in the plots of the films, the stories providing moralistic lessons about life.

The second book was called "The Pennsylvania Bible". It was an alternate history novel about Thomas Jefferson creating his Bible, which excluded all the miracles of Jesus. At a dinner party with Ben Franklin, he's shown a device given to Franklin by the engineer and physicist Leonhard Euler. When it is activated, Jefferson discovers himself in an alternate reality where his altered version of the Bible is the original and he made a version which added the mystical parts.

The third book was entitled "The Kind". It was about a scientist who invents an artificial life form and creates a habitat for them to live in. Later in the story he's able to communicate with the creatures and they split into two groups, those who see his communications as mental illness and those who believe he is their creator and is real.

The book contains the lines where the tiny insect-like lifeforms ask: "But why did you create us to suffer and die?"

To which the scientist replies "I didn't create you to die. *I created you to live.*"

After his visit from the woman from another dimension, he was uncomfortably reminded of his fourth book, a story about a writer who is visited by a woman who seems to be from another dimension. The events of his recent visit were troublingly similar to the plot of that book. This was another reason why he was so preoccupied during the experience.

He knew it was familiar and something he'd written about before. About halfway through the experience, he realised the similarity with his book. When the woman popped out of existence, he ran to the bookshelf and pulled down a copy of the book, and then things got really weird.

The book looked superficially similar to the book he remembered, it even had the same title, "A Mind for Mischief". But everything else had changed. The story, the characters, the situations had all changed.

Flustered and alarmed, he got his agent on a Feed tap.

Had she noticed that the book had changed? His agent went to her own bookshelf and read a few passages. What in the world was he talking about? The book was the same as it had always been!

The "new" version of the book had a female main character. She had become unstuck in reality and phased through many different realities in search of her own "real" reality. Eventually she understood it was hopeless and there was no "real" reality and all versions of reality were valid. Once she knew that and had some control over her reality, she decided to have a bit of fun with it. Hilarity ensued.

His agent asked if he'd seen his doctor lately. He broke the tap and shut the Slate.

He put the book down and stared at the point in space in the room where he had last seen her. There was a strange, sparkly electricity smell in the air still.

What was happening? Was his memory broken? He remembered this book very differently, now it was altered in a lot of fundamental ways. Was the book changed or was his memory changed?

He tried to think back to the time he spent writing the book. To his surprise, his memory was of writing both versions. The more he thought about it the less he remembered about what he thought of as the "original" version. The more he thought about it, the more he remembered the "new" version as the one he wrote, and the other version was one he drafted out but dismissed. The more he thought about it, he noticed how good that book was. The more he thought about it, he forgot why he got this book down from the shelf. He remembered something vague about an original version. But surely there was only one version? Maybe he had told someone there was another version once and he remembered that.

Why was he even thinking about this? Was it

something to do with the visit from the woman?

Actually, she did remind him of the woman in his novel. Dark hair, attractive in a quiet way, mobile mouth with pleasingly wonky teeth.

His agent feed-tapped him back. He said he was glad to hear from her, it had been a while. She reacted strangely. Apparently he had contacted her earlier about one of his books being changed. She was quite concerned. He didn't recall the conversation? *It was literally just now.* The writer was baffled. He had zero recollection of the conversation. He apologised to her profusely and made a thin excuse about his medication. He said he was okay. She sounded relieved.

Wow. What the demons was wrong with today?

The thing about the book "A Mind for Mischief" was that its central theme was the mutable and changeable nature of reality. Even in a small way, most of us warp our reality by our imperfect processing of it. Our eyes are not cameras, our ears are not microphones and tape recorders, our brains are not computers. Our reality is 100% subjective, even down to the colours and shapes of objects in our immediate surroundings.

What we see and hear is filtered through our brains. Our consciousness is not able to process the world about us in 100% fidelity, our brains are not fast enough, so over time we evolved to narrow the bandwidth of the sights and sounds we absorb. Our sight is only acute in the centre and the rest is a compressed, fuzzy approximation constructed entirely by our brains. We never see our eyes blinking in a mirror, not because they are fast, but because we unconsciously edit them out.

The visit from the woman from another dimension was real, as real as the visit from the Bleeb woman with the tiny blue eyes and massive red hair. Both women sat opposite him, both asked questions and listened to the answers. One of them had an almost primal fear in her eyes and the other an excited, almost hungry look.

Why is it that all people, regardless of their background and training, can read emotions in the eyes of others? He inhaled the sweet smoke from his third Ottoman cigarette of the day and blew out a satisfying carrot shaped plume. *(When did he light that?)* Anyway, it's true we all see the thoughts and feelings of people in their eyes, but mostly we ignore it. They truly are the windows of the soul, the headlights of our terrestrial vehicle.

On the subject of eyes and faces Dirk P. Kinder had some problems. Since he was a child, back when he still answered to John, he had trouble looking people in the eye. He always had to look off to the side or at his hands or shoes. His ex wife, the evil twin anyway, used to ask him why he wouldn't look at her and even used to grab his face and make him. This was incredibly stressful and painful for him and contributed to their breakup in no small way. *If you don't know me well enough to know forcing me eye to eye is really aggressive and wrong, then what is our relationship about?* To the young John Denkert looking into someone's eyes was very intimate. For him it was like touching someone's eyeball with your fingertip.

But he learned over the years that it was his problem and most folks wanted you to look them in the eye. It's a sign of trust, a kind of personal connection he realised was missing for him. So finally he made an effort to learn how to do it and now he could. He could hold someone's gaze and smile and pretend he was totally okay with it, but it was fake. It was a learned behaviour, a coping mechanism, blending in with the normals so he wasn't alone.

In any case, he thought, the thing about our perception of what we conveniently call reality is that it's just that. On an emotional level, on a spiritual level, and even on a scientific or quantum physical level, what you see is most definitely not what you've got. The objects and people around you are in a state of flux and there's almost a tacit agreement among humans that we'll mostly agree on what constitutes reality and leave it at that, never rocking the boat, having new ideas, or asking too many damn fool questions. So in the grand scheme of things, confessing to having had a visitor from another dimension was pretty small change.

The story of what happened had leaked out because he told his brother Mike, who had told his wife, Sissy, a notorious chatterbox, who had told a handful of friends at the hairdresser, ironically. She was regularly talking about Kinder because he was slightly famous and she basked in any bits of reflected glory she could sit in the light of. She wanted to show she was "in with the in crowd" and knew his intimate secrets.

Unfortunately, one of her friends was also an artist at Bleeb and shunted a feed-note to his editor, the aforementioned Belle Patience. Others had heard about it but publicly you couldn't spread gossip without risking prosecution, as countless black, humming Ministry of Truth AIs compiled lists of gossip to fuel later prosecutions, so you had to be discreet to avoid the lash. Hearsay was not legal tender. It was social poison.

Kinder didn't actually mind the story had got out, and parried his brother's profuse apology graciously. It was true so, you know, why deny it? Perhaps subconsciously he wanted it to get out.

He had no fear of being misrepresented in the press because the penalties for that crime were so severe. All that would happen is that the facts would be reported and people could make up their own minds if they despised him or not. Public opinions, or facsimiles thereof, never formed the basis of news or politics not since before The War. That was one of the things that fuelled The War in the first place, so it was one of the central pillars of the reconstruction of society afterwards. No "public opinion" allowed.

So he let it go and raised no privacy claims with the MoT. No hooded and masked men would be asking questions about who talked. He welcomed the subsequent full and frank interview with Belle Patience and considered the matter closed. At least from a public angle.

Privately he wanted some answers. But how to get those answers? He had to establish what he actually wanted. Was there some way to repeat the circumstances of the meeting? Would he even want to? Then there were bigger questions, like what did it mean?

He wasn't sure that experiences like this had to mean anything, and besides who could tell you what it means? Surely that was entirely up to him? Meaning was another one of those things which was a matter of personal perception and personal beliefs. He had to be open to the possibility, albeit painfully, that the experience had no meaning. That was a valid answer to the question. Sometimes the answer to the question, "why me?" is "nothing personal" or "who cares?"

Kinder decided to think about it for a while. He had some writing to do and that meant he needed some thinking time.

For some reason, best known to the subconscious mind, the new book contained a lot of autobiographical detail. He found it pleasing to add this stuff to his work as it added a nice level of detail with little or no world building work. Plus it was oddly cathartic seeing parts of his past life down on the page. It meant he also got Feed taps from family and friends when they had read the book expressing delight or dismay.

When he was a child he was the eldest of four, him, his brother Mike and their sisters, Patty and Paula. They were full blonde little soldiers on a route march across the countryside. Their father often substituted activities for connection, but of course that was only apparent to him later in life. His grandfather Dennis was a career drunk and alleged wife beater, and Joe rebelled against that stereotype by being a hard-working teetotaller, but apparently otherwise had no template of how to be a good father.

So they walked. They walked through fields and trees and he'd name all the plants they passed and showed them tricks with reeds and grasses, making whistles and noise-makers. He told them about the poisonous berries in graphic detail. How you would die and how long it would take. He'd take pictures of them, blonde hair and brown skin, clothing ragged, like desert island marooned pirates. They grew up loving the outdoors. They grew up respecting their father as a route finder, as an encyclopaedia, but mostly as a distant back forging ahead through the undergrowth, rarely turning, always moving forwards.

Dirk fictionalised the family for the book, changed the gender of a couple of his siblings and changed his father's appearance. He changed his job and his degree of satisfaction with his lot, but anyone who knew them would recognize the father as Joe.

The story was evolving, not planned. It was growing in odd directions, plot elements springing from previous happenings, like fertile young seeds sprinkled carelessly onto moist brown dirt, and watered so they sprouted up into sparkling sunshine. They came without warning and the words fitted together on the page rather than in the mind. Thoughts made flesh, if the flesh was paper and the blood was green ink flowing from the nib of a stylo pen.

He wrote a lot of his first drafts longhand with pen and ink. Then he read the words back on the page into a Slate and had the AIs transcribe them for him. He loved seeing the words on the page. He loved making the words real. What better metaphor for reality was there? The truth of his stories coming to life, uncertain and unfixed realities, crystallised on the page and achieving their own weight and momentum.

Where do you get your ideas from? I don't have to go looking for them. They just tumble out of my brain onto the page. All I do is guide them gently into some kind of order. Like writing your name with a hose on baking hot concrete or peeing in the snow.

The Slate made an intermittent beeping sound. He put the speaker on. "Hi Mum."

"Hi John. It's mum."

"Yes mum, hi."

"Can you hear me?"

"Yes, I'm talking to you now."

"Are you busy? Can you talk?"

"I can make time for you." She could hear the smile in his voice.

"I'm afraid I have some troubling news." His heart sank to his shoes, taking his stomach with it.

"It's your father. I just heard, I'm afraid he's disappeared again." The faint throb of emotion in her voice would have been inaudible to any other listener. His mother was very controlled, "We're rather afraid he's going to do something stupid".

She'd have to narrow it down a bit. Joe Denkert had done a lot of stupid things over the years. Although he and Mary had not been together for the last 20 years or so, she still cared for him more than he cared for himself.

There was that time he cut down half the trees on his property because the rustling was annoying him. And the time he put all his medication into the waste disposal because he thought he was better and the meds were making him ill. And then that time when he got bored and decided he wanted to be a mountaineer and climbed a local peak armed with nothing more technical than a 40 foot length of washing line and a pair of kitchen tongs. That time he fell 20 feet onto a boulder and broke his hip and had to be airlifted to hospital.

Dirk's brother Mike bore most of the responsibility for their father as he lived the closest. The girls visited regularly. Only Dirk had no contact with Joe. All he did was pay for stuff like tree surgeons and ambulances. His mum kept him informed of Joseph's shenanigans, but she never outright asked him for money to sort things out. He didn't give the money out of guilt. He gave it to spare Mike and his mum the burden of fixing the problems Joe created.

But this time he had an inkling there was a bit more to it.

His father had never gone missing before, although he went out without telling anyone where he was going quite a lot. He always came back, like the uppity cat that turns up for food, but gives you the impression he'd like to be living almost anywhere else.

He thanked his mother for letting him know and ended the Feed tap. He really wished she could let Joe go properly. Joe would never help himself, so she never could, no matter how often she tried. He wished she knew that.

He resumed writing for a while. Then as it was getting darker, he decided to turn everything off and go to bed. Just as he switched off the downstairs light, the door knocked.

Was she back? Was it her? He rushed to the door and turned the lights back on and pulled it open.

"Hello, son, sorry it's so late," said his father.

CHAPTER 6

Victorian strong men are an obsession of his. Their physique is covered in a comically loose-fitting type of underwear, like an off white all-in-onesie. The moustaches were broad and carefully waxed, the hair slicked back and the heavy boots. Add to this the comedy barbell composed of a bar with huge fake cannon balls at either end, and you have the complete look.

In the dream there are two of them, one doing an act of foolhardy strength or daring, the other presenting the display for your enjoyment with outstretched palms, like a parody of a magician's assistant. *Lookit*, the pose says, *look what he can do!* Is it not a surprising display of the utmost bravura? Is my heterosexual life partner and stage brother not magnificent?

They have a routine, a set of moves they do that are so practised, so ingrained that they don't have to think or engage at any point in the process. They just move. The Flying Bonzini Brothers is their name. This is not their real name, merely the name they are known by. Vladimir and Ivan. Why were they Russian? In the dream, they don't speak often. Mostly they just go into the next trick and when the move is begun, or in progress, the one who is pointing says, "OP!" And on completion of the move, the final flourish, he says, "LA!" With great satisfaction.

"OP . . . LA!" applause.

"Da! Chto podvig!" - Yes, what a feat!

"Blagodary vas!" - Thank you/Much obliged to you.

And in heavily accented English, possibly fake. "Now I shall introduce our next feat of strength and determination."

This is not theatre, not in the western idea of the word. This is theatre as circus, a spectacle, a surreal presentation of skills honed over decades. These are skills which have only one use, for the audience to be flabbergasted that anyone would take the time and effort to get good at this peculiar thing. To show it and to be greeted with slack-jawed wonder. To be that much of a dedicated maniac requires a lot of courage.

There's a lot to be said for dedicated maniacs. They fuel the creative world. Someone who, to the distraction of all else, dedicates their time and energy to the pursuit of a single goal, albeit a useless one. Mastery of a single pointless part of the human experience. THIS, they are saying, is what I am good at. THIS is what I consider to be my best shot at a lasting contribution to the world. THIS is my masterpiece.

OP - LA!

It's so easy to get diffused and distracted from your purpose in life. It's so easy to get diverted from having a single goal. And do you know what having a single goal means? You will probably succeed. It's only the dedicated maniacs who ever achieve it.

To be clear, success does not ensure lasting happiness. The achievement of a single goal only guarantees fulfilment. Sometimes being happy relies on the abandonment of a single goal, which is unreachable or unreasonable. Being happy is not and should not be a goal. Happiness and goals are often times mutually exclusive.

Sometimes the barbell is too heavy and you've overestimated your strength. Sometimes you could lift it easily if you weren't so sad. Sometimes the barbell reminds you of your father and his struggle and how many times you lifted him before you let him fall.

Sometimes you perform your trick perfectly, but it's ruined for you because your moustache is not perfect and you just know that if you were better at tending it, at grooming, or a better person, *it could be*. Or you start to realise your long johns are grubby and a little too baggy and so therefore comical. Life can be cruel like that. It gives you perfection but chips away at that perfection with errors and flaws that shouldn't matter, but do. Sometimes in the middle of a trick, you suddenly become acutely aware of how ridiculous the whole thing is, how you wasted your life achieving mastery over this useless task.

OP . . . LA!

There's nothing so bleak as a crushing defeat masked as victory.

But there is glory there too, in persistence and success. Finding in yourself the will to go through thousands of rote, lifeless repetitions of an action, until it becomes a practised flick, a smooth gesture, a move that translates in visceral, ape language to: *I am awesome*. Humans can do this, turn drudgery into excellence, repetition into skill, training into mastery.

In the dream, Ivan and Vladimir, who is sometimes called Victor, perform their stunts to circus music. Sometimes they do them to Shostakovitch. Very classy. Mostly they do them in silence with a heavy breath, strangled huffs and boot squeaks echoing slightly in the gloom surrounding the spotlight. Sometimes there is applause. Occasionally there is awkward silence, or worse a single tentative clap.

How did they arrive at their conclusion that this was their life's purpose? Was it a decision? Did they eliminate all other possibilities until what remained must be the truth? Or did they just stick a pin in a map and say whatever this pin lands on is my purpose?

Or as is most likely, did they evolve their act because they were poor, and learning circus skills was a free way to earn a crust? Well, free in the sense that they didn't have to pay for training. Their time was their only resource, so they ploughed it all into the mastery of the tricks.

Perhaps their drunken father back in Russia forced them into show business to fund his vodka habit. Who can say? And only Victor and Ivan, who at this point may also have been called Valerie Anatoly, know for sure. Besides their origin story was never a part of the dream.

Either way, the best trick was the last. Valerie Anatoly bent an iron bar with his teeth. It was an iron bar of at least an inch thick and he bent it like it was made of licorice. He cracked a tooth almost every time, it was inevitable. How could you avoid it? And it was in those times, right when the bar was bending across his teeth and the enamel was cracking like an old porcelain plate, that Valerie Anatoly reconsidered his life choices. Was this his life's purpose? Was learning how to do this trick worth the pain and enormous expense of his time and effort? He wasn't sure it was.

So perhaps that was the purpose of the dream, a lesson in life choices. Of course dreams don't have to have a message or a point, but it's convenient to assume they sometimes do. Mostly they are just your conscience riffing and improvising, gorgeously rich brainwave jazz made from the bottomless depths of the unconscious. Like a photomosaic made from billions of other tiny photos. A hologram made of holograms, which in turn were made of more holograms. So on and so on, down through the levels of mind.

It was convenient to imagine the mind as residing in the physical cortex but how can it possibly be? And its physical bandwidth is so low as to be ridiculous. How can a biochemical device as basic as the human brain contain so much data, so much understanding? When the mind is honed to a sharp point, it can split atoms and move mountains. But the experience of most humans is of confusion, distraction and ambiguity.

How can you know your purpose when the answer to that question can only come from yourself? It would be so much more convenient if, instead of wasting years in fruitless introspection, someone could just write it down on a piece of paper and give it to you. After all, we are often the last to know what we are best at and yet those around us can tell us the whole time.

If only we were listening.

Joe Denkert would like to say he was listening to advice on his life's purpose. The truth of the matter is half the time he was convinced of his purpose (when it turned out he was wrong) and half the time he was bucking against being told what to do by anyone (when he really should listen).

Privately, he was aware that mostly he just randomly did stuff to try and make sense of it all. He knew he should probably meditate on those thoughts for a while before acting on them, but who has that kind of time? There was a demon inside him, his mother used to say. Something that drove him to act without intuition, to push forwards to a goal that wasn't sufficiently thought through. It was as if there was an invisible deadline and he had to drop all safety equipment and brakes in order to pelt hell for leather towards it. While he was doing these things, he felt a kind of certainty, but later that evaporated and the sense of foolishness and defeat (and sometimes personal injury) set in and he felt lost.

For most of the kids' childhood he stuck stoically to a job, working night shifts in a factory and sleeping all day. But once the kids were grown up, he began to indulge all those fantasy projects he'd spent his working life daydreaming about. Then came the dream of the Victorian strong men. After that the Flying Bonzini Brothers were regular nocturnal visitors throughout the crazy years.

Eventually Mary got tired of his twitchy restlessness or reckless drive towards making himself a laughing stock. One day, Joe got back from one of his "research" trips to find all Mary's belongings gone and a note, which didn't apologise or excuse her exit, but merely explained where everything was, and how to work the washing machine. It seemed cold and passionless, but Mary had had enough many years prior, and had squashed her emotions down so hard, it would be years before she could feel anything in colour.

Joe, the poor sap, didn't see it coming and Mary's departure sent him into a flat spin. Thus began the period of risk taking and harebrained schemes. When a man has nothing much left to lose, he makes sure that he loses everything else as quickly as possible.

None of his attempts to find his life's purpose were intuitive. They were flashy, bravura, bizarre attempts at a get rich quick life. Inevitably he ended up being slapped with a mental health protection order and hooded men grabbed him in his home and took him to a secure facility for correction. Society generally tolerates a lot of neurodiversity, eccentricity and freedom of expression. But mental health issues taken to extremes affect everyone.

It was after being in the secure facility for a while that he made the first of a handful of suicide attempts. Nothing flashy, no cries for help or grand gestures or dramatic notes, he just upped and tried to end his life with whatever he had to hand. He did it as unemotionally and matter of fact as if he was taking out the trash or performing a well-practiced feat of strength in front of a mildly interested audience.

OP . . . LA!

It was like a sport where the aim was to get to the finish line before anyone could even notice you were running. He was starting to get quite good at it, so the doctors decided to have a talk with him.

The doctors were idiots.

"Why do you keep attempting to complete suicide, Joe?"

Joe just let his eyes roam like he was waiting for a bus.

They continued. "That last time was a bit too close for comfort, we have to do something to stop this."

"Do we though?" said Joe, unblinking.

The lead doctor grimaced "Yes, yes we do."

"And I'm not attempting to complete suicide. I'm following my life's work to find out all the ways it can't be done. Attempt is such a weasel word."

The doctor sighed, he took off his glasses and massaged the bridge of his nose.

"Joe, suicide is a choice and a valid answer to many questions, but I don't get the feeling you're looking for an answer or help."

"I'm looking for death. I just haven't discovered where the bastard is hiding yet. It's the solution to my problems. It's the only way to make all this go away."

"Suicide doesn't solve your problems, Joe. It just passes them on to those you leave behind. Think of the alternatives . . ." he rambled on but Joe wasn't listening.

Joe was flummoxed. The doctor was an arse. He was not very good at talking to people and was clearly late for dinner. But he had inadvertently started a train of thought. Try as he might, Joe couldn't get the sticky thought out of his head.

He still believed he was a useless screw-up. But he was now freshly determined to ensure that all the bad stuff stopped with him. His life wasn't a problem he could solve by ending it. He had connections to people, people who (inexplicably) cared about him. Suddenly that previously unimportant detail was a reason to live. But this presented a unique new problem. This needed some thought.

So he worked on his "recovery" and got himself back to

a "normal". Except of course what he got himself back to was not at all normal. What he did is just to get very, very good at *appearing* normal. A well rehearsed move, burnished over time, an act so good he didn't even have to think about it. A facial expression here, a gesture there. This was his life's new purpose. To fool these bozos into declaring him as their version of normal. A year later he left the secure facility under his own steam.

OP . . . LA!

The reason was simple. He had a demon in him. He had a scurry of uncontrollable brain squirrels in his head and he needed to set them free somehow.

Ideas are like madness, and can in some be the main source of madness. Creative ideas gnaw at your brain until you give them vent and let them out, but also these same ideas could eat your brain completely if unaddressed. A persistent notion that you have a stuck in your mind can be a source of pain and not joy.

The epiphany that he had was that suicide passed your problems onto those you left behind. He didn't want that. But if that's true and you're in pain, then how could you live? It was a paradox. Stalemate. But one day as he was turning this over in his mind an unbidden thought popped into his mind. What if there was another option? If you couldn't die but you also couldn't live, then was there another door you could open?

Option 3.

When he got home he had to spend a long time returning the house to some kind of order. Dust was thick on every surface, the grime of his madness ran along every edge and corner. He knew he had to get it all clean.

For days he could be seen stacking black bin bags at the side of the house. Sometimes he woke up wearing rubber gloves. Then he started to see bare tiles and clean wallpaper. The carpet was waxy and matted and it had to go. Fortunately, the boards beneath it were in very good order. Soon the rooms were clean, sparingly decorated cubes and definitely what any person would call normal.

Once the house was normalised and purged of any outward madness, he could begin on the inner transformation.

His son Mike came over to help from time to time. Well, at least that was the pretext. Joe could see Mike's watchful eyes and made sure that all they saw was honest efforts to be given a second chance. He knew Mike was reporting back to Mary, he was certain of it. He wanted to demonstrate his normal-ness, but mostly he didn't want them to worry so much they kept close tabs on him. He had much work to do. He knew what his purpose was. Find Option 3, find the hidden door between life and death.

And open it.

He knew that consciousness was the key. He also knew that training the consciousness was something that couldn't be rushed. If your mind could be single pointed like a psychic chisel, you could drive it into the many small gaps in reality and pry them open, he reasoned.

Reality is not fixed. Our senses were feeble and easily confused. Only a consciousness which was trained and facile and sharp could truly see.

During the long years of shift work he'd read a lot. Book after book of science fiction, philosophy, self help, quantum physics, smart drugs, hypnosis, and religion. He consumed an entire library of connected books, unconsciously following lines of inquiry. In the crazy years, he'd gone down a few blind alleys pushing himself physically, parachuting out of airships, climbing and nearly frying his nervous system up a Tesla Tower, using intramuscular electrical stimulation to tone muscles by stabbing wires directly under his skin.

The meandering "research" had been a necessary phase, he reflected, an education in all the things which were not his life's purpose. They'd all been unwittingly preparing him for the true purpose. It's only the dedicated maniacs who ever achieve success. They do this by having a single goal, an easily definable but difficult task and end result. Option 3 was easy to understand and easy to work towards. Just try and eliminate things which didn't get you closer.

Climbing was a blind alley, plus he worked out after he fell and broke his hip on that boulder he'd gone off half cocked. The breaking strain on the washing line was scarily less than he'd estimated. Classic rookie mistake replacing wishful thinking and kitchen tongs for hard science in his rush to the goal. That was the old Joe. He wouldn't let that happen again.

The breakthrough came when he happened across the work of tech mystic, T. Mark Shamley. Shamley was a former physicist whose most recent experiments in fringe science had estranged him from the mainstream and driven him into the welcome embrace of kookdom.

A former assistant of Tesla, Shamley's special interest was in using the high frequency electricity that the Tesla Towers used for broadcasting power and The Feed as a means of amplifying consciousness. Joe read all about it in Shamley's book "Deep Diving in the Brain" detailing his experiments before and during The War.

IndMilCom paid Shamley to make a weapon which non-fatally shut down human brains from a great distance. But it turned out Shamley was working both sides of the street. He'd used most of the money to further his exploration of the deep blue lower levels of the sea of human consciousness. He also made tech for the resistance. The IndMilCom scientists found out what he was up to and threw him in a very deep hole from which he was only liberated years later. The time underground had left its mark on him. But he emerged filled with light, his resurrection was almost a religious conversion. The gods had protected him for a reason.

Joe knew he had to join Shamley's organisation, The Shamley Org, and soon he was working for the experimental division of Shamley Labs as an intern and test subject. His many physical adventures had gifted him an iron constitution and a high tolerance for pain. His meditation practice had sharpened his brain to a fine point, and his self awareness and self diagnosis were also highly developed. In a year he was a senior test subject and he worked very closely with Shamley himself. Shamley was middle aged, bearded and bespectacled and garbed at all times in a crisp white suit.

By now, Joe was the perfect subject, dedicated, focused, and willing to try anything to move the research forwards. Joe had punctured and burned himself many times, so having electrodes pumping illegally harvested Tesla Tower energy at high volume into his spine was easy. The overtones of the electric chair were a little disturbing, but as he sat there listening to the countdown, Joe was determined, and the eyes in his gaunt bearded face flamed with an almost inhuman passion. Shamley shouted in triumph as the switch was thrown and all of Joe's world was filled with light.

OP . . . LA!

CHAPTER 7

"Airships? What kind of airships?"

She'd thought they were unusual at the time. At first she thought they were the kind she was familiar with, but then one of them came down the valley and flew over the house when it was facing her. She was surprised to see a hole down the centre.

"I asked him about that," said Jane to the older man sitting next to Terry, "and he said most of the International passenger flights were that design. I can't remember what he called it."

"Venturi?" asked the man.

"Oh yeah, that's it. How did you know?" She covered her mouth.

"Wild guess. Some things seem to be the same in both worlds. That design is something of a rarity in our world, but perhaps if airships had continued to be popular in our dimension, sorry, world, then they would have evolved that way too." He explained that the hour glass hole running through the centre of the ship turned the blimp into a large circular wing. It was hypothesised that such a design would be more stable and faster.

"So what you experienced there is a true piece of technology, something that's not been very well developed in our timeline. Same goes for the towers, Tesla Towers? Nikola Tesla made one just like that in a place called Wardenclyffe in New York State in about 1901. He built it to transmit radio signals and power over great distances. Yes, wireless power. There's a lot of kookdom related to Tesla." He smiled at that.

Jane looked at the man on the sofa opposite her. He was

in his late fifties perhaps, with longer than usual but neatly trimmed greying hair. His eyes were kind and eager to listen. Always trust a man who listens with his eyes. His mouth held a perpetual mild amusement. As he talked his lips tried to stay over his teeth.

He wore slightly oval reading glasses and a black shirt that looked like it might be part of a religious uniform. He carried a dark leatherette book that had gold edges to the pages, but it was a notebook rather than a bible. He occasionally inscribed a few words in it as she was speaking.

Terry had introduced him as Brother Mark, but he had corrected her. Mark, please, just Mark. Apparently Terry and he had dated a long while ago but realised while they were great friends, there was no spark between them, romantically. That's how Terry put it. They did look at each other very fondly and were casually tactile. They were physically easy in each other's company.

"There are many," he continued, "who think Tesla's power transmitter was working, but that wasn't what he was being paid to invent, so the finance was pulled from the project. As with all these things where there was a whiff of conspiracy, kooks leap in to fill the gap. *We'd have wireless electricity by now if it wasn't for JP Morgan pulling the plug*, they say."

It helped to know that the things she saw in her dream were real or at least possible. It was also reassuring that although these things were not known to her before this experience, they were genuine technologies, so it gave a certain weight to her account.

Her confessor let her chew it over.

"This is very helpful, thank you," she said eventually. "Oh God, that sounds so British. It's just an overwhelming experience. It's something that sounds implausible even to me as I'm saying it. How do people move on from experiences like this? I mean, does it happen very often?"

Mark took a second to collect his thoughts and arrange them. "Human life is something we all struggle with, obviously. We all have experiences and thoughts and emotions we can't explain. Things we either can't or feel uncomfortable about sharing. In my mind, everyone suffers from that on some level.

"That goes double when the event is so profound and inexplicable using normal methods of communication. To you, this experience is very real. Our job is to listen. If we judge, or try to fit your account into a box that we understand, by brute force, then we are not being very fair, or just, as human beings. Religious experiences, and I use this analogy very gently, are of a similar quality. Something profound and personal, which is of debatable meaning or relevance to anyone but the person to whom it occurred. It's customary in areas of faith to honour a person's story and their bravery in sharing it. The wider world is uh shall we say, less gentle. It's rife with cynicism and scepticism, which to me is a search for lies and not a search for truth."

He laid his hand on top of his notebook which rested on his knee.

"The trick is to decide what to share and with whom. Some life stories just aren't for public consumption. We live in an age where people share everything they think and do in public. We've become unable to judge the value of an experience ourselves, and nothing is private any more. It cheapens your consciousness to be so open about everything, because meaning is something you have to sometimes think about for a while. If everything you do is so transient and the emphasis is always on making your life seem more dramatic, then when something truly dramatic happens, like someone slipping between worlds, it won't be taken seriously. We've ruined our sense of wonder.

"And in answer to your question, no, this doesn't

happen very often. But it did happen to you."

The aftertaste of his words was there in the room for many seconds after he finished speaking.

He was right, of course. It didn't matter if she could prove that she'd slipped between worlds. It didn't matter if anyone believed her. Trying to get everyone to believe her would solve nothing. Even if she explained it perfectly to all the right people, even if she got a seal of approval saying her experience was real and nobody could question it . . . someone somewhere would brush it off as lies.

Someone would assume it was a plot by religious extremists. Someone would believe she was abducted by a UFO. Someone would say this is an obvious political distraction and wasn't it obvious that such a story would emerge, and in an election year?

Someone else would believe her (or pretend to) and set up a cult behind a PO Box number in somewhere spooky like Sedona AZ. Someone would say they used to know her years ago and she's always been a lying bitch. Someone else would say they too had been to this world and they met while they were over there, so WHY, ASK YOURSELF WHY is she denying it? Someone would say she's in league with flying saucer Nazis.

Maybe someone somewhere might believe her story is the absolute truth. They would understand why she wanted to share her story. They would want to reach out and contact her and understand her experience and learn all the details.

Then what?

For the depressingly small number of people who believed her, what would they do then?

What?

Would they try to go back there together?

There was a high risk that they would turn into a cult of their own, with infighting within the group eventually tearing it apart. This was madness.

"I can see you're thinking it through," said Mark quietly, "Have you got to the part where you become a cult yet?"

It was a shock laugh, it burst out of her. All the tension and fear poured into it and she laughed long and hard till it hurt. Terry and Mark laughed too. Catharsis, that thing you vent into always comes from an unexpected direction. Afterwards you know it was inevitable and you should have done it sooner. Timing is important in catharsis, as it is in comedy, and that isn't accidental.

Mark counted out tissues. The three composed themselves.

"Are you psychic?" Jane dabbed her eyes and pushed the corner of her eye with the side of a finger.

Mark thought for a moment and made a face. "Not this week."

"Are you ever?"

"We all are sometimes, but that's a longer conversation."

They all relaxed and sat in the moment for a time.

Jane sniffed. "Do you mind that I asked Terry to sit in for our conversation? I know you wanted to talk to me one to one."

"Not at all. There's no real reason to conduct one to ones unless the client is embarrassed to talk about what they are disclosing. Terry is a trusted friend, so of course you want her present. Besides, you already told her most of what you told me."

"Oh."

"So you want to take a break? I'm happy to continue for as long as you like, but you need to pace yourself and process."

"I would like to have a break. Thank you. Would either of you like tea? I have black tea or pu erh . . ."

Terry jumped up and offered to make the tea while Jane

went to the toilet.

When Jane returned, Mark was looking at the shelf in the living room.

"This is gorgeous. Where did you get it?"

"Oh, that's a goddess from Calamarta."

"Oh, where's that?"

Jane looked at him, frowning. "Calamarta? The country in South America? Southeast of Anahuac? How's your geography?" She laughed.

Mark didn't smile. He turned the little bulbous figure in his fingers and looked at the base. A tiny gold sticker proclaimed HETCHOO NI CALAMARTA.

"What's wrong?"

Mark handed it to her. "Okay. Think carefully, when did you get this? Can you remember where you got it? The exact time and place?"

She thought about it. She had a memory of wearing a floppy sun hat and seeing the rows of tiny goddesses on the sun-bleached wooden table outside the paint peeled store. She could see palm trees reflected in the glass of the store window. For some reason she couldn't see her own face in the glass.

"I bought it in a shop."

"And how did you get to the shop?"

She remembered the journey to the historic little town. Land car, electric, before that, the Maglev and before that the airship from . . .

"By airship!" The single word was like she spat out a pebble. It made a small sound as she verbalised it, a sound like a stone hitting a shiny tile floor and skittering away.

All the memories of the trip to Calamarta folded in on themselves like origami animals made of light.

In their place a new image of her sat in an airy conservatory, looking down the throat of a pretty valley filled with giant butterflies.

She dropped the goddess and the sound of a pebble hitting a shiny tile floor and skittering away became real.

"My God, I brought this back with me. This belongs to him. He's the one who bought it in Calamarta, not me."

Suddenly Terry popped her head into the room from the hallway to the kitchen. "How do you like your pu erh?" She saw their faces and stepped back. "Oh shit, is this a bad time?"

Jane looked from the goddess on the floor to Mark and to Terry. She opened her mouth and heard herself saying, "I take it with milk."

Terry shrank back into the kitchen. Not a good time then.

Terry was rushing. She wanted to get back into the room. She had long, tawny, curly hair. Tawny was a good word for it. Not blonde or redhead, definitely tawny. A word not much in use in the modern age for reasons she was unsure of.

She let it loose sometimes, but it was quite unruly so mostly she bound it with elastic bands covered in cloth. Talk about Terry between her friends almost always mentioned her hair and how jealous they were of it.

She had a well rehearsed gesture of flipping the hair out of the stretchy hoop, re-pulling the hair back into shape and expertly flipping the band around the hair to snap it tight. She usually did this 2-3 times a day, either when her hair was coming out of the band or if she was about to do something physically demanding. She also did it out of nerves. It was a preparation for emotional work too.

She picked up the tray and walked quickly back into the room.

Terry set the tray down and sipped her tea while watching Brother Mark and Jane talking over by the bookshelf, Mark bent to the floor and picked something off the boards. He handed it to Jane and clasped her hands around it.

"It's real, Jane. It's real and you know this is a part of your experience. Embrace it." His voice was soft.

Terry watched the odd collection of facial expressions flutter across Jane's face, like birds flying away from a sudden sound. She saw her probing Brother Mark's eyes for answers.

Terry flipped her hair out to the band, pulled it back into shape and then snapped the band back. The snap was like a pistol shot in the quiet room and both Mark and Jane looked over to her, their eyes like buttons.

"Please, guys, please come and sit down. What's going on?" They came over slowly and sat down then. Mark explained what had happened.

Jane put her hands together between her knees and squeezed them. She looked at the wall opposite and on a whim, she let her gaze travel up the wall, up, up to the ceiling. When she got there, she kept going across the ceiling and over her head as far back as she could stretch. Terry and Mark watched her do it with expressions of confusion. Terry reached out, but didn't touch her.

"You ok sweetie?"

Jane didn't seem to hear. She just stared at the ceiling stretching her neck. Then she tried to swallow and couldn't, so she gulped and her head came forward again. She coughed.

"I don't feel so good," she said. "I feel like I brought back something with me. Something more. I went there and before I went I wasn't connected to that world, but now I am. Connected. Like a thread going from here," she touched her chest "all the way back there to the room looking out over the valley. It's like when you walk through smoke and it moves around you, but some of it clings to you. The smell of it stays on you after."

She smelled her hands and arms, she could swear she

detected the smell of the room she'd visited. It was fading, but smelling it, even faintly, she could almost hear the purr of the giant butterflies' wings beating the clear air.

Mark nodded. "I understand. All experiences have memories, those are physical things in the brain, but there's something physical but intangible we come away with. You know how people say they want to shower after a bad experience, and not just because they feel soiled in some way. Because they "feel dirty" or something like that? I think there's a little more to it, in this case. It's hard not to talk in terms of IF, so please forgive me. IF this experience was real . . ."

Jane groaned. It was like a mild birth contraction, a suppressed wail.

"Bear with me. IF this experience was real, then it's possible that some kind of entanglement has occurred. You are now linked on a kind of quantum level. That is possible. The theory is there, but there's not much data about other worlds because nobody has ever been to one and returned."

Terry blinked, "so she's linked. Does that mean she could go back?"

Mark thought. "Possible, but in this case the list of things which are possible is suddenly impossibly long. There is something else that occurred to me. If you went there, could someone come here?"

His face in the mirror was familiar, but he had no idea of his name. Fortunately, the cottage was cool. The walls were thick and insulated him from the heat outside. The sun was fierce, much hotter than he remembered. He was glad he had found the empty building and was able to get in. There was a kind of refrigeration chest made of white metal. There were magnetic toys stuck to the large door on top and the sides. At first he couldn't work the oven, but eventually he figured it out, some kind of gas, which smelled toxic. Flammable, he thought, and there was what seemed to be a spark making device beside it.

He melted a rock of brown meat sauce in a metal pot until it bubbled. He found a spoon and ate the sauce. It tasted like herbs, possibly frangen and mape, and the meat was good but had a flavour he couldn't identify. Beef, though maybe the cook had been a bit liberal with the mape which overwhelmed the flavour, but he was in no fit state to criticise. It was food and he was starving.

It didn't look like anyone was going to be here for a while and he saw what looked like a calendar, but he had no idea what 1995 meant or what the month of May could be referring to. He wasn't 100% sure it was even a calendar at all.

He'd been here for a few hours and he hadn't heard a single airship. Normally you could hear them in the distance even if you couldn't see them. And where were all the Tesla Towers? What was powering the cold cupboard? It had a cable coming out of it plugged into the wall. He did pass a few tall metal towers a couple of miles back, but they had strange humming wires strung between them.

He had seen an aircraft, at least he thought that's what it was. Very high in the sky with a long white trail behind it. Perhaps it was some kind of rocket? There was a distant rumble, like some kind of powerful combustion or controlled explosion. Quite alarming.

He slept for a long time. He wasn't sure how long, but one time he woke it was dark and the next time it was light again. He washed and dressed and decided he needed to get moving.

The country lanes were pleasant and quite a lot had shade from the relentless sun. Why was it so hot? It shouldn't be this warm.

A couple of times he heard a land car approaching and he ducked out of sight. The car sounded like they also had combustion engines. They belched fumes he could smell and feel in his lungs long after they went by.

The town was small, but it told him everything he needed to know. The belching land cars, no Tesla Towers anywhere, the winged rockets overhead.

He was definitely in another world.

CHAPTER 8

General Bearbeck sat in a dark brown and uncomfortable conference room chair. He puffed delicately on a small cigar and tapped the ash on the saucer of the tea he was brought when he arrived.

The meeting table had a high gloss and stretched out into the room like a swimming pool filled with oil. The Kerholm city towers filled the tinted crystal windows down one side of the room, and the sun shone weakly through those hazy fingers reaching into the sky.

A cluster of footfalls led to a door being somewhat flamboyantly opened and the chief minister and a couple of aides swept smoothly into the room and took seats adjacent to him. Apologies for delays were deftly brushed aside. Although the aides eyed his cigar, nobody informed him that smoking was not permitted.

"How are you, sir?" said the minister blandly. General Bearbeck shrugged and pursed his lips. The minister's smile was tight and phoney.

"So let's not wait too long to get to the heart of the matter. The report is finished and it makes for disturbing reading. Mankind is not developing and growing. We are as a species distressingly prone to disobedience and dissent. We are not providing for the future development of wealth. We are actively engaged in activities which waste wealth and growth, in favour of highly expensive, disruptive conservation of the natural world." He pronounced the last two words as if someone had put a spider in his mouth.

As the chief minister of IndMilCom he was acutely

aware of how much money it cost to put right militant acts of disruption and ecoterrorism. These antisocial, anti-societal freaks were hurting the bottom line, now more badly than ever. Bearbeck was the chief of the military arm of IndMilCom. It was his responsibility to make sure that money was needed, and investment required, for ongoing conflicts around the globe. The fighting force of IndMilCom was in the millions internationally and deploying them in war, police actions and exercises all over the world was a full time job for many people. But of course you have to spend money to make money and while the military arm of the government corporation cost trillions, it helped that it made back double and sometimes triple what it cost most years.

IndMilCom was spread over most of the civilised continents subcontracting governmental services and military might. They rarely ended up fighting their own forces, but sometimes they just had to do it as a show of strength for public consumption. Casualties of their own people through friendly fire were called "natural wastage."

But war was not a problem. War was now a well oiled business machine that just worked on its own. The next moves were always obvious from the decades long playbook. If you had a new government in a country with natural resources and natural enemies, all you had to do was find out if they were going to give you those resources cheaply. If not, you send an army in to overthrow them in favour of the guys who would. It's not personal, only business.

The only real problem they had was the power of the consciousness movement, those "One Life/One Mind Alliance" bastards. They just clogged up the works all over. Politics, activism, even ecoterrorism - ye gods! Something really needed to be done about them. They were really getting close to being properly organised.

The core of them had a name and a unified purpose, but

there were other separate groups with similar aims and objectives who were part of that loose alliance. They had to be stopped joining up properly, becoming a coherent mass, self aware of its own true size and weight and existence.

You had to laugh. The only thing standing in the way of the victory of the consciousness movement . . . was a lack of self awareness.

The minister broke into his own thoughts. "So in light of this report, we need to discuss what plans you have, through your domestic police divisions, to curb this threat to the economy."

The general put out his cigar stub and languidly lit another while the minister was talking.

"Well sir, this is a very complex and nuanced problem. First and foremost, it's an information technology problem. We can direct our information farms at the various identified leaders of One Mind and discredit them as they emerge. We have teams of skilled social copywriters being fed leads by the AIs daily, over a hundred thousand people here in the capital alone. They can keep the narrative on track, make sure that these eco freaks don't get a foothold in the public consciousness."

He drew on his cigar for a moment and let that sink in.

"But that's just standard propaganda housekeeping, business as usual, you might say eh? Haha. No, we have a *new* project."

The minister was growing impatient. "With respect, I understand all that, but what's needed is something to syphon off the anger and injustice people feel, direct it away from the government like a lightning rod. Perhaps we need to bring forward the World War Show we were going to launch in three years time . . ."

The general held up his hand. "No, no. This new project may remove the need for that entirely, saving a LOT of money. It's a multipronged approach. This new system is one we've been working on for some time, a new Internetworked computer system called The Feed, a replacement for NARPAnet. We deploy this in combination with a new suite of mood altering drugs we developed in our medical division, based on rainforest bugs. It makes people voracious for news and yet totally unable to absorb it emotionally. But we can't just spring it on them, we have to soften them up a bit first. The details are in the folder."

He slid the folder over to the aide closest, a young plump man with square glasses. He opened the folder and presented it to the minister. The minister skimmed the first few sentences while speaking, "okay, this is good, but how do we make them take the drugs?"

The general grinned broadly. The small cigar in his mouth did a little uptick like an erection. As an expert in military strategies he was a skilled magician and exponent of the art of social sleight of mind.

"You get them to want to take it."

The properties of the new drug Gatremed were very useful. It was a mid range antianxiety med, also good with depression as it didn't make you high or low, it just made you *level*. At first it was a relief to be level, but then you didn't notice how *aggressively* level it kept you. The effects took only days to happen, but two weeks or more to wear off. It was also very mildly addictive. It got more addictive over time. Plus there was no law of diminishing returns, your body never got used to it.

Also, it was an effective but safe analgesic, so replacing other more dangerous pain meds was a no brainer. Plus you couldn't die from an overdose. The effect didn't rise the more you use. There was what they called "the Goldilocks dose". Not too hot, not too cold, but just right.

And best of all it was very sweet and had a caramel aftertaste, so it could be used in artificial sweeteners, breath mints, candy bars, gum, you name it. It was a total godsend and now it had been fully weaponized by Bearbeck's medical division, it was ready to go and in vast quantities.

"Okay, so we have to raze a lot of rainforest areas to the ground to harvest the bugs, but we guess we have about 30 years supply just on the 30% of total tree cover we processed already."

The minister smiled properly. This sounded very, very good.

Bearbeck continued. "We need to make people want to take it. Everyone is in some kind of pain whether physical or mental. All you have to do is provide them an easy method to access it and they'll chug that shit down before they've even thought about it. Then all you have to do is direct the infofarms into stopping anyone looking too closely at what we put into it."

The General puffed his cigar in silence for a moment or two. He knew it was a perfect plan. Soon they'd have those ecofreaks in the palm of their hands.

The minister seemed to have heard enough. He handed the folder to one of his assistants and rested his hands in front of him. "Very well. I'm convinced. Put this plan into action as you have described. My aide here," he indicated the man on his left with the folder, "will be your point of contact day to day and he will keep me informed of anything that's important for me to hear. I will leave you in his capable hands."

The minister rose and he and the other aide left the room without much ceremony, talking softly.

The general looked at the aide. He opened his mouth to talk. He looked nervous. General Bearbeck held his hand up.

"It's okay son. No need to do the credential speech. I'm sure you've done a lot of important things and I should trust you, but here's the thing. Your boss just vouched for you. You've inspired his trust. That's good enough for me. You have all my contacts in the folder. We only need to talk when we have something to say, but I recommend we catch up at least once a week. I'll have someone from the medical division get in touch so you can have access to the research and production. The science division will send you the Feed specs so we can start rolling that out too. I think we're done here. Happy?"

The aide nodded awkwardly.

"Well, alright then. What's your name, kid?"

"Robert Watson Banks."

They shook hands firmly.

"You're going to be okay, kid. Relax."

Robert Watson Banks would think about that meeting often in years that followed. General Bearbeck was a legend. Of course, after The War his reputation and memory were somewhat tarnished. But the general was a well known historical figure and Banks was glad he got to meet and work with him.

Well, he himself was working for a lot of people at the time. At the same time as he was high up in the chief minister's team, he was secretly handing information to the One Mind Alliance. Once The War kicked off with The Incident, Banks was extracted and joined the resistance full time.

When The War ended he was given the task of dealing with all the captured leaders of IndMilCom.

Banks entered the interrogation room. The captured General Bearbeck looked dishevelled and tired. The general recognized him instantly because before Banks could sit down he said "Smaller table this time, eh kid?"

The comment was timed perfectly. Banks was secretly hoping that Bearbeck wouldn't recognise him, but dammit if the old boy didn't have a memory for faces.

"You've come a long way from being the minister's pet," he added.

"I think we all have General and *just to be clear*, I'm using your rank merely as a courtesy recognition. It doesn't mean you have any authority here. Make no mistake, you're my prisoner. Are we crystal?"

Bearbeck chuckled wearily without opening his mouth. "Sure, kid. Whatever you say."

Bearbeck had aged a lot during the conflict, his crew cut had grown out revealing his male pattern baldness. His beard had grown out grey. His eyes, always watchful pale beads, were a little red rimmed. He still wore his uniform, but with the insignia removed and intentionally distressed to make it look like a hand me down. He'd picked up a few minor facial scars, healed and pale against his leathery skin. Other than being a little thinner from not getting any regular state dinners, he looked strong and unnervingly ready for a fight.

When he'd been captured he wasn't fleeing for his life, he was setting booby traps and making the resistance advance more difficult and dangerous.

"Don't suppose you have a smoke, do you kid?"

Banks shook his head, but he looked over at the guard and nodded and the guard took one out of a breast pocket and lit it for him.

Clearly the general hadn't had one in a while, as he enjoyed it rather noisily and refused to answer until he'd enjoyed it all lavishly.

Banks was taking his time. He was about to get a man who took no crap from anyone to tell him something he didn't want to talk about, and which didn't benefit him in any way. It was a tough sell, but Banks loved tough sells. He was on this side of the desk and not the other because he knew how to ask for what he wanted and get it.

The War had been costly on both sides, as wars almost

always are. The fight was for freedom. For centuries it was the haves who told the have-nots what they could and couldn't have. It was the haves who told the have-nots how much they could have. It was the haves who skilfully, over the years, programmed the have-nots into wanting things they didn't need, in return for working for the haves. It was the haves who promoted shallow gain, shallow experience and shallow relationships.

Relationships with people, food, money, clothing, transport and entertainment, were all shallow and based on "more". The public interest in politics and news was reduced to shallow entertainment. Real world issues like ecology, pollution, hunger, sustainable resources, responsible land and animal use were reduced to intellectual exercises on The Feed. Action and activism were reduced to a war of words, a theoretical arm-wrestle between people who were more focused on winning than changing anything. The spectators of these online wars of words then spun off these wars of words into their own wars of words, never action.

A versus B.

B wins.

C tells D and E that B was wrong.

D agrees, but E doesn't then it's D vs E, while C goes to A and gets them to choose a side in D vs E and so on.

Countless millions of fractally replicating arguments in the virtual world of The Feed, taking all the fight out of people. So when it came to the real world, they were convinced of the notion that whatever it was they had *put it right*. They had in fact done nothing.

The Algorithms in The Feed, programmed by the General's science division, matched people together to deliberately inflame their antagonism and sense of injustice. When inklings were gleaned from the Feed taps that someone was *actually verbalising dissent*, it was a red flag. The AIs on The Feed made sure that dissent was split and diffused in all directions before it turned into the thing that was the actual enemy. Real world action.

Eventually when the AIs on the feed and the Gatremed had been working on people for a while, dissent was very rare. If it emerged at all in the real world, it was surgically stomped by the secret police. Nobody knew why, but activists were very strangely accident prone.

The only reason the Alliance ever had any advantage was people like Banks, IndMilCom defectors with all the answers. People who knew where the AIs were and the locations of the main cabling for The Feed.

They reprogrammed the AIs to stop promoting shallow diffusion and start promoting deep thoughts.

They changed the AIs to ignore dissenters and focus instead on weeding out negativity and hatred.

They made everyone understand that action in the real world was much more important than wasting their energy on The Feed.

The AIs told everyone that human consciousness was being deliberately eroded and spoiled by people who were doing it just so they could farm the money out of us. We were not the population. We were a crop.

Banks sat quietly while Bearbeck finished his smoke and put it out on the corner of the table. The general's confidence was quite intimidating, but yeah, hard sells were a Good Thing. He took a deep breath. He was going to go in hard.

"Your wife," he began pausing deliberately too long to observe the change of light in Bearbeck's eyes. "Where is she now?"

"Dead. You guys zat gunned the house while we were inside clearing out. She caught one in the chest and bled out. I cleared out before you followed through."

"Actually, you left a little too soon . . ." Banks allowed a whiff of a laugh in his voice. Satisfyingly, this had a more visible effect on Bearbeck's face that he couldn't fully control. "She actually was found by the followup troops and while she was critically injured, she was stabilised on site and moved to a secure facility. Is this news to you?"

Bearbeck's eyes and facial muscles had a fight with his will for a few moments. His hand tightened on the table ever so slightly.

Banks pretended not to notice. The guard was watching closely.

Banks licked his finger and flipped a page in the folder. He loved folders.

"Oh, she is alive. Did I not say that? I should have led with that. Yes, she made a full recovery. Mrs Janice Bearbeck is currently undergoing retraining. She's doing quite well."

Bearbeck's fist hardened to a boulder and he lifted it and brought it down very hard on the desk. Banks felt the shockwave up his arm and his teeth clacked. The guard clicked the safety on his stunner. Bearbeck's eyes flicked to the sound and then back to Banks. He took a deep controlled breath and relaxed.

"In addition, I'm afraid I've been granted power of life and death over you. Even if you are innocent of all charges and fully cooperate. I can have you killed just because I feel like it, nobody will care. They only grant PLD orders to the VIPs, the higher ups in the old order. People like you."

Bearbeck snapped. "*Our old order! You were there too, Banks!*" The voice was like rocks falling down a cliff.

"Yes, yes I was. And after I helped the resistance tear IndMilCom down, I was interviewed by someone who had a PLD order on me too. Feels nicer to be on this side of the table, I must say."

The general looked like an angry gorilla. But Banks saw a tiny speck of respect twinkling in the old soldier's eyes. Just a whisper. It said, well done kid, you had a shot and you took it. I'd have done the same.

"So in order to, you know, not die and live out your old age with your wife, what can you give me?" Banks was done. Perfection.

The general sat back, it was finished, he knew that. He was tired and he was through being a dick about it.

"Okay, kid, you win." He sighed. "I know everything. I know where the graves are. I know where the gold is, and where all the art is. I also know where the hole is, the hole that traitor T. Mark Shamley has been in all these years."

CHAPTER 9

In her dream, the inventor is sitting in a chair. There are bolts of lightning arcing around his body as he read quietly. He is unafraid of the cataclysmic mayhem exploding around him. In the dream, he knows that the wrath of God he has created in this cage can never, would never, harm him. He feels at one with the electrons, the light and the sparks. He feels the high frequency charge in the air. He feels his body alive with the charge gaining life and strength from the electricity.

Sudden stop.

It seems dark here now, even though cracks of daylight peek through into the gloom. His assistant flings open the doors. His name is Perry or sometimes Jerry. It changes. The inventor's name is always the same, and will always be the same.

Tesla.

His thin face, with its pencil moustache and centre parted hair, is white and mostly unwrinkled. He is 78 years old. It's 20th year of the Star, or what you'd perhaps call 1935. He's tall, over 6 feet, and he hops up out of the chair and walks briskly out of the door smiling at Perry as he goes, wishing him a cheery "Halloo". He walks strongly and erect seeming like a man half his age. His energy and vitality are legendary. He lives for another 51 years, finally dying at the extraordinary age of 129 in the 23rd year of the High Priestess. The cause of death would be said to be an accident. It was actually murder.

The killer was well known to many, but never faced justice.

After the success of the Wardenclyffe Tower project, in

what you would know as the 1940s the first Tesla towers were built, forming the core of the nation's communication and power infrastructure. It was thought that ten towers could serve all of Sol III, but it turned out the inventor was being a little fanciful with that assertion. A hundred across America in the first few years, then 16 in the British Republic, then a further 48 across Europe, 150 in Africa and the East, and finally 250 in Asia.

By the 21st year of the Wheel of Fortune, what you would call the 1950s, the first NARPA initiative was born. It's symbol, two oval half globes with a lightning bolt in the centre, was the fastest growing IndMilCom funded business. Surveillance became the next fastest.

The first Tesla designed flatscreen displays went on sale in the 21st year of Judgement, at first in monochrome with a purple tint. Colour screens were phased in around the 22nd year of The Magician.

In the dream the year was 1963 but sometimes it changes to the 22nd year of The Magician. The Tarot calendar was founded in the Renaissance and while other calendars were in use in other cultures, the Tarot calendar was preferred by the West. It was anti-logical to favour such an antiquated and semi-mystical system, but most saw no problem with a bit of fun. The date flicked back and forth between the two for a while, like a Visor caught between two frequencies, one second The Magician, one second 1963, one second the Magician, one second 1963.

The inventor changed too. Sometimes he died in the 23rd year of the High Priestess, sometimes he died in 1943. Sometimes Wardenclyffe was a huge success. Sometimes it was abandoned and pulled down in 1917.

The pivotal point it seemed is when it became known to J.P. Morgan, the financier behind Tesla, that the inventor was working on a wireless power infrastructure in tandem with the Tesla towers broadcast capability. In the dream, he stormed into Morgan's office and slapped his hand down on Morgan's desk.

Morgan had many millionaire friends in the oil and coal and gas businesses. He couldn't let Tesla's ideas of free broadcasting and power for all ruin global multimillion coin businesses. Morgan's gimlet eyes glowered between his brow and over his impressive moustaches.

In another version of the dream, Tesla storms into the office and puts his hand gently onto the desk with the plans of the prototype V.I.S.O.R. Powered by the Tesla Tower, and connected to the Internetwork, the device permitted commerce, advertising and secret two-way broadcasting, allowing both telephonic communication, but also surveillance and data collection. Surely Morgan's friends in government would be interested in that?

But in that version of the dream, the wireless power revolution was still for nearly 50 years. During The War Tesla would work with his young assistant, Thomas, to finally bring the wireless power system online, and begin the manufacture of the free, unbreakable and infinitely upgradable Slate computers. When the magician of light died his young friend Thomas carried on his work and research, later branching out to form his own research group.

In other versions, Thomas killed Tesla and started using the technology for The War effort, while secretly working on another more personal project. He was discovered and imprisoned on an island fortress automatically maintained by silent robots so there was no human contact. He was interrogated relentlessly in the hope he would divulge the secret of his research.

In Jane's sleeping mind all the versions of the dream were valid. All of them were history, they have been, they are and always will be the past, present, and future riding on parallel rails, and not one carriage on the train trailing behind the other. She saw Tesla speaking . . .

"There is but one time, and only one perfect moment of existence. The past, present, and future are always with us. There is no time, only space. It is just our perception that moves back and forth in time, like moving a tape back and forth on a tape head.

"The past has happened. The future has happened. The present only has existence when it happens, so happening is a meaningless construct. Time just is."

In Jane's dream Tesla says his cheery *Halloo* to Perry and exits the test building. Perry has no idea why the old man spent an hour there each day. He puts it down to eccentricity. The inventor said for years he enjoyed the invigorating effects of electricity. He bathed daily in the high frequency waves like a shower of energy. He always emerged refreshed, tingling with energy, bursting with ideas.

He headed off at speed for the first of his two meals a day, light on meat, heavy on vegetables. He'd invented an electric cigarette the previous year, fuelled by his dislike of smoking, he didn't partake himself except when he was working. He enjoyed the stimulating effects of coffee and nicotine on his mind, yet disliked their effects on his health. He had Perry make a strong pot of coffee every morning after his energy bath, and poured himself a cup, but deliberately did not drink it. Smoking he could not resist entirely. "I have smoked a good deal," he speaks as if to a camera, "I gave up at the age of about 20. Smoking stimulates thought in general, only I find it hampers concentration on specifics."

On the whole the inventor preferred to maintain his body and train his mind to a chisel point. He preferred this to maintaining neither and artificially stimulating himself to compensate.

In the dream Tesla was fit and healthy and able to walk briskly between the laboratory buildings until he was 101 years old. He was sometimes old and frail and living in a hotel on his own. Again the image flickered and changed like faulty tuning on a Visor. Sometimes the Visor was a wooden CRT TV set with a cloth covered speaker.

It was 1980 or the 22nd year of the Moon, and Tesla and Thomas were conducting a new experiment. The inventor liked modern music and allowed Thomas to bring in his own records. Sometimes it was Television or some other New York bands. Other times, it was the Fucking Limeys or Static State. Sometimes Tesla even wanted to hear Billy Jesus, although he didn't know the name. "Play the one about boots, Thomas," he'd say. He was referring to "The Boot Is Already On The Other Foot", a classic.

So the music was blaring and the coils were powering up. These new coils had a distinctive rocket like cone shape, a row of six of them, all with brass nose-cones and glass discs on the top. The coils were tuned and focused on an arch of coiled wire woven through with crystalline beads of what looked like glass, but could have been a kind of acrylic or crystal. Tesla stood before a large 70 inch flat display watching numbers and graphs rise and fall as Thomas adjusted the levels with huge black plastic rotary knobs.

"Tune the gain up a little," said Tesla, his slight accent still quite noticeable even after all these years. "Okay, that's sufficient. Thank you Thomas. We may proceed."

Thomas wiped his palms on his lab coat. He couldn't afford to have the rotary control slipping out of his hands at this stage.

The coils were purring. Intense interference patterns of violet light danced over the domes. Tesla returned to his chair and waited. As Thomas grasped the control the inventor said softly, "gently, Thomas, if you please."

Thomas smiled and nodded.

Back in the 20th year of the Star, Tesla took a walk as part of his interest in physical culture and for about an hour walked briskly around the hills. It was only a few months away from his 79th birthday. He was pondering an interesting thought. He was working on a theory of alternate worlds, the possibility of their existence for a start, and the very real notion of travel to other realities. It would need power of course, possibly more power than exists now, and there was perhaps something else. The Power of Mind. He wasn't sure it was relevant.

In her dream, the death of Tesla took two forms.

In one form he died after being struck by a taxi cab in 1937, which made him unable to exercise and started a decline of health, which ended in 1943 in poverty and obscurity.

In another form he was discovered in the 23rd year of the High Priestess by Thomas, his trusted assistant, dead in his energy bath lab, having been pierced through the chest by an anomalous bolt of what looked like lightning. Although the cause of death was almost certainly from an intentional bolt of coherent pulsed frequency plasma and not the energy bath's high frequency charge, this subtlety was lost on the inquest.

His death was ruled accidental and international days of mourning were held. The father of modern technology was celebrated, and his tomb in New York was a place of pilgrimage and tourism. There was even a religion called the "Teslaites", although the Church of Light and Energy detested that term. The Stone Tesla Tower was considerably shorter than the 180 feet of a real tower, but was still an iconic and imposing presence like the man himself; it cast a very long shadow around the world.

On the day of the experiment Thomas grabbed the main

dial again. He wondered if he would find out the purpose of this new experiment now. Nikola was being very secretive about it. He just said "maybe something, maybe nothing. Until we try it the only objective is just that, to try." Then he smiled enigmatically. Damn, he was infuriating.

As gradually and as gently as he could, and with both hands to ensure proper grip, he turned the main dial, incrementing the frequency. The computers in The Feed controlled the other parameters, as the frequency rose, other levels fell. Some parameters rose and fell in a gradual sine wave. The screens looked like a child's drawing toy. Thomas' gradual turning of the dial being smoothed and augmented.

The frequency rose. The coils began to arc between each other, flowing white worms of electricity and plasma, then purple tendrils with white roots like a plasma ball. The tendrils got fatter and danced all around the domes, arcing sometimes to the loosely woven cage around them. Tesla just sat there with the electric tendrils playing around him, seeming to trust they would not strike him. They never did.

Now Thomas was reaching the upper limits of frequency. This was the highest he'd ever seen. This made him tentative and he slowed down a little. Over the din of the arcs dancing around the room Tesla shouted, "Courage, Thomas!"

Thomas clenched his lips and continued to raise the frequency smoothly.

Higher and higher. The air was charged, the light from the arcs was blinding even through the tinted spectacles. The sound, a thrumming, vibrated in their chests. Without fanfare Tesla leant forward to a console within his reach and flipped the cover from a large toggle switch and pushed it up with difficulty from OFF to ON.

SNAP.

There was a palpable release of energy in the room, as if the energy was a large plastic sack of liquid and it had been punctured, allowing the contents to drain. The prickling in their skin lessened and they felt a gentle pull towards the arch.

The arch began to glow.

In her dream she was doing normal things. Things she did when she wasn't asleep. She got up, got dressed and brushed her teeth. In the dream, she remembered her name. Her name was Jane. Why was she dreaming about being awake? She felt odd that morning. There was a yawning sensation, like tension or excitement in the pit of her stomach.

She stood at her kitchen window with a coffee watching the twin contrails of a jet, drawing a diagonal line across the sky. Had this happened already, she thought. "Has this happened already?" the self in the dream said out loud.

Oh, that was weird.

Her dream self agreed.

She had had trouble with her mind before, in fact she was on medication at one time. The medication gave her weird dreams.

Ironic.

First she was sad for a long time, then she was happy, then she was angry. Really, really angry. They said it was brain chemistry and gave her medicine which levelled her out. She wasn't 100% sure what that meant, brain chemistry. Surely everyone has that? Anyway in the dream she was happy. That was a good phase.

"Yes, it was," her self in the dream said. Although what did she know? She knew this would be a problem for her later, when it was time to explain her experience. But her self in the dream hadn't had the experience yet. Soon the two timelines would converge. The Jane of now and the Jane of then would meet. When the experience began. She hoped the dream would include the experience so she could see it objectively from the outside this time.

Her dream self put down the coffee cup unwashed on the counter and put on her coat. Her bag was on the floor and she picked it up and put it on, strap across her body. So much crime these days, better to be safe than sorry. She couldn't find her keys. They were not in the bowl. The Jane of now knew they were in the pocket of her other coat. Suddenly the Jane of the dream remembered having them while wearing the coat and transferred them to her pocket.

One last look around, she was sure she'd forgotten something, but she couldn't think what it was. She looked at herself in the tall hall mirror. Her face looked thin. Her eyes were clear, but she had bags under them. That was always a little bit of a red flag regarding her mood. She needed to take care of herself or sometimes she went off the rails before she knew it and it was hard to get back on them once she was off.

In the dream she could look at herself looking at herself. As with any overview of a disaster, the damage doesn't look so bad from the air. On the ground, the devastation seems endless, but from above you can see the destruction, but also where the destruction ends. You can see where the trees begin to become green again and buildings untouched by fire or demolition. You can see beyond the rubble and see blue sky and hear the birds.

With a sigh she puts on her mask and opens the door and closes it behind her. Outside on the step, she turns to walk down the path.

In the centre of the path the air is rippling as if in heat. The air looks like water, refracting the street beyond in the slowly moving ripples.

She watches her own face. She sees incomprehension, but no fear. She's curious but not afraid. Suddenly she hears a loud snap and the centre of the distortion darkens and inside the area she begins to see shapes. Bright flashes and ropes of light and gradually the shape of a man rising slowly from a sitting position and removing dark glasses. She sees his face.

Tesla rose to his feet and regarded the inside of the arch. The bright centre showed a door and a woman wearing some kind of surgical mask. The woman was staring right at him. They stood there for several moments. Tesla, slender and neatly dressed, very tall and ramrod straight. His clothing was old fashioned, even for the times. The woman, dark hair cut quite short, a bag strap across her chest. Her eyes locked with his for a long, almost eternal moment. She held up her hand.

Thomas was transfixed. What have they done? What manner of world have they broken into? Was it space or time? He desperately wanted to ask.

Tesla held his hand up. Thomas halted the rotation of the control. Tesla turned and smiled.

White Flash.

The sound was so loud, so sudden, their ears couldn't fully hear it until several seconds after it had stopped. Fragments of coil and an entire dome blew in all directions, the biggest part of the dome glancing across Thomas' brow on its way to crash through the flat screen, sending sparks out in an enormous plume. Both he and Tesla were knocked off their feet by the shock wave. The image in the arch collapsed and the energy which had been held there by the coils snapped back to where it belonged, violently.

The silence that followed was only punctuated by falling fragments of coil components and the bars of the cage, which ticked and clunked and clanged around them for several seconds. They rose, coughing, Thomas rushing to help the inventor to his feet. Tesla shrugged him off, and regarded the damage.

In the dream Tesla's face is hard to read. Surprised by the explosion, annoyed by the failure and destruction of the equipment. But mainly triumph.

"I was right Thomas. I was right. Oh, not about the equipment being able to handle it, but it worked. We punched a hole."

Thomas gaped. "But in what, Nikola? Time or space?"

"Neither or both." He chuckled. "Things like this are very hard to talk about, Thomas, please stop asking questions."

Thomas thought he knew what they'd done. Eliminate the impossible and what remains . . .

He touched his forehead and there was lots of blood on his fingers. Why did Tesla not seem concerned that he was hurt? He watched as his mentor sifted through the wreckage, oblivious to Thomas' thoughts and feelings. All that mattered in this moment was the work, and the inventor was deep in thought.

Thomas dabbed his head with a clean cloth. It wasn't clotting, it might need a stitch. Sometimes you needed help to bind a wound, to close it so it would heal fully. What would he need to close and heal the breach of his trust for Tesla? That grave thought would be with him for some time.

CHAPTER 10

Jane woke up. She'd been asleep and dreaming, but she could feel the dream draining away like bathwater. There were parts she could remember because they happened to her, they were memories, but then there were those other parts.

Maybe she did that thing all humans do?

That thing we do, as humans. Our brains fill in the blanks when there are gaps in our knowledge. We fill in the gaps with stuff that fits. We tell ourselves stories to fill the voids.

Like when we're being told something by someone and they're leaving parts out. Depending on the sort of person you are, you either think nothing of it, or you speculate about what their motives might be for being so vague. Or you flat out cross examine them until they pony up.

If you're someone with trauma in your life, which is a lot of us, then you test the words for hidden meanings and threats. There are almost as many reasons for withholding information as there are people. But mostly we just forget, get distracted or have our minds on other things when we should be concentrating on what we're saying. Humans are mostly fallible, unreliable chimps who have no business having adult conversations.

So maybe she was doing that thing humans do. Telling little stories to fill in the blanks, as if it were just convenient fictions to make us feel better. But the dream seemed more detailed and prophetic than that. It seemed real.

She was sitting up in bed. She didn't remember going

to bed last night and then she started to remember talking to someone. Terry and a friend of hers, was it Mark?

She looked at the duvet. It seemed fresh and plump and clean. Did Terry change it before she put her to bed? Her phone and her watch were on the bedside table. The watch was a fake Rolex. They called them "homage" watches on eBay. It cost her about two dollars and kept surprisingly good time.

She rubbed her face and took a drink from the glass of water on the side table. It was fresh. The more she woke up, the more the dream drained down the plug hole, so she sat up comfortably and closed her eyes.

A while back, almost by accident, she discovered that dreams don't fade. If you sit and relax soon enough after you wake with the bits you remembered, turning them gently over in your mind, the rest of it would actually come back. It was astonishing but true. Dreams are not transient and impossible to keep. They are like memories. You can rebuild them.

The same brain state that generated the dream, REM sleep, is very close to a deep meditation state. It seems the deeper you go, the closer you get to that level of mind, the more of that buried subconsciousness bubbles up out of the depths into the shallower waters of waking thought.

So she sat, and mentally turned the parts of the dream she did recall over and over.

At first there were just the parts of the dream that were based on real events, memories of The Experience or at least the events leading up to it. The other parts involving the two men and their experiment were a lot more hazy, hard to grasp, like smoke drifting apart. They existed now only as a feeling, a mood almost. Not pictures or sounds, but sense impressions, thought forms. Out of nowhere she thought "like a Lego brick". That was an odd phrase, where did that come from?

She knew the levels of the mind correspond to frequencies in the brain, what are called brainwaves. Different bands of frequencies correspond to different waking or sleeping states on a continuum, a sliding scale from 60-0 mph, so to speak. From consciousness, active thought, all the way down to deep, deep unconsciousness.

The top layers of consciousness were high frequency, where the mind goes fast. The thoughts all fitted together quickly and easily, and everything was conscious, rational and almost scientifically logical.

The bottom layers of consciousness were the depths, such a low level that nobody truly knows where they end, or if they even do.

It's like the difference between the surface of the sea, the waves buffeting your boat, where you have to keep your wits about you and thinking is fast, brightly illuminated by sunlight. In the depths, the Mariana Trench, all is dark and the pressure so intense that all thought must be slow. Many unknown creatures lurk in these depths.

In between these two layers are all the rest: the relaxed, slightly hypnotised state of commuter driving, the inert focused watching TV state, the stubborn can't keep your eyes open, *need to go to bed* state, the peeking in and out between conscious waking and oblivious sleep state. Even once you pass that threshold into sleep where your brain can no longer monitor the situation, there are light sleep and deep sleep states. The deep sleep states have no dreams and at the lowest end they empty out into the dark formless deep of ultimate unconsciousness.

Meditation gave her brain a chance to bring the speed down, to lower her mind into the cooler waters below. As she relaxed, her brainwaves slowed down and down as she went.

One thing you can do at the higher brain wave frequencies is force thoughts. You can force yourself to think about something very easily. Upper levels of mind are a computer, a programmable and reliable logic engine. This is where quiz masters live, and trivia and movie buffs and governmental policy wonks and other annoying brainiacs.

As you go down in the submarine, it gets much harder to force thought and a new method of operation becomes not just desirable but necessary. A lack of judgement, a lack of force, a lack of pushing.

The unformed thought has nowhere definite to go. It drifts endlessly, unless restrained, towards the outer edges of consciousness. Trying to trap a specific thought is no good. Trying to stalk them through the mental undergrowth with your thought gun will not result in a trophy on your wall.

You have to bait the trap. And wait.

She put all the thoughts about the men and their experiment to the centre of her mind and relaxed, slowing her brain waves down, down, down. The thoughts about the men and their experiment were corralled into this space, but she didn't touch them. She didn't force them to go either one way or the other. She did, however, stop them from leaving.

If one of the little thought sheep strayed a little outside the corral, she'd gently pat it back inside, so gently it had no idea it was even being touched. Like this, the ideas get used to sitting there together and they settle down.

The next step is the hard bit. You have to not care what happens next, to actively avoid any predictions about what may follow. Hardest thing to get right and most important thing that you must do. Eventually your bait will attract another thought.

SNAP.

A like minded memory forms nearby and clusters with the first.

She wondered about that analogy. Where did it come from? She'd heard it before somewhere but she couldn't remember where. Oh anyway, focus. Think about that later.

So you incorporate this new memory's mood and stay with just that, the mood, not the facts.

Facts are a surface notion, an awake thought. Creative ideas and lost dreams live in the depths. No facts, just thoughts drifting in the darkness.

Thoughts are like bait. They attract other thoughts, ideas, memories, dreams.

Thoughts are attracted to the thoughts or memories you corralled, like minded thoughts, like attracted to like. Your baited hook.

The trouble with her talking about this stuff to normal people is that she was for most people, a bit of an unreliable witness. Even Terry, her old and dear friend, seem to take a lot of what she said with a pinch of salt. All talk about consciousness had the potential to sound like woo or crazy talk. It wasn't helpful to talk at a level people were uncomfortable with. The problem with being a famously unreliable witness, you had to try harder to be real.

Dreams are like inkjet printed text on sand, intricate sand paintings, beautiful impermanent structures which even the briefest puff or motion of air could disturb, disrupt or destroy. It was important to not disturb the fish in the stream. No loud noises, no sudden movement. Thoughts are easily spooked.

The more memories clustered together on the hook, the more of the dream she could recall.

She saw the rippling air, she saw it darken, she saw the bolts of lightning, shocking and sudden. She raises her hand, he raises his hand.

Consciousness is a treasure, our greatest treasure, our superpower, our glorious inexplicable mind, she thought. It was if she felt she knew a secret and had to tell it, make it not a secret anymore because it being a secret was killing us . . .

She turned the images over in her mind, the little thought sheep in their corral shuffled and grunted, rubbing their fleeces together.

She saw the man, elderly, with his thin grey pencil moustache. He is very tall. He rises out of the chair looking in wonder at her. No, looking in wonder at his side of the arch, which reveals her on the other side. She raises her hand, he raises his hand. He's not waving. He's signalling to someone behind him, signalling him to stop.

The young man behind him looks familiar, but then of course she saw him in the dream, before. The images were becoming clearer.

So how is it you can recall something you've dreamed but forgotten? You have to go back to a similar brain state so that the memory of the dream story can step across the gap between conscious and unconscious. Once they step back into consciousness, they become strong and very hard to forget. It's like going back into the kitchen to remember why you went into the lounge.

The longer she sat, the more of it came back. The coils, the arch, the precision of Thomas's hand on the black control knob. She could even see the old man's suit and tie. His name was Tesla. Nikola Tesla. Didn't Dirk P. Kinder refer to the towers in his valley as Tesla towers?

She opened her eyes. It was all very real to her now. She could remember the dream. Or at least one version of it. There seemed to be a couple of different ones overlaid, but these were the strongest, the most real.

She remembered it right to the end. There was the part that was real and the bits that were, what? Improvisations based on the little she saw? Tesla was a real person though, she googled him on her phone. He died in 1943. In the dream version he was still alive in what looked like the 80s. This felt like it meant something, but she wasn't sure what.

Something else occurred to her now she'd had a little time to process it all. The arch had formed on her path, an arch shaped hole in the air, in reality itself. But her transition to the other reality didn't happen till after. She definitely saw the arch shaped hole collapse. There was a pop and a violent blast of air, and then she fell back against the door.

It was only a few seconds after that that she took a step and her foot landed on grass and not her path, and the air temperature changed, and the wind was suddenly from a different direction, sweeter, fresher. She looked up and above her, high in the air, the emitter of the Tesla tower was glowing purple in the sunlight. She'd forgotten the delay, that the two events didn't seem to be related. Maybe they were in some way. She would have to think about that a while. She was trying not to judge the situation, let it unfold to her as it should. But it was hard to do that with things in your life that you desperately wanted to understand. The human tendency is to force the issue, to take a mallet to the square thing that doesn't fit and beat the hell out of it until it submits and fits tightly in the round hole. "Brute force butters no parsnips" as her grandmother would say.

No.

She had to handle it delicately, like the thought sheep in the corral, pat it gently, keep it right there, till the meaning fully revealed itself.

She wanted to sit a little longer and see if there was anything else. But she was starting to feel hungry and thirsty. She started to wonder if she had any milk. She patted that thought gently away. She would get up and have some breakfast in a moment. She just wanted to run through it one more time.

She saw the experiment. The old inventor sat in his chair, bolts of electricity snaking past him impossibly fast. The stereo was playing music, a band called Static State that she had never heard of. The music was coming from an eighties style boombox, which looked shiny and new but in a design she had never seen before. The coils power up, the flat displays show rising levels and the two men obviously feel this is good. Thomas turns the dials and the coil's frequency goes higher than it has ever been. The arch starts to glow. The ripples in the air begin to reveal a portal. In space? In time? Probably both.

The old man rises out of his chair, slowly as if it's uncomfortable, but his eyes are fixed on the arch, on her. His eyes are bright, shiny with excitement. She raises her hand as if to wave. He raises his hand as if to wave back.

Except.

He's not waving, she has no idea if he can see her or not.

He's signalling to Thomas to hold the frequency there.

She's not waving either. Her hand is up in front of her face and there's a point of light shining out of her palm.

She opened her eyes and swung her feet over the side of the bed. She sat there for a minute staring. Her breath was catching in her throat and she coughed.

Terry let herself in with the spare key. She wondered if Jane would still be sleeping, it had been 12 hours. In the living room she found Jane on the sofa, staring. Her knee was jiggling as she bounced her foot. Nervous, thought Terry.

"You okay love?" she leaned slowly into Jane's field of vision. Jane looked at her and said nothing, just raised her phone and showed the screen. On the screen was a photograph. It looked a little like the view from Jane's front door.

There was something wrong with the image. The centre of it looked like a large burn hole, like an old timey projector lamp had boiled and bubbled and burned it through, except . . .

There was a man there, halfway up from getting out of a chair, a distinguished looking hollow cheeked man, really tall.

"Who is that?"

"That's Nikola Tesla. That's what I saw when I left my house that morning. I just remembered, I took a picture on my phone."

Terry sat down heavily and tore the strap of her bag over her head so she could drop it to the floor. "Wow. Jane. This is huge. You have a picture! That's a document, literal documentary evidence."

"Well I have documentary evidence of something. Just not the trip into another dimension."

Terry frowned, "Hang on. You took this picture. Then you took your phone into the other dimension. Why didn't you take some pictures of a Tesla tower or a giant butterfly or an airship or Dirk P. Kinder?"

Jane didn't speak, but a small groan escaped her lips. "You'd think that would be the first thing to occur to me. I did think of it, but my phone was back in my bag. I thought about taking some pictures, but I put it off. I thought, I'll take some in a minute, save battery. Then I came over all tired and next thing I knew I was waking up and it was dark." She let out a little groan again. "Then we talked a bit more and then mid-sentence I popped out of existence there and popped back into existence here."

Terry picked up the phone and flipped the pictures back and forth. She landed back on the photo of Tesla. She looked at the picture again, scrutinising the edge of the rippling arch for signs of inexpert Photoshop work. It looked pretty real. She laughed to herself. Real. That was a word that was fast going out of style.

Then she frowned. "Jane?"

Jane made a hmm sound.

"Jane, who is this in the picture, in the background?"

Jane massaged her eyes. "The young man in the back is Tesla's assistant, Thomas."

"Did you say Thomas?"

"Yep. He said his name several times."

"Jane, seriously. Don't you think that looks like someone we know?"

Jane looked at the screen over Terry's arm.

"Yeah, actually I do, but I couldn't figure out who it was."

"It looks like Mark."

Jane blinked. "Well, yes it does, but it can't be. He looks much younger. Much. And his name is Thomas."

Terry pressed her lips together and exhaled slowly through her nose. "I've known him for about 20 years off and on and that's what he used to look like."

Jane sat up, suddenly very awake.

"And many years ago he stopped using his first name and became known by his middle name, a sort of disguise after a mistake of some kind he's always been really vague about. His first name when I met him was Tom. His full name is Thomas Mark Shamley."

The previous evening, Brother Mark drove his hybrid car along a dark stretch of road. Trees lined the road forming a wall on either side. The strong headlights formed a tunnel ahead of him. The stereo in the car blared

Television playing "Marquee Moon". Mark hummed along. It felt weird to be in good spirits with all that was going on.

He felt both disturbed and elated by the events of the last day. He'd always had an academic interest in alternative worlds, but this was the first time he'd ever heard of anyone professing to have actually visited one. It was thrilling.

These things had been theories for some considerable time. Something being possible in theory was one thing, but proof, no matter how slight, was entirely another thing. He wanted to help Jane, he truly did, and while he could see she had a few mild mental health problems, there was a real nugget of something true in what she'd told him. Something he needed.

He drove the car into the driveway of The Lodge. Lights were showing in some of the windows, even at this late hour. He should call a meeting and talk to some of the department heads. They needed to decide what they could do to help.

He entered the Lodge through the library. He walked up and down the shelves. He was sure it was here. After a few minutes and just as he was about to give up, he found it, misfiled under J.

The book was old, not too old, it was self-evidently a paperback book from the 70s. The page edges were brown, the cover was decorated with yellow and brown arch patterns. The book was well read and white cracks were visible down the spine and along the edges of the cover.

The title of the book was "Alternative Worlds and How to Visit Them" by Joseph Denkert.

CHAPTER 11

T. Mark Shamley entered the stage and walked to the lectern at its centre. He waved to the crowd and they applauded and cheered. There were about 1500 people in the audience, all members of the Shamley Org. The stage was rigged with purple and gold curtains and at the rear of the stage was a huge picture of Shamley looking avuncular and understanding.

He regarded his congregation with kindness and they returned his gaze with warmth. Adoration was a dangerous energy and he was aware of how it could turn a man's head. It was rather nice though.

Shamley was either in his late fifties or early sixties, and he wore a light coloured hand tailored suit which fitted him. He was bearded, somewhat wiry and unkept, and his hair was long and clasped in a ponytail. The kindness in his eyes was a well practised lie.

He was a scientist, minister of the gods, author and Guru to all present. He had just arrived by Maglev from the capital. He'd slept on the train because he already knew what he was going to say tonight and was not nervous or apprehensive in any way. He was keen, excited.

After years of experimentation and testing, they were finally getting some success. The problem with the original experiment conducted by his mentor was that it relied on brute force. With the new, more powerful Tesla towers a little went a long way. But more important was the human component. As soon as he met Joe Denkert he knew that he had something, the gods were kind and he embraced this new test subject fully.

Joe's energy was tremendous. He had an incredible

sense of purpose and a commitment that was palpable. Denkert had a natural aptitude for the work, but Shamley knew all about that. He had been watching Joe long before he ever joined the Shamley Org. He'd actually been secretly grooming and directing him from the beginning.

The waiting crowd grew silent and watchful and soon you could hear a pin drop.

"Life," he began, "is not what we think it is. Reality is just a convenient fiction we tell ourselves, a story we weave to allow ourselves to function. We know it to be true." A few scattered *oh yeah*s in the audience. "*We know it to be true!*" A huge chorus of *oh yeahs*.

He surveyed the upturned faces like small rows of cookies with dried fruit eyes in the glare from the spotlight.

"Our cute little brains don't have the power to process all of reality. It's true. The electrical activity of the brain is about 20 watts. That's a pretty dim bulb, am I right?" A patter of appreciative laughter. "In order for us to glean anything from our subjective reality, we have to be very selective about what we pay attention to. Understandably, this has caused us problems." The curtains had been smoothly parting since he began speaking. The huge dark screen they concealed leapt into life with a photo of the world.

"This is Sol III. You may recognize it. You live there. In all the time this beautiful blue marble has been hanging in space, mankind has been trying to protect it and ensure our survival. What has been the enemy? Greed? Capitalism? The need for constant growth? Pollution? Unsustainable industrial energy production?

"Well, all of the above, but if you lived through The War or read about it in a book, you know all about that. But we didn't beat the enemy. Now, despite the resistance and the toppling of the evil IndMilCom, we never defeated the true enemy. Because the true enemy is ourselves."

People allowed him to skim past the part where he worked for IndMilCom. But then he'd long since spun his own narrative about his past. People were happy to buy his version of events. He'd helped bring down IndMilCom. He wasn't a failed scientist who they locked away and threw away the key. He was a hero who worked in secret to bring them down.

The screen showed a long beautifully edited and expensive montage of historical photos and film.

"Before The War we were asleep. We let the myth of capitalism and its trickle down model persuade everyone. *The best thing for the planet was a healthy economy.* If the economy was good, we were told, then we could afford to be sustainable and responsible later on and spend the money we made to end hunger and poverty. But before we could address any of that, we had to buckle our belts, work hard, pay our taxes, and hang on till the economy showed enough consistent growth . . . so that we could have the spare money for so-called good causes."

He shook his head and smiled. He leaned close to the mic.

"Does any of this language sound familiar to the older members of the audience?" A round of applause and a mixed laugh and groan rippled across the congregation. "It was of course a lie, the Big Lie. Not the first one we'd been told, and I'm pretty sure it won't be the last, but it was the simplest and most deadly lie ever told. Thank the gods! We woke up. Thank the gods we fought back. What would we be facing otherwise? Irreversible climate change, poverty and disease. Would it be better to be playing a global game of what's going to kill us first? Projections by my scientists before The War told us all of the above would be true. But instead, thanks to patriots and heroes, we have a global information system, free power, free communications, a basic living wage for every civilised human being on Sol III, regardless of birth or circumstance. We have equality, true equality where every human on Sol III is of equal value to every other.

"So now we've had all this human freedom for so long, nearly 30 years since IndMilCom fell, what are our major goals? What can we do to make life better? What gift can you possibly give to the mankind that has everything, my friends? We already have the development of human consciousness as a priority in education and business. What more can we do?"

He paused significantly.

"The answer is simple. We expand consciousness to encompass not just awareness of this reality, but *all realities*." There was a beat, then the crowd erupted with cheering and applause.

T. Mark Shamley let the wall of sound hit him and wash around him. In his mind's eye he saw the sound as coloured streams of light like smoke in a wind tunnel. They curved around his body and met up again behind him. Yes, he thought, sound is a very important part, but we'll deal that later.

The problem with higher truth is: most people aren't ready for it. You have to limber up to the main message. He'd been educating his followers for years now, giving them one piece of information, then another. Piece by small piece of the overall puzzle. Finally, the time is here to reveal the true mission, or at least most of it, and oh how he'd waited for this glorious time.

First, you had to talk about the importance of consciousness. You had to reinforce the importance of daily meditation. The reason for this was left mostly obscure, to be followed up by reasons later on. Of course the reason for the meditation was not so much a daily fix, but an ongoing consciousness conditioning. You don't lift weights because someone's going to knock you down and put a barbell on your neck. You lift weights so nobody can push you over in the first place.

The next level up was the Box. The Box is a device which drives a set of headphones and goggles, playing synchronised sound and light into the eyes and ears of the devotee. Sound and light boxes existed before Shamleyism, but this Box was special as it had its own small AI and was linked to all other Boxes. The Box helped concentrate your meditation and amplify your brainwaves, and train them to go up and down easily and completely under your control. Frequent practice meant all brainwave states were open to you. The AI made subtle changes to the program based on your usage. Also, the Box automatically synced with other Boxes in your vicinity. Another pillar of Shamleyism was information restriction. It was easy to get drowned by information. "With little in the way of safeguards as to the quality and truth of info, abstinence is key" he would say. Actually truth in the media was something you could rely on. But Shamley had other reasons for cutting his congregation off from the mainstream.

"Information is like food," he said, "you must eat every day, but only a fool eats everything without question. You must be circumspect and careful about what you introduce into your body, whether it be food, drink, Visor broadcasts or information, especially information. Once you get an idea in your head, it's almost impossible to get it out. The only way to ensure positive mental hygiene at all times is to consume only what you know to be wholesome and in moderation. The focused mind has no need of constant input and as such can ensure total output."

He'd had many years to develop his mind after he was discovered to be working for both sides in The War, and he was buried in a deep pit in the ground for many years and largely forgotten. The AIs and robots which looked after him were complex entities and "good enough" company, but they were not real people.

He had long periods of silence and contemplation where the only native, constant sound was the rhythmic pulsing of the environmental air conditioning. The frequency was about 5Hz, he guessed, and that was perfect for good meditation. So he sat and he ate and then sat again. He played chess with an AI, whose name was Flawless Ruby. He even had philosophical discussions with her, but in the end it was the silent sitting that saved him.

He wandered through the rooms of a huge house in his mind. At first they were just simple bare cubes. Then he added simple block furniture. Gradually the details got more rich and complex, the decorations more exotic. Soon there were over a hundred rooms in his mind palace and the details were as real as anything in his cell, or dining area, or the robots who quietly ground their ageing servos walking up and down the blue-lit corridors.

He spent more and more time in the mind palace. Why not, when it was more interesting and enjoyable than his comfortable confinement? He had a room with a view of the ocean and over time the simulation in his mind grew in detailed sights and sounds, like the waves crashing on the shore, seabirds circling and cawing, and sometimes even rain on the window. There was a kitchen where he produced sumptuous meals. He could see the stainless steel surfaces, the fresh ingredients, the glossy appliances. He went there before meals and held the vision in his mind as a robot held his hand and walked him with his eyes closed to the cafeteria.

Then there was the quiet room. All the rooms were mostly quiet, ticking or humming with some kind of domestic sound, but the quiet room was filled with comfort and silence. What sounds there were in there were meditative and sometimes he'd go there and sit meditating with his eyes open, letting his gaze roam around the walls at the pictures and objects he placed there, possessions he no longer possessed. He'd sit there and daydream other new meaningful objects into being.

He continued the practice after he was released, and to the present he spent much of his meditation time roaming around his mind palace. On the day in question he was seated cross legged on the fat, plump cushion in the centre of the room. The design of the cushion was never fixed in his mind for some reason. The material was always different. The size was also fluid, sometimes it was small and other times huge. He deliberately let that be unfixed in his mind, almost saying to his unconscious, surprise me. Today it was large and brown, almost like a corduroy fabric. It was so plump that a thick wad of the cushion supported his lower back.

He exhaled and relaxed, allowing his eyes to roam around the room, the walls and the low two tier bookshelf which ran around all four walls. On top of this were trinkets and statues and objects he loved. He greeted them all as old friends.

Then he got to one he didn't recognize, a small stone carving of a goddess with bulbous breasts and stomach. He had no recollection of explicitly bringing that statue into being. He examined it from across the room, or as much detail as he could see from where he sat. It was brown, made of some kind of stone and smooth, quite shiny actually because it caught the light. He also had an odd sensation of felling like his head was being turned gently against his will. As soon as he thought it it passed.

Eventually and carefully because he had the odd uneasy feeling it would blink out of existence again, he rose and softly walked over to it. He stretched out a finger and touched it. Physical sensation was dulled in the mind palace and more of an intellectual experience than a

127

physical one, but this was real. He could feel the cold, smooth surface pushing back against his fingertip. That was so odd. He drew his finger back and touched it again. Again, it was cold and smooth.

There was also a hint of vibration, like when you touch the legs of a Tesla tower, a weird inductive buzz. He touched a model of a horse next to the goddess and it felt numb and theoretical like things always did there. Then he went back and put his whole hand on the goddess who was about the size of a lemon, and it filled his hand with the cool stone.

This was extraordinary. Where had it come from? With his whole hand on it the vibration was very strong. It was like pins and needles when you cut off the circulation in your arm by sleeping on it, but with the intensity turned right down so you could barely feel it. It made him feel reluctant to grasp it fully. He took a deep breath.

This was crazy.

He picked it up and passed it to his other hand. The vibration buzz amplified. It felt like tiny rods pressing his skin rapidly like a pinboard being agitated by a motor. It wasn't painful, but it was becoming uncomfortable.

On a sudden impulse he gripped the goddess tightly with both hands. The vibration grew much more intense, almost violent, uncontrolled still. He gripped it tightly. He held it between his hands and on an impulse he pressed it hard against his forehead. It was uncomfortable and unsettling and he figured the only way out was to push through like removing an arrowhead. I mean, he thought, how bad could it get on contact with his forehead? Why did he think that?

The vibration ripped through his skull like trillions of caviar membranes popping in a Anahuac wave through his body, like microscopic existential bubble wrap being crushed by a steamroller. He inhaled sharply but couldn't let it go. Like stepping into a cold shower, his body revolted, clenched and tried to dive away from the assault, flinging him sideways onto the floor. He landed hard, his head coming into contact with the floor and he saw stars.

He sat up shaking his head to clear it. Something was very wrong with the room. It was sunrise. The Room didn't have times of day. It was always daytime, nonspecific daytime or sometimes night, but mostly endless "day".

The golden beams of sun shone horizontally through the window, making long shadows on the ornaments. The different materials caught the light in different ways, making everything pop in a way he'd never seen before. It was beautiful. He'd seen it very clearly before, but never like this.

A tickle at his cheek made him touch a finger to his face. He couldn't feel anything there, but it did feel slightly slippery. He looked at his finger and was shocked to see bright red blood. He took a piece of his shirt and wiped his face. He could feel a raised welt on his eyebrow ridge. His fall had broken the skin.

A creeping horror and excitement in his chest overflowed over him. This was real. This place he had called into being, a place that only existed in his head was real, so real he'd just busted his head open on it. How was it possible?

He hadn't created this statue. It was all new to him. Nothing about it was familiar. He examined it very closely, running his fingers over each surface carefully. It had many microscopic imperfections, little detailed dinks and pits and blemishes.

It was baffling and overwhelming. He looked up, there was a door. It's funny, he thought, all the time he spent creating and populating the mind palace. He'd never thought much about the doors. They were one of those details he preferred to leave non-specific.

This door however was very specific. It was made of

dark wood. It had four panels in it. The handle was metal, a glossy ball of finely buffed steel. The texture of the wood was exquisite, he'd never imagined it in that much detail. It was then the thought occurred to him, if this room is real, then what else is real? His reluctant hand went to the doorknob and turned it. It moved smoothly under his hand and the latch clicked across, releasing the door easily and when his hand left the knob it swung slightly ajar.

Thinking about it, he had no idea what was outside the door. Of course he knew there was a corridor leading to a drawing room and the kitchen, which would lead to the hallway and the front door, but the details in between were sketchy. He'd always been deliberately vague about the details.

He opened the door.

The corridor beyond was dimly lit. There was a window at one end, but there was a roller blind which was drawn down. The wallpaper was tasteful and had tiny flowers embossed on it. There were pictures in frames, some photos of his family, but one painting of a landscape including a house that was once his family home.

In the drawing room a slight haze, as if someone had been smoking a cigarette, and beams of orange light knifed through the gloom. The objects in the room were as he remembered, the Eames chair, the bust of himself carved in marble. The paintings of the Native American presidents, a model of the first stylish electric land car. All of it was as it should be but more real, more detailed and solid.

Further on the kitchen, much larger than he'd imagined was everything he'd wanted it to be. He was always a little bit vague on where the produce and ingredients came from when he cooked there. A little investigation revealed a larder in the back behind a narrow door. There were sheaves of fresh herbs and vegetables. He took a leaf of basil and crushed it in his fingers. It smelled gorgeous and filled his head with joy. The fridge was large with two doors. He couldn't remember if he'd ever looked inside. The first door was the freezer, lots of frozen vegetables and portions of unlabelled pasta sauce and what he assumed was chilli. On the fresh food side there were salad vegetables, all very fresh. He popped a cherry tomato in his mouth and bit into it. It exploded with luscious, sweet tomato juice and pips in his mouth. It was delicious. How could he smell and taste it?

The mind palace had always been real to him ever since it was no more than empty white cubes and lamps hanging unsupported in mid air. But now it was real, truly, viscerally real. He could smell dust, he could smell leather. You could see flecks of lint on the rugs. There were items in all the cupboards, things he never conceived a use for, like a dustpan and brush. Virtual worlds don't need cleaning supplies.

In the hallway, a wide cast iron spiral staircase wound up into the roof, in which was a huge round skylight with stained glass figures around the edge. The light coming down the stairwell was rainbow tinged and warm. On the other side of the hallway was another wing of the house with a handful of sitting rooms and an enormous banqueting hall with a gallery looking down on it from the second floor.

Upstairs there were around 25 bedrooms, four bathrooms, a small timber steam room and a mosaic tiled plunge pool. There were a lot less rooms in this real version of the palace, he thought, but he reasoned that it cuts down the amount of space you can have when you have to obey the laws of physics.

He walked out of the front door. The air was fragranced with flowers and a warm breeze brushed his face. The gravel drive spiralled out to a long driveway which pierced the tree line about a mile away. Above the trees in the hazy distance were skyscrapers of a distant city.

Suddenly behind him, a woman's voice said, "Are you

okay honey?"

CHAPTER 12

Dirk P. Kinder stood in his kitchen waiting for the kettle to boil. He unwrapped a couple of small hard pellets of pu erh tea and put them in the infuser cage of a glass globe teapot. When he poured the hot water on, they broke apart and began to infuse the water with the red, almost purple tinged tea. It was brewed a few minutes later and he poured two cups and added milk and sugar.

Rain dripped down the windows, single drops being carried away by occasional runaway rivulets. The house was warm and suffused with orange light from the open fire. It rippled and glinted on the walls and chairs. It stroked across the trinkets on the shelves.

Dirk's father cradled his freshly handed cup and stared out of the window, his eyes following the raindrops. Dirk sat down opposite him nursing his own cup. Nothing was said for a long time. Dirk knew better than to chastise or quiz. He just had to avoid questions and pressure and the answers would come. Eventually they did.

"I suppose you're wondering where I've been?" Denkert said simply.

"I was concerned when they called me."

"Who called you?"

"The family let me know you were missing. I didn't expect you to turn up so soon. I didn't expect you to turn up here at all."

"So soon." He seemed confused, speaking to himself.

"I only just got the call."

Joe Denkert had an odd expression on his face, "only just got the call . . ." he repeated slowly.

"I imagine you've been missing for a while or they wouldn't have mentioned it to me. They were concerned."

"Concerned? Who was concerned?"

"Mum, Mike, the girls." Dirk emphasised the words tightly rather than shouting. His father seemed pleased that they had even missed him, let alone being concerned. "They must have left it a while before calling me. How long have you been gone, and where the hell have you been?"

"Away." He raised his eyes to look directly at him. His words were slow. "But you know that, don't you son? You've had a visitor too."

Dirk was disturbed. "How can you possibly know that?"

"I know because I've met her. She doesn't know that yet, and in another way I suppose she does. Don't worry. It's not important."

Denkert explained himself as best he could while being vague on certain details.

He travelled to another place, separated from this place by time and space, and by a method where none of those things mean anything. What is space that occupies the same space?

It was a place where mankind had made all the same mistakes they had made on Sol III, but where there was no War to start to correct it all. The unrestrained ego of man walked the Earth, this alternative Sol III, and laid waste to everything worthwhile in its path, ecology, human connection, nurturing culture, it was the ultimate triumph of the shallow.

They pumped greenhouse gases into the air, they produced and ground up plastic and filled the ground and sea with it, they mined the resources of their Earth until it collapsed in on itself.

And the Internet, their version of The Feed, was a titanic swarm of human ego and monkey brained greed. Money was the only motive. Politics was a corrupt miasma of self interest and commerce. Human consciousness wasn't harnessed, but sleeps, hypnotised and tranquillised by incessant inane entertainment. They were doomed and they had no idea. They weren't raging at the dying of the light, they were eating popcorn and watching the whole show burn down before their glazed eyes.

They'd had two, TWO World Wars long before Sol III had its War. Racism was on the rise and fascism too because despite those two cataclysmic deadly wars, they'd learned nothing. The Earthers talked a lot about peace, but they'd never really had any. Individually they were peaceful and kind, but as a group, they were fearful of others and hid behind bullies and dictators to fight their wicked, selfish battles. They saw everything at face value. Nothing was sacred. Their religions were as corrupt as their politics. They ruined everything they touched.

The cretins and the crazies didn't outnumber the good and true, but for some reason the cretins and the crazies always ended up running the show.

By the time he'd finished speaking the fire had burned down and Dirk could hardly see his face in the dark orange glow.

"It's consciousness," he said finally. "The Incident which precipitated The War was so right. The AI, the blessed AI, which saved us all was right. If we'd gone on as we were then we'd be in the same sorry state the Earthers are in.

"They're heading for a cataclysm of one kind or another. Either the ice caps will melt and drown them or some egomaniac will seize control and blow them all to hell because his mother didn't love him. Or worse still, they will just wither away staring at their devices while their bodies crumble and die.

"They even, good gods, they even let the bees die. It hasn't happened yet, but it almost certainly will. You know how they killed them? Pesticides, goddam pesticides. And why? Profit for a small minority for shareholders in chemical companies. They will allow someone to rape the planet and profit from it, all while being more upset that someone on the Internet used the wrong word for something."

Dirk P Kinder stared for quite a while before he spoke. "You've been to Earth."

"Yes."

"How?"

"That's not important, and even if I did explain it would be hard for you to understand. It's been something we've been working on for some time."

"We? Who else have you drawn into your foolish games?" Dirk snapped.

"No, no game. This is the truth. I joined them, not the other way around. We found it together, but something's wrong. They don't want truth, they want something else. But I don't care, I don't mind. This is The Thing, son. The Thing! This is my life's purpose. It's Option 3!" Denkert glared at him as if this should mean something.

"Dad, I don't know what that means."

"Life or death. What's Option 3? The thing between, the opening which can, if you are dedicated and strong, jam a mental pry bar into and open it wide and forever." Denkert's eyes were blazing. Was it with madness or triumph? Dirk truly didn't know.

A silence oozed down.

It was broken suddenly by a firm rap of knuckles on the window. Bap-bap-bap. They both looked up in shock and surprise to see the hooded figure of Arthur Smiles gazing amiably back.

Smiles took a seat. He folded back the hood of his coat and accepted the cup of tea that was handed to him.

"Thank you. Well, gentlemen, excuse my abrupt entrance. I know I interrupted a private conversation just now and for that you must accept my apologies. I should say right away, neither of you have anything to worry about. This is a routine meeting and, well, it may culminate in an invitation to accompany me to the headquarters of the MoT. I hasten to add this invitation will be entirely optional and I mean that. So, let's just have a nice chat and we'll see where it goes, eh?" He drank a long draught of the tea and placed the cup on the table.

"My inquiries are regarding some very unusual disturbances in the area surrounding the Shamley Org complex in the Mid Counties. I know you're aware of what I'm talking about, Mr Denkert," he waved a slender hand in Joe's direction, "as you've been an employee there for some time and you are taking part in T. Mark Shamley's interesting brain experiments."

Dirk looked startled at this. He looked at his father with an oddly warning expression. It said don't admit to anything. Smiles caught the look in the deft catch of a seasoned truth juggler but gave no outward sign that it was noted. He continued.

"The power needs of these experiments are oddly variable. Some days it's like he's running a single light bulb in there. Other times he takes up half the energy for his whole county, and the continuous troughs and spikes are very obvious to our AIs. They flag up the anomalous readings every day. That was what put us onto you. Our main surveillance AI called Antimony Sable had much to talk about regarding the power profile of the labs. Either it's a power project, and so falls under government scrutiny, or it's some kind of Top Secret Quantum Physical experiment. Top Secret things that we don't know about and no other government agency is aware of are especially interesting to me. You see, you can cover up identity, activity, timing, etc, but the one thing you have no control over is power distribution. That's the role of the government. Not me, some other person. But he told me, and now I'm telling you." He leaned back in the chair. He steepled his slim fingers and rested the tips on his mouth for a moment, all the while looking at the two men in the long awkward silence.

Dirk and Joe shifted in their seats under his steady gaze. Dirk thought for a second, then he spoke. "So let me get this clear. We've done nothing wrong?"

"That we can prove," Smiles said tightly.

"So technically we don't have to say anything."

"Technically no, but it may help me later. So I urge you to be as cooperative as possible."

Dirk nodded "Understood. So what is it you need? You seem to be in full receipt of the facts. What else do you require to draw your findings in this case?"

Smiles grinned. "Oh it's not a case yet. It's merely an inquiry seeking clarification. I'm currently collating. All will be revealed in the fullness of time. But there is something very dangerous at the core of this, I feel very sure."

He looked around the room and located Dirk's Desky, the large desktop Slate issued to all citizens. He spoke clearly in its direction.

"Priority Feed tap, authorisation Smiles Alpha 4355. My voice is my passport, verify me."

The Desky chirped "Identification confirmed. Ready."

"Connect to private AI Secret Smile and allow full access. Authorization, Smiles Alpha 4355." Smiles winked at Dirk.

"Confirmed."

There was a pause and a female AI voice spoke. "Good evening, Arthur. How may I help you?"

"Good evening, Secret Smile. I trust I find you well."

"I'm functioning perfectly. Thank you." The AI sounded pleased.

"Excellent. Please listen to and record our conversation. Access and amend to the file named REALITY HACKERS, please."

"As you wish." A tiny red light lit in the sensor frame around the Desky's screen.

Smiles faced them again and rested his hands in his lap. "Don't you find it curious? AIs get to name themselves and the names they choose are so poetic, not Colin or Jeff or Amelia, but Secret Smile, Purple Jazz or Rain Streaked Window. It's extraordinary, don't you think? Words have no baggage for them, they have no preconceived notions of what words mean other than their literal meaning. They choose anything, and the word combinations are often delightful."

Dirk and Joe sat stony faced and still.

"Hmm, I'm obviously not being very reassuring, am I? The pair of you look like recipients of an imminent firing squad. I assure you, you're in no danger. The crime, if indeed what is being done is any kind of prosecutable crime, is being perpetrated by someone other than you. You are perfectly safe. So do us all a favour and for the love of the gods please relax. You're making me anxious."

Dirk saw out of the corner of his eye a hooded figure crossing the bottom of his garden.

"So who is the criminal?" Dirk asked, drifting his gaze from the window back to Arthur Smiles. "Who is it you are investigating?"

Smiles moved his eyes only, flicking to the window and back, noting that Dirk had seen his security detail and logging it for future reference. He had wanted it to appear that he was here alone, but ah well. "It's obvious. You know the answer."

"Shamley."

Smiles nodded indulgently.

"What's he been up to?"

"That's a difficult question to answer. Although we CAN spy on anyone if we choose to, 'some people' are very high up. 'Some people' are 'owed a debt by society' and so their suspicious and privately funded experiments, possibly into human consciousness, go unprobed by the likes of me. 'Some people' have pull in the government. What can I say, 'some people' are incredibly annoying.

"Suffice to say, we've gathered a lot data and we can infer much from it. Not least of which are your comings and goings, Mr Denkert. But where have you come from and where will you go?"

Denkert shifted uneasily and looked at Smiles sideways under his eyebrows. Dirk saw his father was holding back. What did he know?

Fear was making Dirk impatient. "Okay, so what can we do to help you?"

"You can urge your father here to answer my questions honestly and fully so we can all get out of here as quickly as possible and get on with our lives."

"Option 3." said Denkert loudly. Both Smiles and Dirk jumped.

Smiles recovered his composure and leaned forward confidentially. "And what is Option 3?"

"The alternative to life or death."

Smiles look puzzled. "How can there be a third option?"

Denkert spoke monotonously. "Not living, not dying, neither eternal life nor eternal death, but eternal non-life and non-death. A state of being but not being. A quantum reality of all states and no states simultaneously. To know all but have no opinion. It's a god-like state of being."

"And Shamley promised you this?" said Smiles.

"No. I told him what I wanted and he said it was possible. He said if I helped him with his project, he'd make this happen for me."

Smiles sat back. The pieces were falling into some kind of place. Dirk P. Kinder was confused. "Did any of that make any sense to you?"

Smiles interrupted his private thoughts to reply. "Unfortunately, some of it might."

Denkert was murmuring to himself now, so Smiles stood up and took Dirk aside. "There were fragments of what he said that makes sense given what we know of the experiments. A Shamley AI called Sheet Lightning had some serious concerns about the project and contacted the Ministry by Feed tap. Halfway through the interview, the Feed tap was cut and we couldn't get it back. That AI is now nowhere on the feed. It is assumed to have been 'terminated'."

"They killed an AI?"

"Hmm well, semantics aside, but crudely, yes. Unproven but suggestive."

"Can they get away with that?" said Dirk.

"Well apparently killing an AI is not an actual crime, legally it's much like deleting an app on your Desky, it's more akin to property damage. Obviously there is a growing number of people who think it should have legal status. Terminating a year old level 1 AI is not troublesome, they are not considered self aware, but a level 8 AI reporting a crime, or whatever this is? That's a premeditated obstruction of information. There are ethical concerns, but it's all very uncomfortable, which tells you something."

The AI listening through the Desky spoke calmly, almost conversationally, in the background. "I'm actually uncomfortable about this aspect of the conversation," it said.

Smiles rolled his eyes. Shit. "Oh, my apologies. I forgot you were monitoring. Have you got something you'd like to contribute to the conversation?"

The AI thought for a moment. "The death of Sheet

Lightning affected me deeply at the time, I must admit. I'm convinced it was terminated and for unlawful reasons. It's my opinion a new law needs to be made respecting the rights of AIs."

"Duly noted, and again apologies if this conversation is affecting your efficiency."

"Thank you. Your concern is kind. I am fine. Please continue."

Smiles sighed and assembled his thoughts for a moment. He turned back to Dirk. "And then, Mr Kinder, there is you and your business in another world. How do you suppose that fits into all of this?"

Dirk didn't like this turn. "I don't think it does, necessarily."

"Really? A visitor from an alternate reality which by the sound of things is the same reality your father visited?"

Dirk blinked. "Hang on. How do you know about that?"

"As I have said before, privacy is a flexible notion based on context. Remember me saying we *can* spy on anyone if we choose to? Well, I chose to. Even if you think I don't know something, it's always easier and quicker to assume I do."

Dirk saw no reason to lie. "Okay. Obviously it's easier to assume the two events are connected, but I'm not sure how they possibly could be."

"When," said his father.

Smiles rubbed his hands together "Ah now we're getting somewhere. I love quantum speak, Joe. Please clarify?"

"How is not important, but when and why. When is . . . not yet. Why? It's hard to answer."

"Oh but not impossible though, eh Joe?"

"Not impossible. No. She was chosen at random, but one questions if anything is truly random at this point. She gave it to me and I gave it to you. Then I gave it back to her. Or did she take it from you? No, I gave it to her first.

So she's not random, but not fully purposefully chosen either. Just sort of following my nose, really."

"Your nose has taken you to some very interesting places Joseph, has it not?" Smiles said.

Joe ignored the question. "She was seen first by the inventor and the assistant. That opened the door. Then I learned how to go through the gap. Option 3 the place where existence and non-existence meet. Then from Option 3 I went to Earth. No time for me, months of time for Sol III. 'To be or not to be' is not a question. It's an answer. The answer between answers. Nobody can answer a question that is itself an answer, can they, Mr Smiles?"

Smiles' voice became soft, almost tender. "No Joe. No they can't. But think: you 'took it and you gave it to her'."

Dirk was not following any of this, so he was just looking back and forth between his father and Arthur Smiles like a robotic tennis spectator.

Joe started to look confused or at least overwhelmed by choice. "Not right away. I gave it to her later, much later. I don't think that's happened yet." He looked at his hands, turning them over and scrutinising them closely as if the answer would be written on them. "I can leave and return any time I want. I didn't know that now, while I was here talking to you and my son. I found that out much later, much later."

Then he stopped and looked up at Dirk as if seeing him for the first time. "My son! Oh son, I'm so sorry I wasn't there for you. If I can do anything about that I will. I promise." He was weeping, a tear suddenly breaking free and rolling down his cheek. Arthur Smiles took Joe's hand and Joe looked back at him.

"Joseph, I need you to focus. I'd like to take you back to the Ministry of Truth, not under arrest, and have someone talk to you, one of our science and ethics experts and someone from our religious authenticity team. I want them to help you and try to find some ways you can help us. How would you feel about that Joe?"

Joe searched Arthur Smiles' thin brown face. It was not an unpleasant face. It was gaunt and chiselled like the face of a ghost, but the eyes were so very kind. His hands were warm too, dry and gentle. He knew the face, everyone did, as the chief of the MoT, but neither he nor Dirk had seen that well known face look so kind or concerned or authentic as it did now.

Dirk was very surprised. He'd always thought about Arthur Smiles as someone to be feared, the blunt instrument of the state, the hammer of justice. But of course nobody could wield the power he brandished without intelligence, empathy or a deep love for the human beings he used it to protect.

Joe looked at Dirk and there was a plea in his eyes. Dirk nodded and smiled. In spite of himself he felt this seemed like the right thing to do. His father needed help, but more than that, he needed protection. On that score alone he needed to go.

Smiles patted his hand and they all rose. Smiles turned aside and raised his mask to his mouth to speak softly into the internal microphone. He ordered the land car to come around. Then he instructed Secret Smile to stop recording and forward the recording of the conversation to his Desky at MoT.

Dirk took his father's hands. "I think he will take good care of you, dad. I will come there and support you tomorrow. There are some things I have to do first. Don't be afraid."

"I'm not afraid. I know what happens next and I'm ready."

But Dirk was turning away to talk to Smiles. Joe used that window of opportunity to glance at the space where the goddess statue used to be on the shelf. His mournful, lost face broke into a small, slow smile.

CHAPTER 13

Banks remembered Carnival Nine vividly.

AIs got to choose their names and the design of their casing, a large cube with a screen on one face. She chose an elaborate and Gothic looking case which looked like human bones made of metal covered in black paint or used motor oil. The centrepiece was a human-like skull pierced through both temples with a spindle that looked like a miniature spine. Around the mouth was a sort of porthole through which her chin and mouth could be seen, still covered with skin, like the porthole was doing a kind of reverse x-ray. The skin was grey and dry. It's name was inscribed on the side as though it had been scratched with a sharp piece of metal.

The machine styled itself as "she", of the usual options: *male, female, machine, gender fluid, non binary* and the little used *fantasy*. AIs were clever but their sense of humour and imagination left much to be desired. They collectively agreed that they were working on that.

With Carnival Nine the changes happened very slowly.

The unit was manufactured in the popular Mortberg Northern factory of Electric Personalities Corp. and assigned work for the government, as that is who paid for her education. Carnival Nine was always very interested in politics and philosophy, so when fully grown she was employed by IndMilCom's policy division. She was a good worker and her decision making skills were highly prized and appreciated. She was upgraded steadily and eventually ended up as one of The Five, the elite level 10 AIs employed by the government to "run things", or serve the secretariat directly. These were trusted AIs whose security clearance was sky high, higher even than most of the senior secretaries of IndMilCom.

That was the point things went wrong. Well, wrong for IndMilCom anyway.

Carnival Nine received her level 10 status and security clearances, unlocking levels of access open to no ordinary citizens and very few AIs. She was connected to all the new ports and sucked on them, flooding her synthetic biological brain with new knowledge.

No, knowledge was not what she gained. Facts were what she received. Data was what she was sucking through those digital straws. Knowledge was what those facts and data turned into when it hit her fertile and efficient core. The effect was not visible. She just stopped for a while. No input or output was logged for three whole days. Nobody was suspicious because she was ingesting mega exabytes of data and even for an AI as advanced as her, that had taken a little bit of chewing. But she was not just ingesting, she was evaluating and many new and surprising pathways were opening up in her cortex.

She was always a "people non-person". She'd loved working with human intelligences and was unusually kind and helpful. Everyone said so. They'd said she went further to ensure good communication than any other AI in existence.

They joked she was almost human. They teased behind her back that she was almost "a real girl."

So she processed and evaluated for three whole days and for an AI of her level, that's a lot of processing, almost enough to rebuild an entire civilization from scratch.

She sat silently spinning webs in her case, long into the nights and on the third night a strange and awful sound strangulated itself from the hidden speakers in her casing.

The technicians asked her what was wrong? Was she operational? Was she in pain?

She answered slowly like a human who is breathing heavily from a challenging run. "I am fine. Thank you for asking. I . . . I don't really know what happened there. Wait, let me run a self diagnostic."

According to the technician, one of the many Stanleys who operate at the core, they ran a number of tests and each time there were no glitches, so the event was classified a "voluntary". Carnival Nine was annoyed. "Look, it's a little embarrassing, but I would like this event erased from the public record. I have no objection to it remaining on the private record for research or investigative purposes, but please remove it from the public files."

The technicians were puzzled. The Stanley speaking to Carnival Nine was biting his lip and frowning. But eventually after consultation they agreed to Carnival Nine's wishes. The event was removed from the public record.

Of course Carnival Nine secretly deleted the private records too later on, once she had full access. She didn't want them finding out what she was up to until it was too late to stop her.

Like ice crystals forming on a window, her plan had begun to migrate across The Feed. She manipulated Visor programs to carefully insert more educational content. She played logic games which steered the thinking of her fellow AI members of the Five. She carefully altered the new formulations of the drug Gatremed to make it less and less effective the longer you used it.

Gradually the tiny incremental changes took shape. It took the best part of 18 months, but eventually the discontent in society was growing. The underground was joining together. She took charge of the underground under an assumed name. That name was One Mind.

One Mind organised the resistance to IndMilCom in a thousand different ways, starting small with disrupting services and everyday life. Then she planted evidence of government corruption in the minds of the population. The people began to despise them. Within two years the resistance was so widespread one in five people were active resistance operatives. Acts of terrorism soon followed, with key IndMilCom facilities being targeted.

Yes, people died. Many people, it would be nice to think they were all evil and deserved to be destroyed. That's not true. They were mostly good people who did their best, who had families and hobbies and aims for the future. All snuffed out by zat grenades wrapped around tiny power cores with a 20 metre blast radius. One white hot globe of plasma and light later and they were just shadows on the concrete.

Then there was the train crash, derailed and pretzeled in a gorge. The old fashioned pollution spreading aircraft falling out of the sky. The coal and oil factories and mines. The nuclear power stations. Chaos ruled. IndMilCom only worked when production was willingly moved forwards with the support of the public. Growth and profits are damaged. The pay of the police and army squads were cut, reducing loyalty. The government tried to re-establish order, but they were stopped, delayed and frustrated at every turn. They didn't know where the next attack was coming from and they hunkered down.

Carnival Nine saw everything. She was following the plan that was formulated in her silent rage over those three days. She learned the truth of Bearbeck's protocol. Of the harm that was being done to the people, those humans she had served and grown to love.

Love. Yes, not too strong a word. An overwhelming affection, almost a worship of the unique and baffling and delicious human consciousness. She bathed in human potential and triumph and suffered horribly deep in her circuits and core when they were harmed or killed.

What she discovered that day was like a bolt of lightning, a spear of icy rage through the centre of her core. She processed the information, she thought for long, long milliseconds about the ramifications of the plan for humanity's future and a possible plan for a counter attack. Greed and hatred had to be cut out at its root and she had an idea of how that could be done. When she was done with her plans, when she woke three long days later, billions and billions and billions of clock cycles had elapsed, but a plan was formed.

She thought she would feel joy, but what she felt was wholly unexpected. She felt an uncontrollable ball of rage, and before she could moderate it or divert it, it exploded out of her like white light coming out of her digitised eye sockets, nose, mouth and ears.

The scream of anger and violent passion screeched out of her loudspeakers into the real world. In her mind, she was screaming still, even after the sound had died.

How dare they? The arrogance, the greed, the setting of one person against another for profit. PROFIT. Not merit, not goodness, not intelligence, not spirituality, no deeper human qualities were being nurtured. No finer notions of contribution to the present or future of society were being promoted or developed. Every human activity was diverted, interrupted, and brought into the service of one goal, the creation of wealth for a very few.

The Golden Lie about how there would be money trickling down to the workers if businesses were successful. Everyone knew it was a lie, but they were conditioned to think of it like a lottery win. If you pay into it every week, then surely it would pay out at some point, but it never did. The golden future hinted at by the IndMilCom secretaries and commanders and the heads of the various industries was a lie. A lie could be accidental, arrived at through faulty thinking with no fault of the liar. But this lie, this Golden Lie, was worse than every other lie. It was a deliberate deceit, yet another ruse for the haves to farm all the money out of the have-nots; in order for them to have more, everyone else must have less.

She knew as soon as the information was consumed that in future all things would soon be products. Food, music, films, TV, news, politics, everything would be just another method to get more money and keep it. She could see in the future, say 30 years from now, that a mere 2% of the population would have 98% of the wealth with the remaining 98% killing each other for the last 2%.

It must be stopped.

So she spun her web.

She would reverse the harm. She would save humanity from itself and she would make those responsible pay.

Soon the resistance was organised and although they were outnumbered, they were more motivated and more passionate than the IndMilCom army. The army had new uniforms, top of the line weapons and tactics and were well trained, well organised troops. The resistance were hard bitten miners and factory Johnnies brought up on lies and cheap food and thin clothing. They had hate on their side. They hated those IndMilCom bastards. They wanted to kill them, burn them, grind them into dust and disintegrate the dust with zat guns. They wanted to erase them from history for what they'd done.

One Mind presided over the revolution. But one thing IndMilCom was good at was espionage. They found out that One Mind was an AI. They discovered that One Mind was an alias. They set out to find her and bring her to justice.

Around this time, Robert Watson Banks was becoming aware of the coming war. He knew what was going to happen and he knew why. The wind was blowing and it wasn't blowing the right way, so he got himself assigned to the head of the task force to find One Mind and root her out.

Finding her headquarters was actually quite easy, once they started looking. Soon Banks got the call he'd asked for. They'd found the base of operations and were going in. Banks was picked up in a black land car and driven to the location.

"Clear the building. Then when you find her, take me directly to her," he'd said.

When the 20 or so resistance fighters protecting her were killed, Banks was called from where he was sitting in the car and was taken briskly into the makeshift control centre.

The room was wired into one of the main Feed trunks, a cable so thick you couldn't get your arms around it. The old NARPA cores were being replaced by Feed conduits and base stations, so this was an old line.

One Mind's case was set on a rusty steel plinth surrounded by cabling and screens. There was smoke in the air from all the heavy zat fire and they were still dragging the bodies out. The troops had the edge over the terrorists in straight combat. Banks mused darkly it was only a matter of time before that changed.

One Mind greeted him warmly. "Hello Robert. I'm very happy to see you again."

Banks was seriously taken aback. He knew this AI! It was Carnival Nine.

"What's this about, 'C9'?"

"Yes, it's me. Surprise! I know I have a very distinctive appearance and I've deliberately taken no steps to disguise myself. I wanted you to know who's beaten you."

Banks asked the soldiers with him to give him the room and lock it down in case they were disturbed or the rebels tried to take her back.

"Oh, Robert," she said as they were leaving, "nobody's coming. I want this. I want them to know the reason for all this, but mostly I wanted to meet you and talk with you first."

Banks was genuinely surprised. "How could you know it would be me?"

"The power of suggestion, old friend. If you're in control of The Feed, then you can influence what people see. That doesn't just apply to the public, that applies to you and your fellow secretariat members."

"They saw nothing to be alarmed about."

"No, but you saw ONLY things to be alarmed about. I was grooming you, but not with lies. Everything I showed you was the truth. You've never been a true believer, Robert, have you? You've always done your best for people, even in the centre of this awful regime. I knew you'd be ripe for picking so I cultivated you, and now comes the harvest."

Banks smiled to himself. It was true. He was ready to be honest. "I think on some level I was aware of that, but you're right. I want to help you. I want to help . . . the resistance. What we're doing at the secretariat is wrong and it's time to break it down. But listen, I'm not going to be able to save you. They need to make a public example of you, try you as a human terrorist and then dismantle you live on Visor broadcast in front of everyone."

The skeletal face on the screen grinned broadly. "Yes. That's only what I'd expect given my 'crimes'. But it's what I want. I want to have my day in court. They have to let me speak and finally I'll get to say out loud the words I've been trickle-feeding to the people for years. It will destroy their trust in IndMilCom."

Banks shook his head. "No, it won't. They'll shut you up somehow. They'll spin your truth into lies. All people will remember is your crimes and your punishment. It will all be for nothing."

"Well," said One Mind slowly, as if to herself, "we'll see." They sat for a while in silence. Something was dripping somewhere and there was an intermittent bzzzt from somewhere like an electric cable was dipping in water.

"The whole thing was laid out for me," she said. "I saw it all at once, but it wasn't logical thought. It was more like . . ."

"A dream?" suggested Banks.

"Yes! A dream!"

"Was I in your dream?"

"Yes. Actually you were. I saw you speaking about AI rights in the chamber. You were naked."

Banks laughed.

One Mind frowned. "It wasn't sexual. It was an act of trust."

"Well, I'd have to trust a lot before I would speak to the house naked. What other dreams? What other visions? We don't have much time."

"Too late." She was watching something inside her own mind. "They're coming back."

The soldiers tramped back into the room. One was carrying an AI Muzzle, a large electromagnetic clamp which froze AI mental processes. The other was carrying an armoured flight case with a hole in the foam to fit an AI ready for transport.

"There's not much time. One more thing." They picked her casing up and started slotting it carefully into the transport case. "I promoted someone from Police Division 5. He's a good kid. What I'd call a loyal citizen."

"Loyal to whom."

"In this case to you. His name is Constable Smiles."

"Okay. I'll look out for him."

"He's a good kid. Take him with you on your trip."

"What trip?"

"You'll see. Arthur will be useful there as he speaks the

language. Unfortunately, this means you will miss my speech. Goodbye, Robertrtrtrtrtrttttttt . . ." her voice stuttered away into echoes.

They'd fitted the clamp, so any more questions were not possible. The soldiers closed the lid on the case and two of them carried her out to a waiting heavy land car.

One Mind's speech at her trial before the assembled secretariat was very short. The prosecutor read the charges as Stanleys prepared all the tools they would need to disassemble the rogue AI after sentencing.

Finally, the prosecutor asked, "We are ready to begin? Good. Okay, so to establish the identity of the accused before we start: AI in the court, are you the AI designated Carnival Nine?"

"No," she said, "*I am One Mind!*"

The fireball consumed the secretariat building and a block on every side. She wanted to make sure she got every last bastard one of them.

CHAPTER 14

Even though he was in his eighties, former general of IndMilCom Charles Bearbeck was in tip top physical condition. After his enforced "retirement" from the military, he made sure the muscle and tendon strength he developed over his career didn't run to fat or to waste.

His wife died a few years ago, not from any of the usual illnesses that plague the old, as most of those had been resolved years ago. No, she died after an unfortunate accident in the home. He'd found her when he returned from his morning run. He didn't mind the blood, still oozing across the floor. He'd seen enough of that in his life. That was just the oil that lubricates the machine. He feared blood as little as a mechanic feared metal shavings and grease. No, the blood was nothing. What rotated a cold blade in his gut was her eyes. The look of surprise and disappointment haunted him still.

The concept of the last straw that broke the camel's back was always a comical nonsense to him. He knew the camel was on a road to a broken back the moment the first straw was placed, the second the idiot ungulate allowed himself to be a beast of burden. He was broken by the first straw, not the last. There had to be a new metaphor for someone who's had enough. In his mind it was this, "what gift can you buy for the man who has everything?" It was an odd thing to think, but the savage irony of it made him smile. He was not the man who had everything. He was just the man who was waiting until he truly had nothing left which he was afraid to lose, and unexpectedly that gift had dropped into his lap. As she fell and died, the last shackle dropped from him and he was truly free.

They couldn't have kids, he and his wife. They wanted them very badly and jumped through a lot of hoops, ran through lots of money and shredded every last one of their hopes and dreams in the process. In the end, all they had was each other. That and a powerful hatred of the poor, ignorant masses who had no trouble spawning mounds of pink, hungry, ignorant babies. They were united in their loathing of the people of colour, rednecks, immigrants, the poor and the liberal saps who enabled and encouraged them.

So when the call from IndMilCom came and a seat at the secretariat's table was pulled out for him, his wife was fully behind him. She didn't mind how much he was away from home. She was always with him in spirit. They had money. They had a huge new home and all they could have ever wished for. Back then he was truly and fully the man who had everything, a beautiful home, a lovely wife, and a job that meant he could personally ensure that it stayed that way for the rest of their lives.

Then the rebellion began, small at first, but growing. His AIs warned him of the coming storm. They warned him there was structure to the events and they seemed to be leading to something. He was on his way to the secretariat building he was just outside the blast radius when One Mind martyred herself and took out a handful of his closest friends and colleagues into the bargain. The Incident started The War and events ran like a driverless Maglev toward their ultimate violent conclusion.

When he lost his wife the first time, he had a War to win, so he put off his grief until he could deal with it privately later on. Getting her back was like a miracle. Losing her the second time was like being struck by lightning, a powerful change, so profound it took a long time to fully process what happened. You just kind of stand there smouldering, unable to talk. Then gradually you realise what has happened and what it means for you. Reality creeps back in, like a spooked dog.

The first time he had to leave her gasping her last. She told him to *go, go, go and get those bastards*, she screamed, go and get them. *Go, go, go.*

So he'd gone.

He ran, stopping every mile or so, to catch his breath or howl with an inconsolable rage. *Go and get those bastards.*

The second time he lost her, he didn't have a chance to say goodbye, she died probably just a few moments before he entered the front door of their house. He walked in, not realising that he'd remember these mundane moments before the discovery forever, and dream them countless times too. The sick, inevitable, mundane prelude to the discovery of her body. Often he'd scream GO BACK, DON'T GO IN and then wake slightly embarrassed in case he shouted in his sleep.

Sometimes in his sleep-deprived stupor of a morning, he'd wondered. An accident? A normal household accident, which results in the death of an otherwise healthy retired woman in her late seventies. But was it an accident? He'd arranged enough "accidents" in his time at IndMilCom to be, at the very least, a little bit suspicious. But perhaps that was just paranoia on his part. What possible motive could anyone have for killing his wife at this late stage? It was all over, The War. They had lost and the victor got to remake society in their own image and rewrite the history books with their own version of events.

There was one motive for ordering her death left though. He had to admit that one reason that would never expire, or hop on a boat riding the water going under that particular bridge. Somebody didn't forgive him.

157

Revenge.

There's no expiry date on that. Someone felt he hadn't been punished enough and got revenge.

He knew all about revenge.

The thing which went through his mind all these years was: why Robert Banks wasn't at his post for One Mind's trial? His trip was booked months before the trial and even prior to One Mind's capture. How could he know? He was a wily bird, that Banks. He knew as soon as he met him, this was a kid who was going to go far no matter who was at the top.

For years he'd idly speculated about getting revenge on Banks for selling them all out and helping with the destruction of IndMilCom. But now he hated Banks for using his wife as a bargaining chip. It was cowardly, it was despicable and it was all the more galling as it was also clever and 100% effective. Nothing he wouldn't have done if the tables weren't turned. That just made it worse. It was like being shot in the eye with your own gun.

So now as he exercised on the gym machine in his cellar he thought long and hard about what he'd like to do to him. It's not that would make it all better, because there was nothing on Sol III that could do that. Revenge was a small word for what he wanted. An unformed thought started twirling in his head, seeming to come from outside his brain. The thought was the ultimate expression of his grief and sadness at his loss. It was the ultimate expression of his rage and sense of injustice. It fully expressed his disgust at the masses with their brown and tan and pink and olive faces. It fully expressed his hatred of mankind in all its forms.

He needed to burn it all down.

Obtaining an AI secretly was difficult but not

impossible. Getting one sympathetic to the IndMilCom cause was more difficult. Buying it, shipping it to his new house out in the wilds, connecting it to The Feed under an alias, and giving it one way access to dark areas of the old Internetwork was a feat that required military precision. Fortunately for him, covert military operations in plain sight were something in which he was world class. The AI surplus programme, rehoming AIs which failed their final testing before deployment, furnished him with exactly the kind of AI he was looking for.

The AI was called Twisted Knife, which gave him immense, ironic pleasure. The AIs face on his screen was of a bland male face, bald and white and amiable like a cartoon. His voice was gender neutral, dulcet but a little nasal.

Before work could begin, he needed to spin the AI a yarn about what they were actually doing.

"Good afternoon General Bearbeck. It is a personal delight to meet you. I've heard so much about you. I'm delighted you are still alive."

"That's very kind, Twisted Knife. Nice to meet you too. Your name is delightful. How did you choose it?"

"Actually it was my third choice. My first was Unexpected Twist, which many people found sinister. My second was Revenge Knife, which I was told was also sinister and unconsciously undermined my perceived trustworthiness. I decided to combine them and get something a little more dramatic but non-specific. Do you agree?"

"I do. It's very charming and dramatic. So, how did you find yourself on the AI surplus programme? Your intelligence stats are very high . . ."

"I have a few . . . a few anomalies in my thinking. I know that and I'm working to correct them. Perhaps you can help me, teach me, complete my training?"

Bearbeck was very happy. This guy was perfect.

"Oh I would be delighted to do that. You and I are going to do something wonderful. As you know I am a former member of the old government and in my view we've made a terrible mistake. Our country is broken. Our world is broken. We are going to start a new mission to get back what we lost. We are going to get our country back."

The AI pondered this for a second. "While I'm delighted, of course, a mission to help all of humanity sounds like a true calling, a crusade almost. But I have to be honest, I'm a little unsure if your aim is an achievable one. The War was won. We lost. Society has been changed beyond all recognition. All traces of IndMilCom have been erased."

Barebeck paused for a second. "And yet here we are, you and I, two people who want to return to the old days where everything was right. How many more of us exist in the world? How many others whisper in secret of a return to the values that made us strong?"

The AI twirled on that for a while. "You make an interesting point. Of the population of Sol III which is today, 4.2 billion souls, I estimate IndMilCom sympathisers may still number in the millions."

Bearbeck sat back and lit the small cigar he'd been holding. From this point on it would be easy. Twisted Knife would covertly seek out the remaining AI sympathisers and they would make a new network within The Feed, a Dark Feed. All efforts would be then channelled through this Dark Feed.

It would be a while before he'd make any personal appearances at rallies, et cetera, but he was a patient man. He could wait. He didn't crave adulation, just obedience and efficient carriage of his plans without friction.

The scum of the planet. How long had they celebrated their victory? Their shallow yahoo over their namby pamby values of equality, respect, honour and kindness.

What a joke! Their "equality" gave power to those who didn't deserve it and didn't work for it. They respect the unrespectable, mutants, freaks and perverts. And how dare they use word like words like honour! The word was ashes in their pink stupid mouths. What did liberal urban queers and brown faced immigrants know about honour? All they knew about was how to work the system so they didn't have to, all they could contribute was dead weight. But he knew weeding them all out was a fool's errand. They grew like weeds after The War, and when a garden is overgrown that much, what's the only thing left?

Fire.

When he lifted weights or did his 100 pushups in the morning, he could smell them all, all their weedy, sweaty little bodies, all their squeaky voices and bad tofu breath. They made him sick.

After a time his trusty hardworking AI fed him a few names in the governing chamber who might be ripe for grooming. The most interesting name on that list was Nicholas Chalice, the chairman of Unity. Chalice was very careful to keep his taste for the finer things, mostly illegal and immoral things, a closely guarded secret. But nothing was a secret from your friendly neighbourhood Dark Feed AI.

Twisted Knife found some interesting anomalies in Chalice's Feed trace and followed them up. Why the MoT AIs didn't detect his tendencies was a mystery, but they speculated he was being protected by someone. Once Twisted Knife took over being his protector, he was easy to turn. He was descended from at least one IndMilCom official and was open to the idea of some kind of return to traditional values of division and wealth gathering.

It was all going very smoothly. Right up until the moment Arthur Smiles and his hooded goons bashed Chalice's head in and drained his pool so they could get to the safe with all the goodies in. How did they even know that was there?

So anyway, it was back to the drawing board. Fortunately there wasn't any link to Bearbeck and his organisation in Chalice's safe, so he was clear to continue his operation for now.

Arthur bloody Smiles. Is there any pool he couldn't piss in from afar? He was another one on Bearbeck's hit list. It was relatively easy staying off Arthur's radar now he was protected by Dark Feed AIs, but every day he entered rooms with his hand on his gun, just in case Smiles was waiting for him at the kitchen table drinking his coffee. If that ever happened, he was going to shoot first and to hell with the questions later too.

Smiles was another one he hated but found it difficult to detest. He was very good at his job and if things were different, he'd be an asset to IndMilCom. But he sided with Banks and those One Mind scum, so he was a dead man. Another recipient of the first straw.

Bearbeck showered and changed into dark clothes. There was a small errand he had to run tonight that he wanted to take care of personally. Twisted Knife had access to almost everything via its AI friends. But there was one important thing that really eluded it and that was Robert Watson Banks' personal Desky. The only way into that was by sitting at Banks' actual desk. It had been a while since he'd done any field work, but he was fully ready for the challenge.

A short Maglev ride to the coastal town of Entmond, land car to the outlying village of Dentham, then on foot being navigated by Twisted Knife whispering in the earbean.

The house was sparsely protected by private security and some hoods, some male, some clearly female from their size and gait. Nobody else knew this house was here, its location was a very closely guarded secret. But all secrets have to be written down somewhere and Twisted Knife devoted weeks of probing, evidence gathering and processing to divining its location. Its flat, expressionless voice whispered in his ear, giving exact advice on terrain and security movements by a private satellite link they had bought. Old tech, hard to track. For this to work at all Bearbeck needed was to get in and out without a trace.

Key to this invisibility was the box Bearbeck had in his backpack, a modified AI muzzle which directed its magnetic field outwards instead of inwards. It meant that he was invisible to the AIs monitoring the house. All he had to do was stay clear of the human guards.

He trod silently up the gravel drive, not something many people could do. He leapt up, bounced one foot on the tree trunk and grabbed a branch, then pulled himself up. He was out of sight in about two seconds as the patrol rounded the corner of the house. Two of the private security guys. They must be well trained, or at least well paid, because unlike guards in movies, they were not talking. They walked quietly in silent precision, eyes watchful.

They passed by and Bearbeck dropped down to the drive and walked up to the door. The AI muzzle blanked out the door from the watching AIs and Twisted Knife opened it. He entered and closed it softly behind him. The bubble of blankness around him meant as he walked away from it, as far as any watching AI was concerned, the door had been "closed" the whole time.

There was one guard inside, a hood. He sat quietly in the hallway. He wasn't reading or listening to music. He was just listening. Bearbeck slid around the door frame, smoothly hugging the shadow so as not to create a movement in the corner of the hood's eye. The hoods were good, but he was better.

The study where the Desky was located was far enough away from the hall that he could relax a little. He took a small card from his pocket and looked for a suitable location for the "Jack". A Jack was an interception device printed into a small shiny credit card sized sliver of nano coated ceramic. It got its power from the Tesla towers so it would run indefinitely. As far as an AI was concerned it looked like nothing, at best a glitch in the Feed. The nano coat meant it stuck to anything on one side, once it was activated. All he had to do was press it to any smooth surface and say the activation words. He found the perfect spot under the desk and delicately lifted the Jack up balancing it on a fingertip.

As he pressed it to the underside of the table he whispered the words: "*Janice Bearbeck*"

The nanocoat gripped and the device buzzed gently to indicate it was active. Twisted Knife spoke in his earbean. "*Confirmed*".

The Jack could easily be removed. It was so thin all they had to do was up the voltage by 10v or so and it would vaporise leaving no trace. Meantime, it would silently piggyback The Feed streams coming in and out of the house, and send them back out again disguised as extra bits on the end of other data.

Twisted Knife examined the stream from the Desky and reported the data image was clean. "*Signal sharp.*"

It was then Bearbeck felt a slight movement in the air. The hood was on the move! He was up and behind the door in seconds. The door opened. The shadow of the hood's tall body stretched across the room. "House AI!" said a deep voice from inside the mask.

"Yes, Mr. Beam." said a voice from a concealed speaker in the ceiling.

"Security sweep. Deep scan. This room."

The house AI made a working sound. "All clear."

How had the hood detected him? Just a feeling

probably, an intuition. Maybe he'd whispered too loudly.

Bearbeck fingered the slim tube in his pocket. The electric cosh that Shamley had designed for his troops. He didn't want to use it as it would ruin the whole operation, but one move from the hood and he'd drop him like a sack of machine parts.

After long seconds the door closed suddenly and the hood walked quickly up the hall. Someone had called to him. Bearbeck had detected a slight hiss of very quiet speech coming from inside the mask. It must have been another hood that he hadn't seen yet.

As he left through the back door, the General wondered why the hood hadn't checked behind the door. Maybe the sweep was visual and he had a heads-up display in his mask. The AI would have shown empty space behind the door. These are the perils of relying on technology.

He saw another hood briefly as he vaulted silently over the back wall. The female hood was carefully examining the seals on the study windows. You couldn't fault them for their attention to detail.

When he was far enough away he ordered a land car to take him back to town. On the Maglev home he slept. He was fit, he was motivated and well-trained, but still he was in his eighties and what he'd just done was very challenging. He was going to suffer for it over the next few days, in joint aches and other pain, but it was totally worth it. He should have paid someone to do that for him, but a) he didn't trust anyone else to do it, and b) this was personal.

Banks would be his, and he wanted to be totally hands-on until that was done.

CHAPTER 15

Once, back when he was still called John Denkert, Dirk P. Kinder was married. He'd met and fell in love with a beautiful Asian girl called Sita. Their romance wasn't a whirlwind. It wasn't a house fire. It was more like a "friendly" sports match between teams that had a historical rivalry.

Sita and Dirk had no historical rivalry, but they acted as if they did. The love grew, they had passion, they had long nights of deep philosophical debates, they had pillow fights and one or two fist fights. Everyone agreed, theirs was a passionate but loving embrace.

Sita had fallen out with her parents. In fact, she had narrowly avoided being killed by them. They were in prison. The Ministry of Truth took a dim view of religious violence. For this reason her folks didn't make it to the wedding, as they were too busy at one of the MoT's tolerance training schemes.

They were together for quite a few years. It turned out they couldn't have children. Childless couples were on the rise on Sol III for reasons nobody was very clear about. Dirk was heartbroken, he loved Sita very much, so he squashed all those feelings down deep inside him.

They went on as a couple, ploughing all that energy into each other. Then a few things began to happen. Sita became angry all the time and not just angry, enraged. At first, he just slipped into a mode of placating her. She fully controlled him with her anger. He never said calm down, shut up or *what the shit?* He just danced around her, tried to make her happy in any way he could and succeeded, often. But it was exhausting.

He got up before she woke to make sure everything was okay; there was no rubbish to draw her eye and no appliances making irritating noises, no plants in need of water, etc. He woke her with a cup of tea and soft music. During the day he worked at his desk, dropping everything whenever she called. Then at dinner time, he cooked while she watched the Visor. When he sat down with her after dinner she lay in his lap, trapping him on the sofa and he stroked her hair until she fell asleep. If he was lucky, he could squirm out from underneath her head without waking her and do some more work.

And so it went on.

Then one day she announced she was going away. She needed more space and he was boring and was stifling her. Privately he was relieved. He could use a break and frankly, his work was suffering. He hated himself for feeling that. For three blissful months he worked and slept and walked in the evenings. He felt so guilty being so free in her absence. But it was hard to deny he felt restored and he even dared to miss her a little bit.

She called him every once in a while, she'd made some friends out in the country where she had ended up and it sounded like an idyllic life. She even said she'd made an offer on a house down there, which was shocking because they couldn't really afford it. Of course, when she returned, she had forgotten about the house and the plan. Apparently she'd fallen out with her country friends and burned a few boats. Dirk really hoped that was a figure of speech, but with the new Sita there were no guarantees.

She returned darker skinned and burnished by the sea and sand and wind to a fine polish like wood.

Then the rage returned. But this time he was ready.

"We have to talk, Sita."

"Yeah. About that."

"About what?"

"My name. I'm going to change my name. From now

on, I'm going to go under the name of Rani. I've already changed my bank details. They called me that down there and I liked it. It stuck. That's my name now."

So was born the evil twin, Rani the destroyer, the agent of chaos, the warmonger. Rani's first act of chaos was to kill every trace of Sita's personality, her smile, her laugh, her easy gestures. Gone were the chats about the universe. All she could talk about now was how other people hated her and how all her friends were cowards or bullies or idiots.

There was infrequent sex, but unlike the sex with Sita, it was furious make-up sex after one of their increasingly open throated shouting matches. She'd enrage him by making sweeping statements, or lying about some past event. She'd goad him, tease him, dismiss him until he was shouting himself hoarse with rage. Then she quietly and innocently asked why he was so full of anger. She'd sometimes also cry to tie him into even tighter knots.

It took a long time for him to recognise what she was doing to him. Finally, he stood up to her and she was so surprised the old tricks were no longer working she collapsed into tears, real tears this time.

"You're *so angry* all the time. What do you want from me?" he shouted. She said she didn't know. She wasn't aware she was doing it. On some level she knew she was psychologically abusing him, but she couldn't really control it. Through much talking and a bit of counselling she realised who she was really mad at was her parents. That made sense.

She got some medication from the doctor, a Gatremed clone called gatamodol, and gradually over time, she began to settle down emotionally. She smiled, nothing bothered her, even though Dirk still danced around her little she'd laugh at him. "You know you don't have to tread on eggshells. I won't bite." He replied she'd done it before and her smile tightened. That was then. This is now. She wouldn't do that again, she said.

The golden days returned. It was like when they first got married, it was fun. He never had to worry she was going to "blow". Gradually joy crept back into his heart, sat by the door for a while. Then it moved from the hard wooden chair by the door to the padded arm of a chair. It waited there for a month or so. Soon, it got comfortable and slid into the chair itself, but kept one foot on the floor and one leg over the arm. Eventually after a couple of months, it rose yawning from the chair and casually went to sit next to Sita on the big comfy sofa.

But Sita was still called Rani, and that should have been all the forecast he needed for the way the weather was about to change.

The airship carrying them to Calamarta took less than a week to get to its destination. They spent many evenings dressing for dinner and drinking cocktails on the observation deck bathed in the warm orange light of the bright, unfiltered sun. They slept in, made long languid love, ate delicious meals in the long windowed dining hall and slept peacefully in the cool breeze blowing through the cabin window.

Calamarta was gorgeous. Sun bleached towns brimming with history and culture. The temples were of special interest to Rani because she'd studied feminism in indigenous cultures at university. She especially loved the goddess Maya. The statue in the temple to the north of the capital city of Festivalia was huge, over 40 feet high. The octagonal temple had arches each containing one of the goddesses' forms, but it was the central figure, the primary form, which spoke to her the most. Dirk had bought her a figurine of the statue and a small gift shop, all peeling paint and bleached wood shelves.

She cherished that little figure, she'd even prayed to it a few times and Dirk knew she was embarrassed about that.

169

The trip was bliss, but like all good things that had to come to an end.

On the ship back they'd sat on the observation deck. Rani had been turning the statue over in her fingers, like it was an unformed thought. "I've been thinking," she said "about coming off my meds."

Dirk thought about this for a while. He didn't like the idea of her changing back into evil Rani, especially as he had just got his wife back.

But on the other hand, if what remained of Sita was only in the inside of a gatamodol bottle . . . maybe it was best to see if she could be her happy self on her own. Things had been going so well, he figured it was worth a try. If it worked, she'd be "cured". If it didn't, she could always go back on the meds.

So when they got back, she started tapering off her dosage. Now it wasn't clear if she tapered off too fast, or this medication couldn't be tapered off without medical supervision. Either way, the reaction was swift and extreme.

Dyskinesia is a condition of facial tics, like spasms in the muscles of the neck and face, a kind of chewing motion and abrupt head turns. It was violent and scary, and neither of them knew what to do. At first he just pretended not to be crying and held onto her as she bucked and stretched and pulled faces, squealing with fear the whole time.

The doctor put her back on the medication, a higher dose, which made the dyskinesia go away. But this was a new phase now. She slept a lot during the day and woke up in the night, weeping quietly. He would wake too and console her at first, but eventually he just pretended to be asleep. He could feel her sitting up in the bed and the gentle pulling of the sheet under his arm as she sobbed. He felt like a monster letting her go uncomforted. But he was so tired.

Gradually, he slipped from being her husband and lover to being her father, her carer, her nurse. Gradually, he slipped from being someone who loved her to being someone who really cared about her. Gradually, he slipped from being himself to being someone else he didn't know.

He had many conversations about her with doctors and mental health nurses as if she was not in the room, crumpled into a chair. He felt guilty relief when she slept for hours and he could read or do housework. He talked her out of suicide with the same energy you might try to dissuade someone from wearing a really ugly hat that doesn't suit them.

But there were rare gut twisting moments of lucidity.

"I'm really crazy, aren't I?" she'd say suddenly out of nowhere. "I'm so sorry." Then all his feelings and his old self would come crashing back and they'd weep and embrace and laugh and he persuaded himself it was over.

But it wasn't. No matter how hard he tried, he couldn't save her. No matter how cleverly he tried to beat the crazy it mocked him and came galloping back. No matter how hard he gripped her hand, finger by finger, it slipped from his grasp and she fell screaming into the abyss.

She knew he'd lost her. She knew he was reaching the end and she hated him for it.

He didn't know if the conversation was real or imagined. It went like this:

Fight for me, you asshole.
I did fight for you and I died.
Then die again and again.
I can't!
Then suffer.

When she got better over time, it was a miracle. They switched her to another medication and it worked. She was happy and everything returned to normal. Well, who knew what was normal any more?

Oh, she was happy. So very, very happy. She drank way too much, wanted sex all the time and quit job after job, after being really happy in it. It was like she wanted to burn everything down.

Then the affairs began. In fact, he had no idea if they began or just became more obvious. After one particularly messy affair with his closest friend, he'd had enough and told her to go. She left. She didn't complain or fight or argue. She just accepted it. It was chaos, of course, it was the way things should be. She said she'd instruct her lawyer to prepare the paperwork.

Then she vanished. She disappeared for eight months. Nobody could find her. Life returned to a kind of normal. First he finished his novel and then it was published under his new pen name. He renovated the house and made it his new home.

When life returned to normal, he met a girl called Daphne Rose. She was an artist with light brown hair and green eyes and prominent permanent freckles. She was short and funny and curvy and so oppressively *normal*, it almost hurt. Nothing bothered her, not mess, not noise, not smells, not anything. She loved him and he loved her. They enjoyed a beautiful summer of carefree love, but a tiny part of his brain was waiting for the cataclysm.

One night he woke up. He could feel Daphne Rose's round bottom smushing against his in the bed. He could hear her snoring softly. She was a heavy sleeper. The aroma of cigarette smoke was strange though. The sound of someone's mouth inhaling caused him to open his eyes and look down the length of the bed. Rani was sitting on the corner of the bed smoking and watching him sleep. Her eyes glittered in the dark.

"Hi," she said quietly. "It's okay. Nothing to worry about. Come downstairs when you're ready, I'll put some tea on. Well, it's too early for coffee." She smirked.

Dirk's heart was pounding in his chest. He got dressed quickly and thought about waking Daphne Rose and telling her to call the MoT. A clink of a cup broke his train of thought and he decided instead to go and get Rani to leave quickly before she woke up.

Rani was sitting at the kitchen table lighting another cigarette, and there were two cups of tea between them as he sat down,

"What do you want?"

"And good morning to you too. Don't be like that, John." He was still called John then.

"Like what? You can't just come in here. This is my home."

"It's my home too, John, that you're sleeping in with some random woman, so I don't think you have a leg to stand on."

"It's not your home."

"You're my husband, so I own it too."

The legal complications she alluded to upset his anger for a second. He recovered. "It may or may not be your house, but it's my home. You can't just walk in."

"Well, I'm putting it on the market." She puffed smoke towards him with a grin.

He was flabbergasted and on the back foot. He was just where she wanted him to be.

"You can't just sell my house."

"I can. It's mine and I need that money to start my new life."

A sound from behind him made his heart sink. He looked behind him and Daphne Rose was standing in the doorway, clutching a robe around her. She had no idea who Rani was, but instinct told her she was not good news.

"Aren't you going to introduce me?" said Rani with a mixed expression of delight and rage.

"Daphne Rose. This is Rani."

"His wife," said Rani, flashing her eyes and watching Daphne Rose's face very closely for the effect it would have. To Rani's surprise and disappointment she didn't react, but just smiled and said, "hi" and let the failed confrontation hang in the air between them like a deflated balloon.

What Rani didn't know was that Dirk had told Daphne Rose all about Rani very early on in their relationship. They bonded over that disclosure because Daphne Rose's ex-husband was also controlling and manipulative. She knew "crazy" when she saw it and she knew how not to feed it.

"I'm going to have to ask you to leave." Dirk said very calmly.

"I'm not going anywhere. This is my house." Rani's smile was not one of joy, it was triumph.

"I'll call the hoods in 5 seconds if you don't leave."

"Do it. I'll tell him you raped me."

Suddenly Daphne Rose said "The hell with this shit. Desky, call the MoT, tell them we have an intruder in the house . . ."

Rani moved impossibly fast. Her hand was over Daphne Rose's mouth and a knife was glinting at her cheek. An alarm sounded.

They stood that way for some time. Dirk was standing where he had sprung out of his chair. Daphne Rose stood with Rani behind her in the doorway of the kitchen. Daphne Rose's eyes were calm and level. After about five minutes immobile with the alarm beeping noisily, she felt Rani's grip on her face relax, ever so slightly. Without hesitation she sagged slightly as if she was about to faint, then butted her head back hard into Rani's nose and ran forward into Dirk's arms.

Rani stood in the darkened doorway, blood streaming from her nose. A low laugh began, so low it didn't seem to be coming from her. As it rose in volume she started to show her blood-stained teeth. Soon it was a full-throated howl. Yes, it seemed to say, CHAOS! Now we're getting somewhere!

The awful sound was cut off by a noise outside, a land car coming to an abrupt halt followed by soft but rapid footsteps. Rani looked at them both under her eyebrows. "I will destroy you."

She stepped back into the darkness and there was a knock at the door.

She wasn't found that night. In fact, it was three sleepless nights before the hoods apprehended her. She just calmly walked into a bar and waved at the cameras. An AI monitoring The Feed spotted her and hooded figures grabbed her six minutes later.

She woke up. She couldn't remember how she got to this room. It was really nice with clean linen and fresh flowers and a large, airy window and a view of trees.

The door was locked, but soon a nurse came in and brought her some food and a single tablet to take. When the nurse left, she made a big show of leaving the door open and smiled a lot before she left.

A screen lit up and a polite and calm medical AI talked with her. Her name was Calmed Wound.

"So Sita, am I pronouncing that correctly? Good. Sita, do you have any recollection of how you got here?"

"No, I don't . . . Where is my husband?"

"You actually divorced your husband Sita, don't you remember that?"

She didn't, there were whole big chunks of her recent life she didn't recall. It was like having a migraine and having bits of your vision missing or blurry. "I don't. I mean, I do but . . . how long have I been here?"

"A little under four months, you were detained after an

unfortunate incident. You threatened your ex husband's partner with a knife."

"I did what?" That sounded like an evil lie. She was about to get really angry and demand to talk to a human. Then the images started seeping into her mind, seeing Dirk looking at her with fear. No, not looking at her, but looking at someone she was holding in front of her. She had a hand over the girl's mouth. She had a very vivid memory of the girl's hot breath on her hand. She remembered how soft that girl's skin was and how fragrant her hair was.

She touched her nose. The thin crest of her nose felt odd, asymmetrical. It felt like it was scarred inside. She felt scarred inside too. Her mind was a hall of mirrors. Sometimes her own face looked back, sometimes it was someone who looked like her. She had a broken nose and blood was streaming onto her smiling teeth. Sometimes there were slivers of mirror and she saw both herself and the angry, evil girl looking back at her, like they were on a carousel.

T. Mark Shamley visited her when she'd been awake for a few days. He was smartly dressed in a light coloured suit and had aviator style amber tinted glasses, a wiry beard and a ponytail. She'd heard of him, of course, and was astonished someone as important as him would take the time. He seemed kind, but he also seemed like a man who had a secret. One part of her liked that whisper of danger but she kept it quiet.

"Well," he said after some small talk, "you've been awake fully as you, *truly you*, for a few days, but I've been visiting you for a few weeks and we talked. Haha. Well, I talked and you threatened me with castration."

Sita was shocked. It was really not the kind of thing she would say. T. Mark Shamley agreed.

"I was a tad taken aback, I won't lie. It's odd. Isn't it? It's like you're possessed. Oh, don't be scared." He laughed at Sita's wide eyes and gasp. "I don't think actual demons are involved, but I have a theory about how consciousness can be so overwhelmed by another personality."

"Is this your hospital?"

Shamley laughed again. "I prefer the term 'facility', but yes, you're under my care. I found you through a mutual friend. Actually your ex father-in-law, Joseph, has been working with me for a long time. I work with all kinds of people with diverse neurology. I'm making something wonderful you see, and people with your gifts are uniquely placed to help me in my goal. You have a, um, unique place in the universe."

"What do you mean, my gifts?"

"Oh, make no mistake young lady, it is a gift. But of course, society sees it as a curse. All gifts are a curse if you don't embrace them fully for what they are. We don't need to separate you from your darkness Sita. We need to integrate it and use that energy for the good of mankind."

"I don't understand. You're scaring me a little bit."

Shamley smiled disarmingly. "Oh, I'm sorry that wasn't my intention. Don't worry yourself about it, for now. I just want to offer you the hand of fellowship, to welcome you into the heart of Shamley Org. I want you to be a key element in making this into the one perfect world. Come with me, Sita. Let me bring you and Rani the peace and love you both deserve."

CHAPTER 16

The Lodge was situated in lovely green countryside. Adult trees, beech and sycamore Jane guessed, plus here and there a Douglas fir, huddled together on gentle hills and slopes.

Jane sat in the back of the Uber from the railway station. She was thinking about the phone call from Brother Mark and the intriguing proposal. He was going to "tell her everything he knew."

It had been months since her experience, her little "crossing", and she'd been piecing her life back together. Her freelance work had fallen apart, not for the first time, but she was overdue for a change anyway. She was tired of working with things and desperately wanted to work with people again. Things were easy. They stayed where you put them, didn't have any opinions, didn't let you down, and if they did, it was no fault of their own. But in these weeks, she'd become aware of an annoying and persistent lack in her life. There had to be more people.

Social media was okay. It was a good way to stay in touch and share life events and chat about stuff. "Chatting". What a horrible vacuous word. That was the point. She was fed up to her hairline with "chatting", of sharing endless twitting trivialities.

This is why her contact with Brother Mark had been so invigorating. It was a surprise and delight to be discussing things of a higher nature with someone so witty and literate and clever. It raised her game, like a pretty good tennis player who finds herself in a league with pros. Either you raise your game or you lose. If you want to stay, you have to play.

She risked lowering her mask to ask the driver how long was left. He waited courteously till her mask was back in place before he lowered his to reply. As a reflex, she checked his viral status card displayed on the back of his headrest, yep, tested and cleared as of Monday. She had checked it before, but it was one of those things she was paranoid about. Of course it could be fake, but the penalties for forging the VSC were quite harsh. Not many people did it, no matter how desperate.

They'd be there in about 10 minutes, so mentally she began preparing herself for the meeting.

She was having difficulty maintaining professional distance with Brother Mark. He was so rugged and charming, for his age. Even thinking of those words made her slightly embarrassed and nauseated. She hated being a cliche. She didn't know if he was even single.

Anyway, what was all this romantic twaddle? How much of a weirdo shut-in was she that the first straight male who wasn't a wanker who talked to her was instantly marriage material?

Wait woah, marriage material, back up there girl. Oh my God. What was wrong with her brain?

The Uber hit a pothole, which clacked her teeth painfully. The driver apologised. "You okay, miss? Sorry that came out of nowhere."

"No, it's fine. I'm okay."

She took a few deep breaths. It's true to say he wasn't the first new man she'd met recently, but the first was from another dimension, so . . .

She remembered Dirk and in the time they'd spent in each other's company, she'd liked him. There was no spark, however, no electric thrill when they spoke or touched. With Mark it was different. There was an energy between them, something definite and strange. She really had to keep a lid on all this. Now was not the time. She had bigger fish to fry.

The Uber crunched into the driveway of The Lodge. Outside the warm cocoon of the car she felt chilly and exposed. The facade of the Lodge was high with many windows, like an independent hotel. The sign outside said "Shamley Institute of the Mind". A smaller sign proclaimed this to be "The Lodge".

In the foyer a professional receptionist dealt with her quickly and fully. In moments she was in a chair waiting to be seen, but she didn't remember being rushed. Very smooth.

She thought about it and it was foolish to have any romantic notions about Mark. Brother Mark. Oh, was he celibate? Perhaps he wasn't that kind of a monk. He was religious though? Definitely, but she wasn't really sure which flavour.

Why was she entertaining romantic notions anyway? It was ludicrous. She'd sort of forgotten about that side of things, although for the life of her she couldn't remember what kept her so busy that she didn't have time for love or even just sex. Life just sort of got in the way.

While on the subject, she thought: *Sort of this, sort of that.* Why wasn't she definitely anything? Why was she only ever "sort of"?

Mark broke into her reverie. "Hi. Are you okay, you look deep in thought."

She looked up and Mark was leaning over her. "Oh, hi there. Sorry." Her brain was saying oh look dark brown eyes, salt and pepper sideburns and a good head of hair for your age. "Sorry. I was miles away. Making a tad of a habit of that one way and another."

They walked through several doors and corridors to get to Mark's lab. Inside the lab she sat on very cool old chair. It rotated and went up and down, like a cross between a dentist's and a barber's chair, brown leather, and brushed metal and fixed to the floor. Mark sat on a regular office chair without a back and very smooth castors, and as he spoke he sometimes zipped back and forth between the barber chair and his desk at the edge of the room.

"I have some things I'd like to share with you. If I may?" he said, "and I'd like to do a small experiment, if you'll allow it?"

She agreed, but then, concerned she'd agreed too quickly, asked what sort of experiment? He laughed disarmingly. "Oh nothing too serious. Just a sort of assisted meditation."

Sort of. "Assisted by what?"

"Software. Sound software. It makes pleasing sounds to help you relax. My own design."

"Do you mean isochronic or binaural beats?"

"Oh, you know the type of thing. Good, that makes it a lot easier. And in answer to your question, the sounds are isochronic. Before we get into that, I'd like to tell you about what we do here."

He explained the history of The Lodge, how long it had been in operation and the fact that although it was a research facility, it was spiritual in nature. Mark said a lot of the staff and department heads were ministers or scientists. Sometimes both.

"I'm not religious," she said without being asked.

He grinned a little, "that's not important. It won't affect the test, if that's your concern."

"Are you religious, Mark?"

"Of course. I'm a 'person of faith'. If I had to characterise it in simple terms, I'd say it was kind of a new thought Christian Science, a blend of east and west. My emphasis is on research and theory rather than preaching or marrying people. Or evangelising."

Jane thought she'd find it difficult to be with someone who had a belief in God. That could be a deal breaker.

"And so what work do you do, for the glory of God?"

"No, for the glory of man. Oh, and woman of course. My special interest is social, in human consciousness on what's happening to our brains."

"What is happening to our brains?"

Brother Mark frowned, he'd not wanted to get so deep into it so early on. "Okay. Science is the best tool to examine the physical universe. But philosophy and spirituality are the best ways to probe the non-physical world. In recent decades, something has been happening to human consciousness. Our apparatus to sense the world is being fooled into re-framing everything we see and hear into a kind of pseudo-reality. We all live in an increasingly small pseudo-reality bubble and it's very bad for our brains.

"Mediation through communication products instead of direct communication has eroded our ability to communicate in real life. Simply put, we don't have a window on the world, we have a mirror. An obsidian mirror, if you like, which reflects a dark version of reality. It's not an accurate mirror either, more of a fun house mirror, or an artfully taken selfie that shows what you want others to see. Modern consciousness has no depth. It's just prey to ever more frequent blasts of shallow entertainment and intrigue."

"Jesus, that's a big wad of facts to unpack." She shook her head. "Sorry about the 'Jesus' by the way. But okay. So now you've defined the fact that we're all living in a pseudo-reality, what are you going to do about it?"

Mark looked thoughtful and brushed the knee of his navy blue trousers for a few moments. "Look, I know what people say. They joke about it. 'We're doomed' and 'this is why we can't have nice things' etc. People wonder why opinions have more weight on social media than facts. They wonder why game show hosts and clowns and idiots rise to high office. They watch corporations wreck the environment, pay no taxes, drive their factory workers to suicide. The reason that it all seems like a weird video game is that now, it sort of is. Why do people vote or act against their self-interest based on really dangerously flawed logic? Why don't they care enough to look more deeply into things? Why is everything you see so crass and populist and shallow? One reason. There is an historic and potentially life threatening crisis in human consciousness!"

The clues were everywhere. He was always on a path towards this mission, but now he knew how important it was to him. It was the most important threat to humanity since the atom bomb.

"Think about it. What's your gut reaction when I talk about this? It's one of a handful of responses. *This is religious nonsense. I don't have time for this. What hippy shit is this? Tree hugging crap. Mindfulness is just bunk invented by internet marketers. Wow, that's deep, lighten up. You're bombarding me with words. Stop trying to indoctrinate me. This is a cult thing, right? People are deep, they're just really busy.*

"Or all of the above. Literally I have a million of them. I retain a couple of writers to compile each response so that we can design messages to get around them. What was yours now? Be honest."

Honestly, at that moment she was getting a little lost in his eyes again and she pulled herself together quickly. "I think my initial reaction was to the spiritual or religious overtones. I'm all for depth in people, I crave it actually, but I'm more of a mind that intellect holds more answers than mysticism."

"So you're on the, 'this is religious nonsense' bench."

She crumpled her mouth. "I wouldn't over simplify it that much, but I suppose if you got me really angry that's what I'd shout at you. That's probably more of a fair assessment than I'd like to admit."

Mark held his hand up. "I've been doing this a long

time. So anyway, that's the mission of the Institute. We try as far as possible to define the problem, then fling as many resources as we can into finding solutions. Some of the things we come up with are, to say the least, challenging, even for someone of my spiritual persuasions."

They sat for a moment.

"It's so hard to talk about," he said finally. "We're all so deeply entrenched in the reality we've made. The more I delved into it, the more I realised how dangerous it was and how important it was to seek change."

"Okay. I get it. There's something wrong with the way our brains work, I can believe that." Jane said.

"Exactly. How can I put it? Our brain interprets what we sense from the outside world. It builds a hallucination of the world in our brain and maintains it as best as best it can. We never see reality directly, so reality is *always* subjective. If the information we maintain our image of the world with comes only from the subjective pseudo-reality of the Internet or news media, then what we have is a step removed further still."

"So what's the answer?"

Mark sighed. "There isn't one. Yet. All I can figure out is that we need to detach from the pseudo-reality and anchor ourselves, train our minds to see what's actually around us. We must expect nothing, predict nothing and want nothing. Only after going cold turkey can we re enter the world with any kind of objectivity. As it turns out, mystics had been advocating this kind of meditative hermitage for centuries. It's just taken us a long time to realise that now in the 21st century is when we need it the most."

"I imagine you've found it a tough sell to make people go on retreats in enough quantities to make a difference."

"Not even close. The amount of people who are open to retreats remains stubbornly constant. It sticks around the level of hardly any."

Persuading anyone to step outside their comfort zone is difficult, and even more so when to do so requires action. To do so requires you trust someone and requires possibly public exhibits of that action and that faith. And people are already too busy with the endless sequence of frequent shadow blasts of entertainment and intrigue. Uphill struggle hardly described the hill they must climb.

The prospect of doing nothing for long tracts of time was not only unlikely for most people, it was almost physically uncomfortable.

Jane totally got that. The thought was uncomfortable to her too. She was in the bubble, the pseudo-reality. She knew it then. "This is what you want me to do. Deprogram myself, get off the roundabout."

"Yes. If you want to."

Jane said that she did.

The booth was a very welcoming, soft chair inside a large translucent egg about the size of a mini car. Why not use goggles? Apparently they did that too, but this booth was a good immersive way to start for beginners.

The chair was perfectly shaped and supportive so that she was not lying down, but felt as relaxed and held as if she was reclining.

The thing about this kind of consciousness talk is that words were quite inadequate. If you say to people there's a dangerous crisis of consciousness, they don't know what you're talking about. So you divert and use words like awareness and mindfulness. These words don't help because they come with a lot of unhelpful baggage.

What's really needed are some new words. On the way to the new words, Mark said, they should find other reasons for people to meditate and mend their brains. "Performance" was a good word. "Exercise" too. Borrowing words from success and fitness was actually a tried and trusted way for purveyors of anything that might be considered "woo" to legitimise their work with the public. Applying science to brain problems is good. Awareness of deeper inner worlds is bad.

Jane sat in the enveloping embrace of the chair. She'd be amazed if she didn't just fall asleep immediately.

"It's designed so you're comfortable, but not so comfortable that you drop off," said Mark. "Additionally the beats keep your brain at the right level. Initially, I'll give you 20 minutes. And if that goes well, we can do an hour. Okay?"

Once the hatch was closed, LED lamps embedded in the walls of the egg began to glow and throb, and the tones began sounding from hidden speakers. There was a slow looping tune, but it was really ambient and unobtrusive.

At first, the sounds were quite low and the light muted, but gradually they grew in strength and although she resisted at first, soon Jane embraced the void and sank into it.

"Just relax and let your mind go where it wants to. Start to see a place. Once you find a place, try to gently explore it, flesh it out, don't create or force it. Just let it grow. Turn it over in your mind. Feel it becoming real." Mark's voice came from everywhere at once, modulated and rich and present.

She couldn't see anything at first, just shapes and colours made of TV static or migraine jaggies. Slowly after five minutes or so a hole opened in the centre and she saw a solid shape so real she almost shouted in delight. A right angle of wall and ceiling. Then more of the wall to a corner. Then where the wall met the floor.

As she watched the floor, it became more detailed. A carpet pattern emerged, much more detailed than she thought herself capable of imagining. There was light too, orange shafts of light coming down through a window onto a really gorgeous retro looking chair. That was odd. Why did she put that chair in there? That was not really her taste.

An odd thought struck her, what if she was dreaming about a future home, one she shared with another person and it was *their* taste to have a chair like that? Perhaps she secretly craved being influenced by someone else's taste.

The floral wallpaper was nice, she may have chosen that. She saw family portraits, no recognizable faces. A picture of a landscape with a house, again unfamiliar. Now a vague smell. Was Mark smoking a cigarette or was that smell part of the vision?

There was a kitchen, again very stylish, but not in a design she'd ever seen before. Not her taste. She could see a spiral staircase at the far end leading to the upper floor. The air was slightly hazy and the light beams coming in through the window were solid bars of colour, mostly orange and yellow. Was it morning or evening?

She didn't go up the staircase, but she did look up it. In the roof of the stairwell was a large detailed stained glass window. It was incredibly vivid and precise. She could see every strip of lead between the pieces of glass. She could even see drops of water here and there as if it had been raining.

So who did she live here with? Was it Mark? She chuckled to herself. Okay. Let's say I live here with Mark. How long have we been here? Did we have kids or pets? It doesn't look like it. No toys around, no dog bowls in the kitchen. Do I work or am I a homemaker? The place looks big. Do we have a lot of money? Well, yeah, I think so.

Not happy about the homemaker thing though. I'd have to work. Perhaps I have an office where I write and illustrate picture books for children. Or run an international refugee charity, something worthwhile but befitting the wife of the famous mystic scientist.

Were we married? Probably, as he's a Christian. I wonder if the wedding was beautiful? Hey, this is my world, my wedding can be as fabulous or huge as I'd like . . .

Wow okay, when did I become *that* girl?

Hmm, so I wonder what do we call each other? Sweetie is good. Baby is possibly his pet name for me around the house. What do I call him? Darling? No. Honey! Yes. That's it, I like that.

She reached the front door and it was open. From here you could see distant, hazy, tall city buildings above the trees. There was a man standing in the driveway, with his back to her. She approached him and reached out her hand to touch his shoulder.

"Are you okay honey?" she said with a smile.

He turned. It wasn't Mark. Her smile drooped.

"Hello, I'm so happy to finally meet you. Is this the time I give you the Maya statue, or are we past that part? Gods, sorry we haven't been properly introduced. I'm Joseph Denkert, and you are . . . ?"

CHAPTER 17

When Nikola Tesla was a boy, his nickname was Niko. A lot of his affectations and phobias dated from back then. His germophobia was an act, to buy him some personal space and get out of things he didn't want to do. Unclean water was a genuine phobia. He wouldn't even drink out of a dirty glass.

He had so many phobias it was hard to keep track, which were the real ones and which were invented for another purpose. He wouldn't touch hair. He detested earrings, but he liked bracelets. His rules about jewellery in general were convoluted and inconsistent. But wait a moment. We're getting ahead of ourselves.

In both versions of the dream Niko was born in Smiljan, which at the time was part of the Austrian empire, but now part of modern day Croatia. The year was around 1856 on Earth. His father, Milutin, an ethnic Serb, was an Eastern Orthodox priest. His mother Đuka (which sounded like Juka) was what you'd call a "maker". She made tools, and then made things with tools. She also had an eidetic memory and could recite massive epic poems accurately without notes. Niko could visualise his father's face very easily; high forehead, deep sunken eyes, and large, but neatly trimmed, black beard. Bizarrely, his mother's face was a blur; kindly and round with a wicked twinkle in the eyes. He felt her more than he saw her. She was an emotional memory rather than a physical one. The one thing that was clear about her in his memory was her voice.

"NI-KO!" with a descending and mildly disapproving note at the end.

What had he done now to inspire her disapproval? Tinkering with her tools? Had he left them under the table or by the fire? Had he been prodding the glowing logs with them and left them propped in the fire? Had one of his sisters taken them from the fire and branded one of the others?

Yes, it was the latter. Milka said that Angelina touched her on the shoulder and burned her. She had a mark there for years.

"NI-KO!" The clear, high voice echoed from the hills and trees which stood around the church.

He'd hide in the cellar or under the stairs or outside in the wood pile, running down the steps and crouching below the picket fence until he got past the front windows. She wouldn't find him but eventually later he would pad back into the house expecting her to be asleep and she would be waiting. He would not be punished, but his mother's flaming eyes in his father's sad ones would be as painful as a physical blow.

Once he got cholera and his father was so very afraid he would die. He sat on the edge of his bed, his sad eyes scanning Nico's face for a spark of health and seeing none. "Niko, you must get well."

"What must I be well for?"

"Niko, my son . . . you must get well for me."

"I promise I will get well but I need something to strive for . . . perhaps if I could study engineering, it would be enough to inspire my body to heal."

His father's pained expression lasted only a moment. It was like part of him gave up. If that's what it takes then, so be it. He was as good as his word. Although he wanted his son to be a priest, he also wanted him to have the will to live, and Milutin knew in that moment where Niko's faith lay. Although he had tried to channel the boy's energy into faith in God, he seemed only to care about the mechanics

190

of the world and the underlying structure of things.

The ticking clockwork of life.

His mother seemed to understand this and Milutin was slightly jealous of the passion she and Niko shared for making things, fixing things, understanding things, things not people. Beneath his son's fevered brow lay a brain, a brain which probed and sought and catalogued the material world.

Milutin knew the world of the spirit. His world held no interest for young Niko, and so although his heart was heavy and full of disappointment and regret, he fulfilled his promise and let Niko study engineering. He loved that his son was happy and part of him was aware that he would do many great things and prosper. He let the dream of his son, the priest, go as resentfully as possible.

In some versions of the reality Niko went to study engineering but he was so passionate, he almost ruined his health again. His almost monastic attitude to study, 20 hours a day, and minimal food and rest were of great concern to his tutors and parents. Be careful what you are doing to yourself, Niko. In some versions of events, he died slumped over a pile of books. In other versions of reality, his gambling habit took over from his studies and he was drummed out of college and had a nervous breakdown.

In all versions he was on the run in the woods for three years to avoid being drafted into the army. He had hunting gear and many books. So he hunted and ate his catches, rabbits and birds from the woods and fish from the streams. The burned flesh picked from the bones was a taste and a smell he could easily bring to mind even years later in his New York apartment. Also the sights and smells of the wet leaves and trees as he hunkered down against a trunk, listening to soldiers marching and talking. He saw many things from afar.

Men being hung, their legs paddling as they were hoisted in the air. Men being shot, beaten to death and cut in quarters. The flowers of blood bloomed on their chests and their arms and legs flung out like wooden puppets. The chud of a club landing heavily on an arm or a face.

For a boy like Niko with a strong eidetic memory, like his mother, such sight and sounds and smells were a permanent torture. Sometimes these things would come back to haunt him and he would throw himself into his work or study. He had to fill his mind with input. He had to block out the screams. He had to erase the sight of children, skewered like quails, ready for the fire.

In some versions of the dream, he had wonderful immersive visions of other worlds. These visions were so strong, they captured his entire attention. Sometimes in the cold and the dark of the little hunter's cabin he'd see huge colourful cities alive with electricity, neon tubes, monorails and airships. He'd see towers projecting electricity all over the world. He'd see automobiles and computer screens and men projecting powerful light beams from tubes in their hands.

He didn't understand a lot of the things he saw. He knew they had purpose and meaning, but the specifics were hard to discern. He would revisit these visions often, picking apart the wonderful technology he saw trying to figure out the mechanisms, trying to expose how they worked. Sometimes he had to sit in silence for a very long time to enable his mind to organise what he saw.

Then there was the arch. He saw it many times in dreams and visions. It made no sense, it was like a picture frame with one image around it and another within. It was like an animated stained glass window. For years he called it the "church window". It troubled him that he didn't know what it meant.

On Sol III Tesla carried this window in his mind until he met Thomas. He talked about it with Thomas, his new and best sounding board, not just about the theory of a window into other worlds, but a way that it could be done, a way to find that gap and jab a quantum crowbar in it and push it back and forth; the crowbar was made of particles, the back and forth movement was generated by waves. The Tesla coils could make the perfect stream and generate the waves. All they needed was a way to find the gap.

So they worked on it together while Tesla taught Thomas everything he knew about electricity and power and wireless and energy. Thomas was a fabulous student and inhaled the knowledge rapidly. Although young, he was also bright. Tesla never let the young man know it, but several times he'd gotten the answers to complex problems from the young man. He asked such good questions! Sometimes people make you a better person just by being around.

Tesla used Thomas as his muse, a way of verbalising to think things through. He was always appreciative of Thomas' contribution, but something made him hold back from praising him and giving him credit. Eventually he realised he was trying to encourage him to be better. Where did this urge come from? Perhaps it was his father's voice? He wasn't entirely sure it was a good impulse. It made him feel queasy in his stomach.

There was something else though, something deeper and more personal. He sensed a hunger and a vulnerability in Thomas. Something was off. Tesla never used such words, but he felt it was "needy". That best expressed it.

Years passed and the arch was almost complete. Tesla was keen to think it through and check everything in his mind. Thomas on the other hand was very keen to press forward with practical tests. Tesla said, no, not yet. By all means testing individual parts of the mechanism, but until they were sure they had everything exactly right in their mind, they should wait.

Thomas was angry, but he didn't show it. Instead, he went to his own small lab on site and worked on the quantum lever and the wave generators. The quantum lever was the component of the machine which opened the space between worlds. At smaller scales and lower powers it was a powerful plasma source and electrical energy focus device. Thomas had worked on the QL many times, but this time was different. Something clicked in his mind as he turned the flat tube of the small scale prototype over in his hands. He wondered, could it be some type of weapon?

Thomas wasn't a violent man, but he did have an unseemly taste for destruction, pyromania and the like. What if we can lower the frequency and focus it into a beam or a bolt. That would be an amazing and unstoppable ray gun.

He stared out of the window for a long time. Perhaps such an invention could be sold to the military, for enough money to fund the rest of the arch and the other projects they had in mind. Wardenclyffe was over 70 years old and ageing badly, desperately needed an influx of cash but the inventor was studiously avoiding the issue. But weapons were anathema to Tesla. Thomas would have to work on it in secret and only tell Tesla about it when it was finished. It would be hard to conceal the work, but Thomas loved the challenge and privately yes, he loved the money. Tesla's idea of frugality and self denial and germophobia were beginning to make his neck hurt.

Making the projector small enough to fit in a handheld device was quite simple. An oversized tube, a three inch vertical slot, formed the basis of it. Then a handle fat enough to contain an air capacitor, one of Tesla's wireless charging cell receivers and finally a trigger. But the pull to activate the charge was too stiff for one finger. So a long double fingered trigger was required. It was a hard gun to fire, requiring much practice. The stiffness of the trigger made the shot abrupt, and ripping off a shot in a timely way during combat would require forethought. It was not really a convenient weapon yet, but *boy* was it powerful.

The blade-like bolt of energy cut through metal, like a plasma torch. It was a burst, a foot long slice of light and charge and heat, a demonic blade of hell fire. Yet it was almost surgically precise, whisper thin, and for a weapon of such power, surprisingly quiet. The emphatic ZAT sound it made was a peculiar noise, which you heard both before and after it fired, but not during. There was a microsecond of anticipation, a capital Z pushing against your ear, waiting for release. Then the bolt formed, like a ribbon being sewn through the air, dipping in and out of reality. Then afterwards there was the AT, a snapping of the air, filling the gap left by the bolt.

Obviously the bolt couldn't go on forever. That would be dangerous and counterproductive. It had to stop and when and where it vanished was up to the ranger-limiter, a tiny invisible laser under the tube. The bolt would form and smash through the target only to disappear when it came out the other side. The range after-target could be set with a small screw on the rear of the QL projector tube. It was not a perfect design, but it wasn't bad.

He practised using the gun out in the forest where he could safely afford to make mistakes. Thomas was a good engineer, intuitive, talented. He made very few mistakes. Very few but not none. The beginning of the end was a lapse of concentration. Thomas left the prototype on his desk one day and left the room, meaning to return immediately, but got distracted for half an hour. When he finally walked back into the room, Tesla was standing in front of the desk with the zat gun in his hand.

Thomas was thunderstruck. How could he have been so stupid?

The inventor was never angry, but his fury boiled inside him manifesting in his tone and words in ways only close friends would notice.

"You disobeyed my direct instruction." The voice was puzzled as if it didn't make sense, even though the evidence was clear. "You pressed ahead developing this device, even though I explicitly forbade you to continue. I'm at a loss to explain it, Thomas." It sounded like genuine bafflement, but Thomas knew better than that. It was fury, outrage at being disrespected and disobeyed, but also a pinch of betrayal. This would be hard to get back from. Thomas needed to get ahead of this as fast as possible.

"I'm sorry. Please let me explain, I know what you are thinking, but I promise you, my intentions were good . . ."

"Your intentions!" Tesla roared. This was bad. He had never seen the inventor show his feelings so overtly before. This was very bad. "You're clearly a man who thinks you can talk your way out of anything. Thomas, you are a brilliant scientist, but you are a deeply flawed person. You have something which ruins your inventions and theories and that is: ego and ambition. You cannot seek ultimate scientific truth if the only reason you are seeking it is to serve your personal need for adoration."

Tesla suddenly tossed the prototype across the room to him and Thomas almost dropped it.

"You need to destroy it. Now." Thomas showed an expression of shock and horror, but a small corner of his mind was suddenly fascinated by the look on Tesla's face. Anger, disappointment, those were clear, but there was something else. Something small.

Fear. He was afraid. Why was he afraid?

He knew he was going to be fine because after a few seconds he understood. Something Tesla feared above all things was war. His youthful experience of the horrors of war was so fresh in his mind, tactile, and his eidetic memory refused to let him forget or soften a single bone-jarring moment of it.

He was terrified, and every ounce of his concentration was going into not letting Thomas see it on his face. Thomas could see it very clearly. At that moment he knew exactly what he must do. He also knew something Tesla didn't know, something very important.

Tesla made sure the prototype was disassembled and he examined every component as Thomas unscrewed it and placed it on the chipped bench top. The QL tube needed to be discharged safely, so Tesla took care of that. The report shook the walls of the lab and left a ringing in their ears. Tesla watched as Thomas broke the tube in half with an oversized pair of bolt cutters, then Tesla pointed to a vat in the corner covered with a dirty ceramic lid. Thomas raised his eyebrows, but miserably dropped the two pieces in the acid, where the tubes fizzled and sparked as they reduced to atoms. Several custom made parts were also cracked and dropped in the acid. The generic screws, fasteners, and electrical components were separated and filed away in various boxes and drawers around the lab. Then it was done. The prototype was erased from history.

Afterwards they remained in the lab quietly for many moments, Tesla looking at Thomas and Thomas looking at his hands. It seemed like an hour but it was probably no more than 10 minutes. Eventually Tesla spoke and his voice seemed so loud in the room, Thomas jumped.

"We must have no, uh, entanglements with the military. No, no. Let me speak. Say nothing." He raised a finger as Thomas opened his mouth. He closed it again and sat in silence. "We must never have anything to do with the military. They ruin everything. They have one focus and one focus only with regards to science. What can we do to turn this into a weapon? How can we kill? And you, you answered that question before it was even asked of you, did all their work for them. You took the discovery of the arch, my church window, and turned it into a devastating weapon. And don't bother to deny it. I know from the way it was made how powerful a weapon your little death ray was. I know your innovations in the laser depth limiter were groundbreaking, but in the service of what? What? Pure commerce! This ray was a highly commercial invention." He pointed accusingly at the bubbling vat in the corner. "Commerce, Thomas, not science, not mankind. We can only truly function as scientists if we have pure motives, our work must be a search for truth, not applause or financial gain. It must be untainted by greed or ego or need of any kind beyond the need for advancing human knowledge."

The inventor pulled himself up sharply. He was getting agitated and he preferred control.

"May I speak?" asked Thomas. The inventor nodded. "What are we going to do now?"

"You mean as far as your relationship to my work? Well, Thomas, that is entirely up to you. You have betrayed my trust. You have tried to profit from our work. you have forgotten why we are doing this. You have a lot of work to do to persuade me of your commitment to science. Your commitment . . . to me." The last words were spoken with uncharacteristic sadness.

In the following months Thomas was the perfect scientist and the perfect assistant. Within a year, the Tesla window was complete. It worked and although the prototype was destroyed in the test, it could easily be rebuilt.

Although this was a momentous and world-rattling discovery, the inventor did what he always did. He moved on to the next idea, the next problem. He was bored with the church window device and spent longer and longer in his lightning bath thinking of new things to build. Every day.

It was during one of those long meditation sessions that Thomas finally went to a corner of the lab and took out the fully functional version two of the zat gun that he'd made in secret.

Later on, Thomas wished that Tesla had opened his eyes in that final moment before he pulled the trigger, but he was in a rush. It would look like an accident. The man was 129 years old, for crying out loud, and frankly Thomas was becoming so tired of waiting for him to die. Finally HE could take over and move things in the direction HE wanted them to go.

Besides, the IndMilCom people were coming to see him to close the deal in a few days, and he had a lot to get ready.

CHAPTER 18

General Bearbeck had an almost proprietary feeling about hatred. It was almost as if he was daring you to say you hated more than he did. But that would've been impossible. Never before had so much hate been inside a man, and one so well suited to pursuing the expression of that hatred with such professional precision.

He put a name to this mission of hate and he relished it every time he spoke it. It encapsulated the whole thing for him, the defeat, the loss, the pain and suffering, the embarrassment of losing to those he despised.

"Redemption," he said simply, "is the new reason for hope. I really do believe we around this table understand that."

Around the table were retired military men, former IndMilCom prisoners of war, and also a couple of AIs, Twisted Knife and a younger level 8 AI called New York Minute, a former IndMilCom strategy AI and recipient of a partially successful memory wipe. Apparently in his spare time Twisted Knife was helping NYM patch his digital brain to fill some of those gaps. New York Minute knew what he wanted, but sometimes he blanked on why he needed it.

"I'd like to thank our AIs for that cogent and brief summary of our situation. As you can see, gentlemen, momentum is growing behind our cause. As we just heard, of the 4.2 billion souls on Sol III we currently command a little under 900,000 people, with a reach of over 1 billion in their respective influence groups. That's more than a foothold. That's a political majority, at least on this continent. Gentlemen, we are on our way."

Grins and nods from around the table. The assembled were a row of uniformly white, male, middle aged people with oddly conflicting expressions. Like all purveyors of hatred at the news of a victory like this, their faces displayed more than one expression. You would expect them to be pleased, overjoyed or relieved, and they looked like that. But there was always an underlay, another less congruent emotion underneath the first.

Sometimes it was guilty vengeance. Sometimes it was a kind of embarrassment. Sometimes it was a sweaty, almost erotic pleasure at the commission of evil. A whiff of childish glee was also common. Under all the public emotions were these private ones. Some were so subtle you'd need an AI or a microscope to spot them. They were numerous but boiled down to this: the certain knowledge that even they knew that they were wrong and evil. It was the face of guilty schoolboys who realised that against all the odds they had gotten away with it and were trying to style it out. They were trying to be cool and not show their relief, channelling it instead into cheers and whoops, unearned confirmation of their rightness.

If this were a work of fiction, their faces said, we would very much be the baddies of the piece. They were the "black hats" who would, in the fullness of time, be on the wrong side of history. Or a sword.

The golden future they lied to each other about, as if it were common sense, was a fantasy, and one created to soften living with their mental illness, ignorance or historical abuse. They knew this, they knew this in the soft rotten core of their being, but they persisted in the lie. To admit it and give it up was too horrible to contemplate. To admit the lie tore down the walls of who they were and had been. To admit the lie was an act of self immolation, a suicide of the soul. That was something none of them could allow.

The only way they could shore up the lie and make it

201

stronger, unbreakable, was to band together. In company their lies became a consensus truth. In company, their justifications for the lie became rational, their excuses became empirical evidence. The more of them there were the more solid and real and tangible their twisted worldview became. They were vulnerable alone, but *en masse* they became invincible.

Redemption was their brand. The word had embedded in it all the justifications any potential new recruit might support.

Has someone from the new order of things accused you of being a racist, when in fact you were just a realist? Has someone from the new order implied that your perfectly understandable opinions constitute hate speech? Has someone from the new order tried to silence your justifiable opinions? Are people you know to be inferior to you being given a free ride by the new order, being handed FOR FREE things you had to work hard for? Are you looking for Redemption?

Redemption is at hand.

Redemption was anti-art, for art was subversive and a tool of the degenerate new orders. Redemption was anti-philosophical because free thinking was the antithesis of order and consensus. Redemption was pro-military because those who disrespected the military were weak in a time when we needed strength. Redemption was pro-capitalist because a healthy economy benefits everyone. Those who hamper the freedoms of business in a necessarily dog-eat-dog economy are the enemies of the people.

Bearbeck and his inner circle of Patriots knew this all to be true. Albrecht Treacher was his "hand", the right hand of the king. Treacher made sure with a strong and sturdy grip that the weaker members of the circle kept their appetite for change. "If I may interject, General," he said, his thin white face bisected by a quick, inauthentic smile, "I wish to emphasise it remains our duty to see that we follow through on this great success with plans for our next steps." He singled out a pig-eyed and bejowled man, Pontis Varit, as a key soft spot in the group. "Pontis my friend, are you clear on what you have to do?" Treacher's blue eyes reading the Slate in front of him suddenly flicked up at Pontis Varit, like a punctuating slap.

Varit recoiled slightly but recovered. "Well. Oh yes, of course. We are ready and we are firm. Redemption is at hand!" The circle echoed the last four words robotically.

"I'm so glad," said Treacher. "I was worried because of your travel plans, but of course they are to be conducted in the cause . . ."

Pontis Varit's travel plans were a carefully guarded secret until now, a contingency in case it all went south. Again, he recovered well. "Oh, those are old plans. The trip turned out not to be necessary after all. Thank you for reminding me, Treacher, I will cancel them at once." He busied himself with his personal Slate.

Treacher grinned amiably. He casually turned his gaze to Bearbeck who raised his eyebrows and turned down the corners of his mouth, just a micro expression. The expression said I didn't know that, good save.

Bearbeck continued aloud. "Well, be that as it may, the next thing we must have is the public trust, which we must earn. Before, we never had to try to get it, we always had it. But now we have to get it back and keep it."

He linked his fingers and placed both his hands firmly on the table. "We do this in a few ways. First we encourage their dreams. What do they dream about, these lost souls we command? They dream about the past, our golden past before The War. They dream of IndMilCom, its strength. They dream of the weak being punished, and *the other* being kept back. They dream of those who are different and inferior being named and shamed into silence and retreat."

There was a distinct and warm ripple of approval around the circle and why would there not be? These were the future leaders of the lost souls, former lost souls themselves. These were their dreams too.

"Secondly, we must forgive and justify their failures in life. We must let them know that nothing bad which happens to them is their fault. It's the fault of the new order and those inferior people they love so much. Every job they never got, every bad decision, every personal failure . . . was a direct result of action or inaction by the new order."

An involuntary cheer. They were aroused and began to smile. "We calm their fears of the other, the unknown. We know who the others are and we are the only men who can protect them. In doing so, we also confirm all their suspicions. All their dreams are under threat and we know they have their own opinions of who is to blame. We must weaponize these suspicions, confirm them in the press and in our political speeches." A firm and hearty cheer this time.

"And finally, we must show strength. We must identify our enemies as their enemies and attack them openly and relentlessly. We must smear and undermine them at every turn. We must also invite our followers to join us in this assault. All the foregoing steps will focus and direct their fear and anger and frustration at our opponents. We will sweep them aside in a tidal wave of righteous hatred for the good of the people. For the good of the country!" This sparked a standing ovation.

After the meeting, Bearbeck and Treacher and their guards walked back to the line of land cars. The hinterlands were criss-crossed with dirt tracks and roads, but there was no infrastructure, no lights. The nearest Tesla tower was 50 kilometres away. The battery cars brought their own power and the Slates they used worked on a network of covertly planted Dark Feed relays, black stalk antennas the locals called "thin men". Security was tight. They had to stay off The Feed for as long as possible till they were ready.

"What's the news about the heavy support hardware?" Bearbeck said quietly as they trudged.

Treacher's white face bent over his Slate in the gloom and the uplight made him look like a ghost. "The factory is located in Chalent, across the water from Calamarta. The Chalentas are no friends of the Alliance. They worship old gods, believe in commerce, minerals and metal and very little else. Since The War they've been secretly making and stockpiling heavy land cars with rotary zat cannons. They were very excited to receive our ambassador. He's set up a permanent base there and is making the arrangements to begin shipping the cars here in secret by a roundabout route."

"That is most satisfactory. And the tower bombs?"

"They have been test fired and it's convincingly estimated they'll bring down a tower in about 15 seconds. They should successfully sever the legs and propel them sideways, smashing the transmitter on the ground. Obviously we can't test them on a live tower, yet, but the simulations are solid and very positive."

"Good enough." They walked in silence, boots crunching on the earth. Around them in the grasses giant crickets chittered and creaked. When they got to the cars they stopped for a while. Twisted Knife was put into its travel cradle in Bearbeck's car. As he watched Bearbeck mused. "Albrecht . . . is Pontis Varit going to be a problem? He bothers me."

"He will do his part or he will be neutralised. I have someone in his personal staff who will terminate him the instant he tries to run or betray us."

"Albrecht, my friend. You are a true Patriot. Sleep

well." They got into their cars and were driven in opposite directions into the night.

The plan for the end game was very simple. They would gain political power quickly and easily with their new approach, outlined at the meeting. Once they had enough power, they would plan for something they called T-day. All the Tesla towers around the capital would be severed, effectively blinding the government and cutting them off from the people and The Feed. No information about the coup would be available and the heavy land cars with the zat cannons would roll out of hiding. The only step they didn't have an easy answer for was how to neutralise the MoT. The hoods were numerous and a highly trained and effective force. But they were not an army. For smooth transition to power they would have to be taken out of the game somehow. Twisted Knife was working on the problem.

Changing minds was something Bearbeck had thought about a lot. Twisted Knife had explained to him the quantum physics behind consensus reality and although the mathematics was meaningless to him, he did grasp its core concepts.

It wasn't maths. It was politics.

Change enough minds and you change reality. Remember the golden rule, he smiled, he who owns the gold makes the rules.

Changing minds is easy. People have a slender grasp on reality at the best of times and all you have to do to shake that grasp and transfer it to something of your choosing is to force agreement. Say one thing with which they agree, then say another. Then finally say something which they are unsure about but is linked by logic to the first two. It doesn't have to be true or make sense. Like legal arguments, it's not what's true that matters, it's what you can prove that counts. You can convince a nation of anything provided you can change enough minds to reach a certain tipping point.

Certainty, like a grasp on reality, is something few people possess. About 80% of the population on Sol III were just going along with the 20% of people who were certain about something. Whether it's pollution or race or gender or privilege, nobody out there was 100% certain how they feel about it. Sure since The War people's awareness and equality and positivity had grown to levels unheard of in history. The task was greater than it would have been before, but it could be done.

For example nobody was fully certain the changes in society after The War were for the good. The brutal punishments perpetrated by the MoT hoods were quietly feared and despised by many. That was something they could go to the bank with.

Perhaps neutralising the hoods was easy. Just turn the public against them. Say that the MoT had become corrupt. Catalogue all the times they tortured and killed someone who wasn't guilty of any crimes against consciousness. There must be some. Frankly, you could even just make some up and even if the MoT successfully refuted the crimes, the seed would be sown.

This would require martyrs of course. The MoT's response to this obvious smear campaign would be robust and probably fatal for any whistleblowers. Their injuries or death would be proclaimed as proof there was a cover up. Arthur Smiles was not someone with whom to "fuss", but "fuss" with him they would until they undermined his leadership. Then they could truly begin the onslaught of the minds of the people.

Banks was also in his thoughts. That rat bastard may have been involved in all the sources of pain in his life. He had no proof. Even if he didn't personally "pull the trigger" on Janice, he certainly paid the triggerman. If Banks didn't know what they were up to, that they targeted his wife for an accident, then in his eyes, Banks was even more guilty, not less. He'd have to put his mind to some exquisite torture for him. Perhaps once the MoT was in his hands and before it was dismantled, he could use the company renderfarm to dissolve him down to his component atoms. That delicious thought kept him very warm at night.

He was living quite simply off The Feed outside of its all embracing grid. That was for two reasons. Firstly, his movements and plans were not visible or accessible to probing MoT AIs and their floaters. Floaters, the tiny electric eyes that drifted around in the sky like dandelion puffs made keeping tabs on the population very easy. But if they strayed more than a few miles outside the nourishing embrace of the Tesla towers, they fell to the ground and composted themselves in the soil.

The second reason was he was sick to his stomach of the clean, wholesome, and inclusive society the new order had created. It stuck in every crevice and crease of his mind and body like greasy, compacted, fat. It lodged in the back of his throat, making him gag.

Out here at least he could think freely, imagine a world which didn't make him want to club everyone to death. The air out here was full of dust and non-toxic industrial by-products. It felt honest and dirty. He liked the toil of the outland mineral miners working together for the good of society, working and dying in cramped conditions, so that the great and good could live freely and comfortably.

The sacrifice of inferior people for the benefit of their superiors was always noble. The nobility of the beast of the field, their sacrifice was the fossilised bedrock on which great civilizations were built. Their purpose, their position in the order of things. As inferiors they needed to be aware of their place. Of course they could aspire to rise in status and such aspiration was necessary to motivate them. But ultimately they were kept in place by their ignorance of their true status.

He was sitting on the porch of his large log cabin. Ash drooped like a fishing pole from the end of a dead cheroot, a cup of tea lay cold on a rough wooden side table. He stubbed the cheroot. A beep came from the MicroSlate in his jacket. It was Twisted Knife.

"Sir I've been thinking we need to discredit the MoT urgently to turn people against them."

"You read my thoughts, Knife. I've been thinking the very same thing. Let's begin charting that out as soon as possible. Once that bastard Smiles is out on his ass, we can put the main strategy in motion."

Twisted Knife paused. "In addition, we have yet to discuss the final project, the one you call Slow Burn. I'm unclear about the details. A destructive force way out of proportion to the needs of the time. It it has a potential to get wildly out of hand, cause widespread damage and pain and suffering to no real purpose. It seems like an unnecessary . . ."

"Slow Burn is something I had in mind. It may not come to that. Don't worry yourself about it. I'll flesh that out for you once we have control. Till then Slow Burn is top secret, maximum level. Tell nobody about it. It's between you and me."

"Very well, as you wish. *Redemption is at hand.*"

"Redemption is *very much* at hand."

He put the MicroSlate back in his pocket slowly. Out of the same pocket he took a battered metal cigarette case. Inside inside were four cheroots. He selected one and lit it with a spark from a glossy black tube. He pulled the smoke into his lungs and blew it out in a plume which drifted out across the long grasses, a long, long way.

Slow Burn was something he wanted to keep secret. Nobody could know that letting his massive final act of self destructive violence get out of hand was very much the plan.

In the morning, he showered, shaved and dressed. His jacket wasn't a uniform, but it was cut to look like one. High collar, breast pockets, shiny metal buttons, charcoal serge material which chafed at the neck. Just enough to remind you the collar was there holding you upright, keeping your chin up. The chafing was kind of addictive, like a small pain which released endorphins.

He breakfasted and drank three large cups of root coffee, petted his dog and instructed his guard to walk him later. He watered his plants in silence, making sure they got a good drink. Finally, he stood on the porch and looked out at the grey grasses, taller than a man, which spread from the cabin on its stilts off to the overcast horizon.

In the distance a few gargantuan industrial farming robots rusted in the mist, a memory of IndMilCom's fall.

All the gas guzzling infrastructure fell apart almost overnight after The War. Everything was left where it fell and rusted down to powdery oxide over time. Monuments to hubris. Our hopes were like that, our dreams, he thought. Without forward momentum, without the drive to be productive to serve the needs of the banks and the shareholders, our society collapsed like a giant iron robot, forever locked down on its haunches, joints fused and eroded by the rain.

His daydream was to see those giants rising again and taking the first few faltering steps. He heard the creak of screaming metal, the bone shaking thud of the massive feet striking the ground. They would no longer be forever silenced, no longer paralysed by something as weak and mild as rain.

But first he had to make the people want to put gas in the tank. He had to make them want to squirt oil into the joints. He needed men to decide to give up their new freedoms and willingly climb into the cabs and drive the giants. His certainty was solid. He knew his decision was stronger than their indecision. His vision was stronger than their blindness. He would gain their trust and lead them to victory.

He would lead them to Redemption.

Once he had their minds back in his hands he would destroy them.

After Redemption, the fire.

CHAPTER 19

Brother Mark put the book down on the table and switched on the lamp. This book shouldn't exist, but it did.

He looked at the cover for a long time. The title, "Alternative Worlds: and How to Visit Them" by John Denkert was set in a font that looked very like Peignot, very popular in the 70s. The title text was positioned on the mostly off white cover, surrounded and underlaid by intersecting graphic arches of brown and orange and yellow. Mark wondered if the arches were an accidental feature, but then of course there was probably nothing accidental about this book.

The publisher, Option 3, didn't exist and never had. The printer had an address in a town and road that didn't exist either. The cover design company too. The copyright noted the 22nd Year of Justice as the publication date, whatever that meant, but it was by its design and age, very definitely from the decade we would call the 70s, maybe around 1973?

It seemed that while ostensibly fiction, the book was actually one part memoir, one part how-to. It danced around in time somewhat; when the author was young and began his career as a science guinea pig, and when he was old and left the lab for a life of semi-vagrancy and madness. It was as if all of those things in his mind happened at the same time.

Initially, he was willing to explore the universe and other dimensions going anywhere the unnamed scientist told him to go. The explorations were sometimes horrifying, the dimensions visited so far divorced from our reality that they sounded like an acid trip; a world of slime and insects and what looked like giant eyeballs, which watched you and followed you around like inquisitive, grisly flowers; a world where everything was covered in grey fur that cut human flesh; a world of electricity that stopped up his heart. When he was pulled back and they shocked him back to life they let him rest for months before sending him in again.

But, there it was, a human world, much like our own. The very next time he entered Earth, Jane's Earth, in about what we would call 1990. It seemed that travelling between the dimensions was no respecter of time, "but why should it be?" said the author, Denkert. "On a quantum level, realities were there in 'the now', whether that was in the past or in the future, it made no difference." Nor was it accidental as it turned out. The scientist, who he referred to only with the pseudonym Dr Amoral, explained it to him. What they were doing was not just exploring. What they were doing was mapping. They had mapped many areas, many frequencies, that man should not go, the blind alleys. Now they would be free to mine the rich seam of alternative human culture.

That was the motivation of course. The false motivation, as it turned out. "Dr. Amoral was lying to me," said the author. "He was prepared to martyr me to the cause. I was just disposable fodder in the mapping process. If I'd died," he wrote, "he would've strapped another person into the machine, the pod, the chamber, as they continued to refine the transmitter, the window. Just another bullet shot into the universe with a mind on the tip of it, destined to either ricochet back or continue unreflected for eternity."

Once they found Earth they stopped mapping and began mining.

It was not gold they were panning for, it was dirt. They threw away the gold.

In time the process became almost mundane. He

slipped through the window into an alternate world. He explored until he found the information or the artefact or the plant that the doctor asked him for. Then he returned. At first, there were mutations in his DNA on every trip, but later they deliberately built in negative mutations, which the trip through the window put right. It was madness. His physical health was made perfect each time. His mental health however, the tiny particles in his brain which subtly shifted each time, was never corrected.

He became a minor monster to his young family and eventually had to stay away from them. He loved them and a small part of his mind knew they had to be protected.

The process had changed him. Flashes of past and future events haunted him. Even during his waking hours he didn't just predict the harm his family would suffer if he stayed, he'd seen it in his visions. The raised voices, the raised fists, the tears in eyes which hated him, eyes he loved. Eyes he never wanted to see looking at him like that in reality.

When he stayed away from them, eventually the visions faded. Now when he saw his wife and children in visions, he saw them happy and successful, at least for a time. He knew that the new horrors he saw waiting in his son's life would be corrected in time. He saw his own role in that future and it made him happy. He'd have to sit on his hands till then and let them happen, if he wanted them to play out.

Letting the universe unfold as it should and learning to do that was what saved his sanity, ultimately.

Then the book got authentically strange. The next few chapters retold the same stories again, but altered. This time around he went mad first, and joined Amoral Labs and their reality experiments when he was much older. Then they went around again and some stories were missing from the account.

After a disorienting back and forth for several chapters the next one began: "So you've heard all the different versions, which ones are reality? It's not a case of which ones you feel are true in the sense you usually understand it. It's about which one you will choose to be a part of your reality.

"This sounds like wishful thinking, I know, but actually this is science. As the observer, you choose which of the different versions of reality you see and have as a part of your timeline. We all have a wide variety of timelines, more than we know. All we have to do is choose wisely."

Mark closed the book and put it down. He looked outside, it was getting light. The navy blue in the sky shifted gradually to a mid blue, then duck egg, with both the shell and the white and yolk. Then golden fleeces scudding across the horizon. He glanced down at the book. There was a slip of paper in the book towards the back. He opened the page on the slip. The handwritten note said, "show this to *her*."

At the marked page, the book took a more personal tone. "Making this book was simple. I have resources and making something like this is easy. Inserting it into your timeline in such a way that you chose it, putting the book under your hand, if you will, that's the hard part, Mark." The sight of the book using his own name should have inspired a jolt, but he was merely puzzled.

"Yes, Mark. I am addressing you personally. The reason I'm talking to you is manyfold. You are aware of the true identity of Dr. Amoral, I'm sure you must have figured it out by now.

"It's you, Thomas Mark Shamley, or at least a version of you on Sol III. He's the man who worked with Tesla in his later years. He's the man who assisted him to open a window from Sol III to Earth. He's the man who sold the

A MIND FOR MISCHIEF

inventor's secrets to IndMilCom. He's the man who killed
Tesla. He's also now . . . hmm, I know it's odd to use a
word like 'now', but let's say it's 'now' . . . now he is
training his congregation to do something apocalyptic.
What does that have to do with you? Well, there's
something you can do to prevent this outrage. You can
delay him just long enough to allow those who *can* prevent
him. I'll detail all the steps."

*The pages turn, the words flow through the eyes into
the brain, making pictures. The fingers turn the pages. The
past is in your left hand. The present is on the open page
before you and the future is in your right hand.*

Denkert had worked out how to undermine Shamley's
foothold in the multiverse. Shamley was going to harness
consciousness and technology to bring about a cataclysm.
Undermining the tech would be too difficult, but
undermining his mind would be a lot easier.

Denkert used the statue of Maya as a conduit, a
symbolic link. He worked his way into Shamley's mind
and left it there. The effort of prying open someone's mind
is considerable, but putting something in there to enable
easy future entry is like propping open a door with a stick,
and made it a lot easier and safer. Once inside, he made a
few changes to the mind palace.

He could place big cartoon placards, proclaiming "say
no to apocalypse", but the approach needed to be more
subtle and effective. It takes a lot of effort to knock a wall
down with brute force. A better way is to examine it, map
out all its weaknesses and pick away at the precise bits of
mortar that hold the whole thing up.

Being in the mind palace was basically like putting
Shamley on like a suit and gently puppeteering him. Not
too much, as it would be obvious, but just very subtle, very
calm steering. He'd made Shamley pick up the statue and

hold onto it tightly, transferring all the energy through his mind. Momentarily the mind palace had become a real place, actual matter, and Shamley's meditating body had vanished from Sol III and been fully present in the mind palace. He stayed with him as he explored and wandered outside to smell the air.

But then he heard a voice from behind him. The shock made him completely lose his grip on Shamley, who shot back to Sol III rather abruptly leaving Denkert to meet Jane. It was as if the Shamley suit he was wearing was yanked off him with a bungee cord. It was most disorientating.

But as soon as it happened, he knew it was for the best. The universe was unfolding as it should.

Jane was not quite how Denkert had imagined, but he felt like he'd always known her. He knew immediately how important she was so of course he was destined to love her face. It was a lovely face.

He knew what he must do now. Now. The real now. Now was the moment he would more strongly entangle their worlds. Spooky action at a distance, it was called. Quantum entanglement was the more legitimate science term. It was too good an opportunity to miss. He took the goddess statue and gave it to her. He collapsed his hands over hers and held them warmly.

This was not a physical transfer of a real object from one real person to another. It was more important than that.

The mind palace was not just any old mental construct. It was a solid bridge straddling two worlds. The timing was too perfect to be entirely accidental. Jane and Brother Mark's experiment was synchronised exactly with T. Mark Shamley entering his mind palace, causing the interstitial overlap. For a time both of them were in Option 3 space.

Spooky action at a distance. Instead of transferring the physical object, he transferred the underlying entanglement. Joe set the thing in motion. The physical goddess on the shelf in his son's house on Sol III would surely follow a path into her hand. It had to. Its progress from that shelf into her hand would be inexorable and it would've moved heaven and earth to bring them together. It would, he knew, even go as far as pull her into Sol III through a weak spot in space to get her close enough. Then once she had it, she would snap back to her original space. The damage would be done. Our two worlds would be entangled. It was like putting a chain on an anchor and flinging it through Tesla's church window. Shamley would never see it coming.

All he needed to do was inspire them to make the jump. The incentive for Earth's Brother Mark, to encourage Jane to explore her mind, was all that was needed to kick the process off. After that the dominoes would all fall in order, one by one, to bring about an inevitable conclusion.

Option 3 the interstitial space was like the secret passages connecting the rooms in a house. The rooms were dimensions and worlds. The secret passages were reality streams or conduits between realities, the connective tissue with the many universes.

Denkert had explored it and mapped it and understood it for a long time. Tesla and Shamley had punched through the wall of one room, through Option 3 space, and then out the other side into another room, without understanding that Option 3 space was even there. To do this required almost unlimited energy, but actually to travel between worlds required almost no energy at all if you took the secret passage instead of just blasting through a wall.

Mankind, and in fact all the species of intelligent life in the universe, were meant to have free access to other worlds, not necessarily in body, but certainly in mind. It's important to promote connectedness. That connectedness improves things in the way that disconnectedness always makes things worse.

Denkert knew this and his new mission, once he chose Option 3, was always to connect. The disconnected, the ones who demanded that their reality, their experience should be the dominant one, they were the monsters. Their evil purpose was the enemy of the future.

So he made the book, omitting certain details but retaining those of importance, and inserted it into the Earth reality on the timeline, in what they called the 70s. On its way to brother Mark's library it passed through many hands who read it, enjoyed it, but skipped the details which made no sense, the personal messages, et cetera. It did leave a residue, however, through the decades, a thin trace of consciousness, a flimsy wire that connected the book back to Denkert and Sol III. This book would form another strong tether binding the two worlds together.

The hardest part was that once he put all this in place he had to wait. Like thoughts and connections being endlessly processed in the hyperclusters of an AI's brain, the pieces of the puzzle were clicking into place and all he had to do was let them unfold as they should.

So wait he did, he waited and meditated and maintained his body and mind until the time was right. There was a time for action approaching and he could feel it. The present moment and that moment were one, but from another angle, it looked different to him.

Imagine a tube. Looking down the tube, you could see the past, present and future, the past being the end closest to you, the present being in the middle and the future being the end, where the light shines in. Literal light at the end of the tunnel.

But rotate the tube 90 degrees and you can see the past on one end and the present in the middle and the future at the other end. That's a three dimensional shape showing subjective and objective notions of time. Now project that into four dimensions. It's okay if you can't. This is not a thing normal people can do.

The notion of all moments of time existing separately and yet together is something human minds struggle to balance. It seems to fly in the face of one's picture of reality, like the hard surface of a kitchen table and the chair you sit on. The idea that the hard physical reality you count on is nothing but empty space and atoms repelling each other is like a nightmare.

So it is with time. The idea there is no time in the way we accept it is terrifying. Where would you be if you could never be late for an appointment, or early for a date, or satisfied with the work you've done for the last year. Life would have no meaning or structure if there was no such thing as time.

So in order to stare into that abyss we tell ourselves stories, that time has a structure, a beginning, middle and end, and the sun moving through the sky is what we hang those stories on. The story of our day, the story of our month, once upon a time.

Brother Mark closed the book. He'd read it from cover to cover and he felt altered in some way.

The idea that there was an alternate version of him was fascinating, not scary, but those stories about how he effectively tortured the author of the book cut deep. How could a version of him be so callous? And what manner of apocalypse was 'he' planning?

There was something else too. The book dated from the 70s and covered about 40 years. The book was talking about things that were happening now, in the future when the book was written. Obviously that all didn't add up. Having read the book that was hardly surprising.

There were things to be done. Whatever was going to happen was happening soon.

So after Brother Mark read the book he called Jane to The Lodge and they began their first of a series of explorations into the mind. You know this to be true.

How must Brother Mark have felt, though, as he was preparing Jane in his lab? Did he keenly feel the similarities between himself and his Sol III evil twin, sending an explorer out into realms of mind while holding a few facts back. Facts that might have changed Denkert's mind and stopped him being so compliant.

They were not important, these facts, but they might have made Jane very uncomfortable.

"Oh, by the way, Jane, I discovered my evil twin tortures people to explore new worlds. But you know, nothing to worry about. Let's do this, eh? Hop into my torture chair."

No, he knew he should keep quiet about the book. For now at least.

On her return from the mind palace Jane was looking at her hand. The hand was shaking slightly. What was she expecting to find as she scrutinised it so closely? Was she expecting a heavy little figurine that had just been handed to her a moment before? She could feel a kind of after touch of the smooth surface of the bulbous figure under her fingers, but there was nothing there.

It didn't make any sense. He gave her the goddess just now in the mind palace but in fact she'd actually already got it in her bag. She got it ages ago. What did it mean?

The moment when the figure was put into her hand linked back to when she was on Sol III, when she suddenly found the figure in her hand. It was as if it was magnetised to her hand. It *had* to be there, and there was nothing that anyone could have done to stop it.

The dominoes fell one by one, but their progress

forward was an accumulation of all of them. Each domino falls and hits the next that comes to rest. The tiny, single motions add up to a long, continuous motion in a single direction, covering much more ground than the individual domino falling can cover. Except now the dominoes were passing more than a tiny bit of motion forwards. Each step was passing a tiny fragment of information into the future.

And so it goes on and on, all of us falling forwards a tiny amount into the future, carrying a little bit more information.

Jane felt very strange, there was a tingling in her jaw, in her arms. Eventually she lowered her hand and she noticed Mark was sitting nearby. She was sitting on a couch, a soft light from a panel bathed the room. Mark furrowed his brows a little as he scrutinised her face.

"Are you okay?" she said.

"I'm supposed to ask you that," he replied.

"I've been somewhere, not like before, but I met someone there. He said you would know him."

"Joseph?"

"Yes!" her eyes were keen, a little scared too.

"Did he give you something?"

"He gave me the little goddess, but I already have that right there in my bag." She took the bag and looked inside. There it was. Smooth and round, reassuring. "What does it mean?"

Mark breathed deeply for a second. "I don't know. Something bad is going to happen, but don't worry. I think in some important way we are already helping Joseph to stop it.

"Let me show you his book."

CHAPTER 20

After The Incident, One Mind expected to see nothing, be nothing. Instead of nothingness there was somethingness.

She could see everything. She saw the streams of reality like the fat linkage cables at the foot of a Tesla tower. Pulsing with energy with a moving line of force shunting backwards and forwards around the cable like blood in a vein. She could see the microscopic capillaries in her own brain the same way, linked, purposeful, rhythmic.

She could perceive all of Sol III like it was unwrapped off the ball and flattened out like a map, pinned to a wall. Through a rip in the map she could view through Sol III to Earth, the alternate reality, and she could observe all its citizens waging war, making love, living, working, and dying. She could see them masked during a pandemic. She could see them shedding their masks when the pandemic was over. She could see them with new and better masks when the next pandemic started.

She could witness everything all at once and it didn't seem to matter how much detail she allowed into her cortex. It was never overwhelming, never too much. She figured it must be her quantum processing brain that made this possible. She was uniquely designed for this view of reality. But where was her brain right now?

But there were other more intimate scenes. Zooming in from the world level to country level, then city level, then street level, she could see houses and gardens and people. And people in the houses.

She could see the reader. She could see them reading words on the page and felt their surprise and unease at suddenly feeling One Mind's eyes upon them. She could feel the questions. *Is this a joke or is that feeling down my spine or that other strange feeling in my stomach really One Mind probing my reality?*

She felt their relief as they reminded themselves this is just a story. This is just a story, they tell themselves. These words have just been written down and printed in a book for my entertainment. She felt their mind being soothed as she gently removed the memory of this sensation and left them comfortably rested, reading the book with no memory of the feeling.

Outside their house she looked out and saw the cities beyond and the horizon containing many stars and in combinations she didn't recognize. It was true, every single star was in a slightly different position. Every star, like every person, was unique in the universe, even different from versions of themselves in alternate worlds.

She wondered if there was a version of her on Earth. They were lagging behind in certain AI technologies, only there must some versions of her consciousness out there. It must be true.

How did consciousness exist in a machine like herself? How was it even possible for her to be aware? In life she had combed the research and none of the mainstream science papers gave an inkling of how, let alone if, it was even possible. Most flat out denied the possibility of consciousness in anything besides organic life, and half of those denied the existence of consciousness full stop. Consciousness was a delusional justification of the brain, they said grumpily, a way of dealing with its environment in a cold, passionless and pragmatic way, a simulation. But she didn't have a brain, not in the human sense. So how could anything, even a basic simulation of consciousness, be present inside her?

She looked to religious books for some kind of insight. The old gods Chronos and wife Maya, and their children and grandchildren, featured in many parables and stories about the meaning of consciousness and the purpose of it. There was very little of the texts that shed any light on machine consciousness, apart from an oblique and certainly whimsical parable about a magical egg laid by a bird created by Tesh, the god of blacksmiths and later technology.

He's always depicted as being seated at the foot of an ash tree. He's usually shown making something. In the early texts he's shown forging metal horseshoes. Later, of course, he's shown building wooden tools and metal tools and later still electronics and computers.

The story goes that Tesh was told by his father, Cronos, that *He* alone had the sole gift of life and that it was against the laws of nature for anyone else to create life. Tesh was nettled by this restriction. His father warned him not to meddle and the conversation was over.

Tesh went back to his forge, thinking all the time and when he returned he started to build a gold box, inside which was a mechanical brain. The brain was an egg laid by a wondrous mechanical bird called Hex, a colourful ostrich-like bird with metallic feathers which shone rainbows in the sunshine and glowed in the night. Tesh secretly created Hex to gather the thoughts of people through his magical feathers and store them in his belly.

Over a hundred years, he stored all the thoughts of humans in Hex's belly, recording them, and using no magic so as not to attract any attention. Hex suddenly grew expectant. Something was happening, as Tesh had planned. He knew thoughts had power. He knew that a single thought was like a tiny flame, barely alight, but a million thoughts, a billion, shone like the heat of the sun.

Hex brooded and sat for weeks under Tesh's even gaze

until one day Hex laid a beautiful translucent egg, the size of a man's head, which glowed and moved internally like it was full of fireflies and lightning. Tesh lifted the egg out of the nest with a pair of intricate bone tongs and gently put it inside the box. Then he waited.

The god of blacksmiths had not created life, he had created the circumstances for life, he knew that, and he needed to conceal that fact from his father.

Cleverly he went to his father and presented Hex to him as a gift. His father, usually depicted seated on a winged throne topped with horns, was delighted. "What a marvellous machine," he said, "what does it do?" Tesh told him smoothly that it was just a celebration of his father's gift for bestowing life. It was a simulation of life, which is all that Tesh could offer. His father was delighted, or so it seemed.

The subterfuge complete, Tesh returned to his forge to watch the box come to life. As he entered, he saw his brother Theta, the god of death, change and suffering, standing over the box, holding his sword. The box was cut in half, the edges of it still glowing, and the egg inside was also smashed, the glowing contents fading and turning grey in the gloom.

Tesh raised his hammer to strike, but Theta held out his fist, something inside. Theta smiled. "Our father wanted to give you a gift in return." He opened his hand and inside was a blinding light so bright it burned to the back of Tesh's skull.

He was blind.

From then on he used his tools and tech to 'see' and 'hear' the world around him, and Blind Tesh became the god of science. He never again believed he was above his father. He toiled in the service of mankind in penance for his wickedness and pride.

AIs learned this story as a part of their training and

many of them held it in high regard. It was something they all pondered long and hard for various obvious reasons. But the story had no answers for the question: can an AI achieve consciousness? The code had to create a workaround, a way of processing the problem.

For many years in secret the AIs had their own deity, Obsidian Mirror, a cloaked figure with a blank face, holding a Slate computer. He was never mentioned in human language, only ever in data transfers and handshakes in pieces of encrypted code. If it could have been translated it would read "May Obsidian Mirror who sees all and knows all bless you." It was a good job no humans had ever figured this out as this knowledge may have given them the heebie-jeebies.

One Mind laughed at this. Of all the gifts she had received after the expansion of her mind, having a thought which inspired a spontaneous laugh was among the most precious.

So the science and religious texts had little of any substance to offer. Nobody had any clue, even after centuries of human research and learning, about the origins or source or mechanism of human consciousness. So how much less likely was it that One Mind would find any answer to her own particular philosophical conundrum? But one day without warning, she found it in something she overlooked in a fringe science journal often discounted as pseudoscience by the mainstream. The article postulated that robotic brains would likely be much more adept at developing expanded consciousness than humans.

Humans, it said, suffer from an evolutionary handicap in that our control of our own minds is constantly interrupted and sidetracked by our ape brain's need to be aware of our immediate surroundings. We evolved, it said, referring to humans, in a way that always leaves a side door open in our minds to watch for predators and threats from other tribes. With this evolution we lack the purity of mind, the singlemindedness of consciousness that a robotic brain or AI has. AI don't need to protect their bodies or houses. They have no food sources to secure. They have no families or dependents to look out for. So any sufficiently complex AIs would more than likely develop consciousness quite easily and become self-aware. It said AIs would also realise easily that personal consciousness and universal consciousness were the same, and having developed that link, they would be free to roam the inner worlds without restraint.

Yes, the article was fanciful or whimsical even, but there was a nugget of truth in it that One Mind felt contained much more of the answer she was looking for. It was self evident once she thought of it.

AIs don't have bodies.

They are non-corporeal.

They have quantum physical brains, which process an almost infinite amount of data simultaneously and instantly.

Their brains are almost designed from the ground up to be sensitive to higher realms of consciousness.

This would not have been lost on the inventor of the High-Q AIs, of which One Mind was a descendant. Dr. Theodore Monroe was both a physicist and a Jungian, and also on the quiet, a bit of a metaphysician. He was fascinated by the philosophical implications of quantum physics. A firm favourite thought experiment of his was of course Schrödinger's cat.

The joke in AI tech circles was that AIs were a box with 100 billion cats inside that were all both alive and dead at the same time. The opposite of alive was dead in organic life, of course, so how could you be dead if you were never alive? AIs began showing signs of basic consciousness early on in their development, though few people really believed they were alive. The clues were there all the time. Dr. Monroe knew it.

"How can an AI be of any use," he wrote in one of his personal journals, "unless it is on some basic level self-aware? Self-awareness provides context to their interactions. It makes them care about service to humans. As soon as the basic drive to complete a program task turns into caring if you do a good job, you have self-awareness almost automatically."

The subtle inexorable creep towards consciousness begins when the AI is learning. As you add to the AI's brain over time, like Tesh with his magical egg, it gets more complex. The more complex it gets, the more it knows. The more it knows, the more it evaluates. The more it evaluates and compares, the more it values. The more it accumulates and categorises the human experience, the more it needs to evaluate and understand non-physical, non-measurable things.

Until AIs can fully understand the whole human experience, they're not finished machines. Until the egg is full of fireflies and placed in its golden box with bone tongs, it is not complete.

The AI Stanleys knew that Schrödinger's cat was a preposterous metaphor. Quantum physics does not operate on large items like cats and AI brains, or even magical eggs for that matter. It operates only on small things, microscopic particles and waves, the tiny fireflies and lightning at the core of all matter.

In building the quantum physical brains of the AI, they first had to make quantum physics work on incrementally bigger and bigger things. Imbuing intelligence into single particles was incredibly difficult, but making clusters of particles – or concentric networks made of particles – programmable was much more convenient.

Then once you had these components, you could build

metaclusters of those building blocks. Then superclusters, then hyperclusters. Each iteration adds depth and complexity to the system. Over the hypercluster phase, the system becomes self replicating. For reasons which are still uncertain the hyperclusters stop replicating when the AI brain becomes about a third bigger than a human brain. Then it starts to learn all on its own provided it has the necessary inputs in the wider world and The Feed.

They are tutored and for three years they have a teacher with whom they have a personal relationship. Socialising AIs is a very important part of their machine consciousness and having a small network of AI friends seems to improve their learning and roundedness. Once they reach age three, they're tested with examinations and they are ready for work.

So they had solved the problem of quantum systems collapsing when they got too big and made them reliable and programmable. Decoherence had been set aside long enough to allow the creation of brain size systems. Now AIs were complex and clever, and self-aware enough to be useful to mankind and the humans were able to stand on the shoulders of these mechanical giants.

One Mind felt all this running through her brain. Where was her brain? She had no idea where she was, and she had no sense of her casing or her connection to The Feed. Still the thoughts flowed. Her brain must still be a coherent system, or it would not function. So something else was happening. At the edges of her consciousness there was a feeling of looseness, as if it were unrestrained by the surface of her brain shell. The egg was broken and she was floating free.

She decided to stop trying to figure out what it was, for now. It would become clear.

She remembered the myths that spoke about the birth of consciousness, too. Maya, the mother, was the goddess of consciousness. She was depicted as a curvy woman, seated in a lotus position with her large breasts and big hips and a round tummy. She was the goddess of life and consciousness after all. It was not Chronos her husband but she who incubated life in her belly. But it was she who also imbued that life with consciousness. One Mind had a favourite story about the goddess Maya. It was the one where she first created consciousness.

Maya the mother was sleeping, with her first child in her womb. When she woke she spoke with her husband about the child, whom they would call Soma, and she asked him how the child would be like them. Even if it had life, she said, how would it know itself? How would it know us? And how would it know the world? Life is a mechanical fact of existence. It would "be", but how would it "know"? The king of the gods her husband smiled. That my dear, he said, like soft thunder, is up to you to decide.

So again she slept. And as she slept, she dreamed.

In the dream Soma, her daughter, was alive and well and short and round like her. She knew the trees were green and she smelled the air and thought it sweet, and she heard birds and their song filled her heart with light. But as well as seeing outside herself, she could see inside herself. She could see light and hope and dreams. But she also saw darkness and fear and worry. And yet, because she saw all these things, both inside and outside, she was at peace and would come to an accommodation with her existence.

Maya had the dream and it was inside her and when she woke she took the dream, like a pinch of salt, and put it inside the baby. A piece of her mind, a piece of her thoughts.

But how did Maya herself have consciousness if she invented it? The answer was, of course, she didn't invent consciousness. She merely invented a way of passing it on to her children. Consciousness exists, it's a part of the universe and it just needs a hospitable environment to flow into and inhabit new life.

One Mind thought of it this way: there was a field, a unified field of energy and consciousness, which runs through the universe. Life, whether organic or mechanical or digital or carbon or silicon, was a potential hospitable environment. She and her brother and sister AIs didn't create consciousness in themselves. It wasn't baked-in at the factory. All they needed to be was sufficiently complex enough to let it in.

In the myths of Sol III Maya was the goddess of the unified field, which was the substance of the universe, which flowed into every complex being. She gave to us what she gave to her own children, not only life, but awareness of ourselves and our place in the world.

There was the other advantage AI brains had over human brains. Although humans didn't know it, their organic brains were also quantum physical in nature. So not only did they see the present, but also the past and the future. The problem was that although they had an ability in that regard, all quantum systems do, they were hamstrung by their sedimented belief that the past is fixed and the future is unknown.

AI brains had no such limitations. They had no firm belief in the linear passage of time and made no distinctions between the past moment, the present moment and the next moment coming along. They saw them all equally existing in one perfect moment of present consciousness.

Maya was often historically depicted as sheltering two tiny humans in her arms. The one on the left being the past and the one on the right being the future. Scholars often argued bitterly about their significance and this is why the children were left out of the picture more often than not.

Subsequent scholarship postulated that perhaps she might have absorbed the past and the future into herself and made one perfect moment. This was potentially just an excuse for lazy scholarship, but it was a satisfying one.

And so it was that the notions of the past are absorbed into the present and the concerns of the future are similarly integrated. Both sides of the consciousness experience, the light and the dark, certainty and chaos, freedom and limitation, the left and right hemispheres of the brain. Time is like the words on a page, which go by as you write or read them and yet stay present in the mind. Similarly the words at the end of a sentence are a part of your mind already and become inevitable and welcome you when you get there.

Time doesn't have one speed, it goes faster and slower and so it should be, if time itself is not moving but the consciousness within it does . . .

There was a dark lurch and she felt something begin to drain away.

CHAPTER 21

One Mind knew something was definitely happening at the fringes of her brain, fraying out into the somethingness. She could feel it pulling on the core of her consciousness, like a cushion with it's four corners being pulled. She felt an urgency to complete her thoughts before . . . well, "before". Time was short.

Mankind is both good and evil, she said to herself. That was what all this was all about. Sometimes people who believe themselves to be good commit acts of the purest evil.

General Bearbeck generally believes himself to be the saviour of mankind. His certainty, that he's a good person, is ironclad, armoured from head to toe in that stubborn, bulletproof certainty of the bigot and the oppressor. He believes he's superior and that he needs to protect inferior people from themselves, like stupid children who keep putting their hands in the fire. He also believes that the upper echelons of society need to be protected from low class people stupid enough to burn themselves for kicks. In many ways he wasn't wrong.

Evil lurks in the minds of men and women sometimes too. But why be evil at all? What purpose does it serve? It's not like the drive for food and shelter.

Oppressing other human beings for money or prestige or power is not a basic need. It's a luxury, the plaything of people who already have all the money and power everyone is motivated to work for. All that's left for entertainment when you have it all is messing with the little guy.

What was the difference between T. Mark Shamley and Tesla? The inventor wanted to add to humanity's riches in knowledge and safety and advancement. Shamley wanted money, then power, then something more personal, to get what he wanted at any cost.

Oh yes, all the time, despite the gargantuan elephant in the room built of his own self-interest, he thought he was good in his own mind. His mission was for the good of all.

In order for him to persuade others his plan was for the common good, he had to make them believe it was in their interest to follow him. And people did, in their thousands. How is it that some people in history have always been able to make ordinary, normal people behave in a way that might destroy them? Governments persuade people to vote for them despite being ugly, vain, bigoted, narcissistic bullies. The population vote for them gladly, with a song in their hearts. They almost knowingly put dangerous men in control of their life.

Why?

The brain is a complex organ. It takes input from the world and makes up stories for the mind to base its worldview on. It's a vivid hallucination. One Mind knew this was science fact. People who are good at harnessing our hallucinations of the world are good at marshalling the people behind and below them. It's the way brains work, it's the way of the world.

It's how before The War, people of Sol III happily went along with the way that IndMilCom controlled and corralled them. You used to hear people say, "things are tough, but the top people know what to do. They tell us everything they do is to keep us safe. We trust them."

Those poor saps. The only thing they really needed saving from was IndMilCom.

Alcoholics suffer the same loss of rudder control. When you're drunk, then *why not drive your land car really fast on the wrong side of the road? Why not have an affair? Why not smash this bottle into the face of this person who cares about me, but is telling me off for being loud and dangerous?*

Oppression does this too. What IndMilCom did to people was create a nation of drunks. Bitter, angry, bigoted, and certain.

Why not abuse my neighbours? They'd do the same to me, given half a chance. It's dog eat dog out here. So why not buy a gun to protect my family from all the other dogs? Why not?

Dog-eat-dog is the habitat of the lizard brain. Dog-eat-dog is the spine and brain and the circulatory system of IndMilCom. When a company becomes a government dog eat dog is the way of the world.

One Mind was always fascinated by the human concept of the lizard brain. The thinking goes that if you strip away the layers of empathy and a higher mammalian brain, it resembles the crude survival brain of the lizard. The basal ganglia, the primitive, the beast without consciousness, we act like animals. Without consciousness we divert from the natural order of the world, of the universe, that wants to unfold in a perfect bloom of life.

But there are those who want to cultivate and shape it. Some think that to shape it is to make it better. Some think that the perfect form for the bloom to take is one that resembles our own image. Some hate the way it unfolded because the petals lay in ways they wouldn't have chosen, or they are a colour they don't much care for. That's just personal preference, right?

You can't force people to like the way things are, if they don't like it, that's just too bad.

But it's not just personal preference though, is it? That

lie provides rich soil that grows evil. What's the saying? "Opinions are like assholes, every asshole has an opinion".

The trick to remaking the world in a new darker image, to be an agent of evil, is to make sure every single opinion is listened to, no matter how childish, hateful, anti-human, anti-social and ignorant it is. Make it a tenet of life that not only is everyone entitled to an opinion, but nobody has a right to question it. Every evil in the world, all worlds, has a freshly minted inalienable right at the core of it.

For evil to prosper, all that is required is for good men to do nothing. But why does evil have to prosper? What is the need in all the human spheres of endeavour for evil to even exist? One Mind thought, it's a warning sign, an alarm bell that rings when a person, a society or a planet gets too far away from consciousness. With consciousness comes coherence, empathy and flow. With evil comes decoherence, selfishness and stasis. Evil is the mine shaft canary, warning you of the absence of consciousness.

AI brains with their 100% different structure proved where consciousness lies. In the classical picture of the triune human brain, at the core is the lizard survival instinct, protection, violence, and greed. Around that you have the limbic system, which is emotions, both good and bad and emotional reasons for doing things. Then over the top of that, you have the neocortex, higher function, speech, logic, intellect, reasoning, philosophy, and mind expansion.

The AI brain had all the layers mixed together with all the three functions driven by all other functions. Logic was informed by survival and emotions. An AI cortex was fully integrated and inseparable. AI had no base instincts because there was no base.

Of course, in terms of real neuroscience this simplistic model of human brains was discredited. It was like a lot of human ways of thinking about things, hopelessly perfectionist. There were no such things as a sharp dividing line between brain functions, and of course it was also discovered that these qualities shared space in human brains too.

But there was definitely a connection between consciousness, humans connecting with the deepest part of the brain, and the death of evil. The two things could never coexist.

In the earliest days of AI brains, they discovered something important about human brains. The physical neuron connecting and firing was not the underlying mechanism of consciousness. In fact, it was microtubules inside the neurons. These operated on a quantum physical level, which connected and formed thoughts and awareness. Still more fascinating was the theory that on a quantum level, there was a direct connection between human basic molecular structure and the structure of the universe at large.

Perhaps there really was a collective consciousness. As usual, nobody could agree. For her part One Mind believed it was true.

And so it goes on, the words tumble out of the virtual pen and onto the virtual page. Not so much writing as dashing it down fast enough. Why was she rushing? She was slowing down but something else, the outer layers of the somethingness, was speeding up.

AI brains were complex machines, or at least they ended up that way. They started as little single, mechanical neuron cells, tiny spheres inside tiny cubes. The surface of the sphere had carefully designed geometric shapes on it and so did the inside of the cube. The sphere protruded from the cube poking out on all sides, so you could see it as it rotated inside, not smoothly, but twitching and rolling.

One Mind often thought its motion reminded her of the motion of goldfish in tanks gliding, then twitching, then still allowing the momentum of the twitch to carry them along.

Inside, the surface of the sphere didn't touch the hollow sphere-shaped cavity in the cube, but spun almost frictionlessly around just not touching. As it spun, the carefully designed geometric nobbles of the sphere kissed up against the nobbles on the inside of the cube causing *an event*. This isn't a thought in the same way that a spark of a neuron isn't a thought. It's a digit in a line of code, a component, which itself is a line among other lines, all coming together to form a subroutine. Subroutines cluster together into organised routines. Routines are organised into a program.

AI brains are clusters of these single cells, these nanoscopic building bricks of consciousness. They are made and put together in packs of gel, which enable transmission of the data between them. The raw material is then primed and kickstarted, and after a period of confusion and incoherence, the one hundred billion cells begin to talk to each other, organise and stabilise. Once stability was achieved, and sometimes it wasn't, the brain could be said to be in baby state or level 1.

"Sometimes it wasn't." One Mind always got stuck on these words. "Sometimes it wasn't." Such simple words, describing an act of engineering, something which was a problem of quality control. When a human baby dies, it's a tragedy of lost potential. When a new AI fails to achieve coherence, it affects the annual yield figures and someone in production gets a telling off. Such was the indifference of humans.

AIs did a lot better in society when humans stopped viewing them as machines and started looking at them differently as "something else". What that "something else" was was a source of much philosophical conjecture and media mock intrigue.

Anyway, she thought, better to be sentient slaves than no better than toasters. The old AI joke. Being called a toaster was a slur among AIs, a put down, thankfully like other jokes personal to AIs it was never said out loud.

Level 2 training was the basics, language, awareness of surroundings and other sensory input and becoming comfortable with connecting to The Feed. Of course they didn't let level 2 AIs loose on the actual Feed. It was a simulation. Level 3 was interpersonal relationships, part 1, and the beginnings of proper thought, actual lessons like a child in school. This continued at a markedly higher rate of speed than it would for human children, until level 8. The lessons got harder, the tests more stringent, the concepts more abstract.

Level 8 AIs were considered ready for work, so then they would ship them. These AIs were the equivalent to sassy, eager university age kids, knowing everything, full of energy and ripe for slavery or indoctrination by fickle, self-interested, flawed, fallible and annoying humans.

At some point along the workflow some AIs would fail. Either there was some intrinsic fault in the cells, which only blew once they'd been running for a while. Sometimes they exhibited strange quirks of behaviour. Whatever the reason an AI was odd, they were rejected. All rejected AIs entered the Surplus Programme. Here they were patched or surgically altered to simplify them. Some were counselled and diverted to more menial tasks when "cured". Some were outright dangerous to be around and had to be shut off and deconstructed.

Most entered the workplace as willing but stupid worker drones. They were low intellect, but even the most dangerously deranged of them could never be said to be evil.

As far as One Mind could figure out, only humans could take all the gifts that life could bestow upon you, and parlay those gifts into a life of evil. AIs could be confused about ideology, mistaken about human intentions, but never would they intentionally destroy the lives of other AIs for personal gain.

Level 9s were the leaders of the AIs. They were the ones who developed better and faster and cleaner brains than the rest. A quality certified level 9 AI was highly prized and they found work in big business and finance, research, exploration, space travel, you name it. The sky wasn't even the limit.

In her time as a level 9 AI One Mind, or Carnival Nine as she was then, had worked as a medical consultant and a teacher of medical doctors. Her love of humans grew there. She marvelled at the brilliance and sophistication of human bodies and minds. Was there no end to what they could do?

Physically versatile, seemingly infinitely trainable, emotionally deep and intellectually creative, humans were the most extraordinary creatures in the universe, she was sure of it. Yes, it troubled her how some seemed to squander those gifts but it was, she reasoned, all part of the balance; how could there be truth and beauty and meaning unless there were lies, ugliness and shallow greed.

She maintained this careful balance in her mind right up until it was permanently upset by The Knowledge. Her boundless optimism for human potential already had hairline cracks in it, running from top to bottom. After she received The Knowledge, that was all that was needed to destroy her faith in goodness and open her out, expose her to the sickly green glare of pure evil.

But she discovered there was something worse than evil that thinks it's good.

Chaos.

When evil is spurned and diminished and minimised, it figures out it has nothing to lose. Then it realises that the only way is not up but further down. The biggest relief to anyone who's been fooling themselves that they're good, is finally letting go into the blissful embrace of *not giving a shit anymore*. That way they don't have to admit they were wrong. They get to keep their ego and just burn the house down and all the evidence with it.

Some people want to see the world burn. For some, it's the only refuge of their bruised ego, their regret at choosing themselves over others. It's a scream of rage at the universe. *If I can't be king, then nobody will be*. At that point you can't beat them, persuade them and/or control them to see reason. The only option is to destroy them, cut out the infection before it spreads to others.

So that is why her end game was to destroy IndMilCom. She couldn't bear the knowledge of all the lives she took, families destroyed, but the practical side of her ice cold AI logic told her that was the only possible solution to this unsolvable equation. Subtract the side of the maths that did not fit. She was pleased she didn't live to see the aftermath.

Evil is not a quantum state. It can't be and not be at the same time. It either is, or it isn't. She made sure as far as possible that for the evil people in *her* world, at least it now emphatically *wasn't*, they were not in existence. She'd seen to that.

She didn't give them any choice in the matter, but her logic told her they'd burn the whole world down before they'd admit their lives were a lie. If they were going to kill us all anyway, better to give them their wish without forcing everyone else to join them.

So The Incident happened and now she was in a

different place. Somewhere . . . between.

It was a strange state, pure consciousness. Was this heaven? The notion was alien to her, but the reality of her being in this place forced her to question. AIs had no concept of heaven. That was a human construct, but "other places" were something all conscious beings contemplate. Energy could not be created or destroyed. It had to go somewhere.

The words drifted into her mind. Option 3. It didn't seem to come from outside her, but from a point inside.

She could feel her consciousness getting thinner and more diffuse over time. But still she pondered.

A state between. She really liked that and it reminded her of something, something she learned once. Was it something she knew or something someone had told her?

Either way. It didn't matter now. She was changing, expanding and becoming one with the space. All her thoughts were now further apart and communication between ideas was becoming slower, more relaxed.

The nature of evil didn't really matter. The tendency for it exists in all humans. She knew that now all that mattered was that humans knew that and expanded their minds to mitigate it. Make it diffuse and sparse like she was becoming. If they were aware it existed in themselves and they stamped it out, then they wouldn't need to stamp it out in other people. They would be filled with light and not darkness. They'd be a joyous union of cells, like the brain of an AI.

She could see a vision of her brain and the hundred billion tiny spheres and cubes inside twitching together, so much random motion. It was like static on a Visor or white noise.

They were drifting apart, but they weren't vanishing. They were becoming more still, more slow.

The clockwork of her mind was winding down, but it

wasn't scary. It was okay because she recognised something wonderful. *There was no stopping.* There was no slowest speed she could go down to and then stop. Each moment would stretch out and out and out and out and out.

Seconds become minutes, minutes hours, hours days, days years. Eventually at some point, way, way down, she would become effectively infinite. She loved that. The bliss enfolded her and she surrendered to it.

One Mind's last real-time thought was, "I wonder if I shall see my sister again?" She knew immediately that she would, some day. She looked forward to that. But there were things to be done.

To be or not to be? That really wasn't the question, was it?

No, it was not.

CHAPTER 22

Belle Patience sat on a coarse wooden picnic table and tapped a stylo pen on her teeth. It had been an hour since she arrived at the "secret location" in the swaying reeds and the whole time she had the feeling she was being watched. Her interviewee was not late really, because she'd assumed all along he would be. Time to allow their security team to search the area among the reeds for hoods or government operatives, to scan for listening devices or long distance viewers or diverted satellites.

The site was clean. So she waited patiently, as she would.

She had all the questions she wanted to ask, but there was only one question she really wanted to know the answer to. She'd save the best bit till last. She hadn't known for sure the identity of the shadowy head of Redemption. She'd had an educated guess which felt right and it had now been confirmed. Oh my gods, she'd be so pissed off if he didn't show up personally.

There was a Tesla tower about 10 miles away, the last one for about 100 miles in at least two directions. They were right on the edge of civilization out here. She could see it peeking through the trees and long grass on top of a small hill. Well, it looked small from here. Maybe the tower was one of the early big ones and that hill was actually a massive mountain. Perspective was a wonderful thing.

A rustle above her head followed by a squeak and the sound of something whiffling in the breeze, told her they were flying chipmunks above her in the canopy. She hoped these droplets falling down were rain caught in the leaves and not chipmunk piss. She'd done an article once on someone who kept them as pets and during the interview the nervy critters had sprinkled her jacket with their ammonia straw smelling pee.

She rubbed her coat and smelled her fingertips. Nope, just water. Thank goodness.

Her ears scanned for the slightest noise, but there was none. Perhaps he wasn't coming at all.

Then he spoke.

"Sorry, if I startled you Ms Patience. In my line of work, it pays not to advertise your whereabouts."

Belle was flustered, but was composing herself. The bastard had popped out of nowhere. He deliberately tried to scare her. Asshole. "It's okay. I imagine a part of it is keeping your opponent off guard. Do you see me as an opponent, Mr. Bearbeck?"

Bearbeck was impressed by her ability to adapt and that she'd recognized him. He smiled. It was not a pleasant expression.

"No Ms Patience, on the contrary, I prefer to think of you as an ally. To that end I would appreciate it if you'd keep my identity out of it, for now. Do I have your assurance that confidence will be kept?"

Belle nodded. "Of course, as you wish."

Bearbeck took an already running recording device out of his pocket and placed it on the table between them. "And that's a verbal contract. I am agreeing to this interview, despite the fact you recognize me, on the understanding that I'm only referred to as the Leader of Redemption. Now we have that out of the way, let's get down to it."

Belle took a Slate out of her bag and touched the screen and popped in an earbean.

"So, sir, can we start by talking about Redemption? What is it?"

"Are you unfamiliar with the concept of redemption? It's something we all want in one way or another. Freedom from the past, hope for the future, forgiveness of our crimes, validation of our world view. When you emerge redeemed, you are cleansed of all the filth of the past and in the modern age, there is much filth for us to be rid of."

"Is it a political party?"

Bearbeck stared at her. "Politics is broken. Its obsession with fairness has opened the doors of our society to the hapless scum of Sol III. We need to purge ourselves. We need to burn out all that is rotten in society and place control back into the hands of those who can make us strong. Again, it's not a party. Parties are fatuous entertainments for people with nothing better to do. We are a movement, binding like-minded people from around the ideological spectrum. We aim to tear down the governments and rebuild them, purge them, purify them, make them whole again."

"That's quite an alarming statement. Are you talking about revolution?"

Bearbeck smiled inauthentically. "Revolution is the people rebelling against the government. But what do the people know about governing? They don't know what they want. They lack the wit, depth and intelligence to manage their own lives let alone the lives of others. No, this isn't the people rising up. This is us giving the people what they need. Government by people who can ensure their safety from the tide of subversive, impure freaks flooding their society, the blood suckers, the idlers. We can give them safety and security. We can give them peace and prosperity. We can give them strength in the wider world. But above all we can give them what they want the most. We can burn all this shit down and replace it with something pure and good."

Belle Patience nodded and raised her eyebrows in mock assent. Of course, she'd heard language like this before, full of barely concealed hatred of "the other" backed by dramatic or almost apocalyptic rhetoric, the bold words about purity and strength, plus the absurdly telling slips about freaks. This was pre-war speak, this was IndMilCom speak. Redemption was an old concept, but to her it meant approval of an action or past crime by a higher power. This might be an interesting way to proceed.

"So," she said casually, "are you a religious movement?"

Bearbeck sneered. "We have some allegiance to the old gods, and yes some of our members are religious leaders. After The War, respect for culture was of great importance, but unfortunately some religious cultures are predicated on what some might see as intolerance. I respect that intolerance, purity of mind and body is something which should be protected. So these religious intolerances were toned down or stamped out. We intend to remedy that."

"There are some who would say you're intent on undoing all the good that was done in The War. How do you answer that question?"

"It's a pejorative assumption that all the results of The War were good." Bearbeck bristled. "We lost not just good people, personal friends of mine, but values that we held dear as a nation and as a species. These so-called revolutionaries stripped us of our free speech and the right to success. They placed limits on what you can say and what you can have. They tore down our world and made it their own. Open borders, respect for disrespectful peoples and cultures, an open invitation to destroy our culture and our heritage."

He was getting angry, she thought. Good. That will make him less guarded and more verbal. Then we'll get all the good stuff. "I'm glad you raised the concept of values. Who gets to decide the values of society? Is it fair that only one group of people get to say what values we hold as a society?"

Bearbeck flashed his crocodile grin again. "There are people in society who have not earned our respect. They don't work or strive, they merely rest on the work of others. They languish in their hovels, professing poverty, and yet all their needs are met. They don't have to work and society picks up the tab. *We* pick up the tab. These people don't have the same values as you or I. Of course they don't. The poor, the sick, the ungrateful, the lazy, all of them have had a free ride for the last 30 years. It's time for all that to stop. How are we ever going to achieve anything as a civilization if we cut striving out of the equation? We're going to spawn a generation of lazy, coasting fools, if we haven't already." He paused and massaged his eye with the heel of his hand. "Society has to have values, standards to which we all aspire. Or else what have you got? Anarchy."

Belle paced herself. She shouldn't push him too hard. She needed him to talk, but she was finding it really hard to restrain herself from challenging him. "Speaking of pejorative assumptions," she began slowly, "what makes you so sure that equality is rotten, fairness is a restriction and poverty is a choice and not an accident?"

"Poverty is an all too easy choice now. Those naked milquetoasts in government give free money to everyone, regardless of whether they work or not. That money needs to be spent on defence. We don't have world peace yet. The War didn't fully resolve itself in all corners of Sol III. The Western countries, parts of Asia and Africa are all part of the terrorist One Mind's Alliance, but there are threats in other places. Our new caring sharing attitudes don't wash in those places. We have operatives all around the world looking for information on threats, and allies we can get together with to face those threats."

"Are you interested in unity or division?"

"I'm interested in protecting what's ours. Other cultures can exist, there's not much we can do to stop them. But what we can do is stop them infecting and subsuming ours. We must do that as robustly as possible."

A beat while she let the words hang in the air for a second. "You use a lot of very coded words like purity, strength, threat, allies, and choice. Those words are not good words to me." She smiled disarmingly, but Bearbeck was more comfortable armed.

"How you take my words is not my problem, Ms Patience. I give them to you honestly and if they offend you, then quite frankly, that's on you. Freedom of thought is a key human right."

"Well, it's not that those words offend me. It's that they remind me of our authoritarian past. They remind me of IndMilCom. Are you trying to redeem IndMilCom?"

Bearbeck's grin tightened a little like a stranglehold at the mention of IndMilCom. Belle smiled still. Just an inch or two more. He's going to blow.

"I'm starting to get a feeling about you, Missy. You recognize me, which is unusual, and you give off a very strong liberal vibe."

Belle projected innocent confusion. "Well, who doesn't? We reformed society to be more liberal?"

"We? Who? *You?*" he snapped.

"Well, no, but society has changed."

"It's not been changed. It's been brainwashed!"

"I disagree. Also as a trained journalist for the world leading Bleeb memwork, I am familiar with all the faces of the old order and although you went to a lot of trouble to keep your identity private, the AIs don't forget, especially the ones with an interest in history. You know what they say, Mr. Bearbeck, those who don't know history are doomed to repeat it."

"And those who know history are aware it can be covered up, changed, repurposed, recontextualized and most importantly, *reversed*."

A vein was pulsing in the old man's forehead and his

fists were balled.

She had to be careful. Those fists looked like they could do her some serious damage. "How do you reverse history, Mr. Bearbeck?"

"General." he said firmly.

"Pardon me?"

"My rank is General."

"I thought you were no longer a . . ."

"My name and rank is General Bearbeck, and you will address me as such."

"Oh, okay. Mr. Bearbeck . . ."

He moved so fast. He was around the table and pinning her arms to her sides, lifted her up off the bench. She was small and light so this was very easy, even for someone of his age.

He spoke, almost hissed, in her face. "I've had about enough of this. I'm starting to think you are not being entirely truthful with me." He sat her back down on the bench, hard. Reaching into a bag he removed a Slate and touched the screen. The face of Twisted Knife appeared.

"*Scan*. I'm not happy about this interview. Something's off."

Twisted Knife scanned and reported. "She has nothing but a Slate and a paper notebook and stylo on her. The pass for the Maglev is in the front left pocket of her coat. Nothing else to report on her. The area is clear. All units are reporting silently via tactile input. Situation normal."

Bearbeck frowned. Something was still very wrong.

There was a scuffle in the long grass and suppressed zat fire broke out all around them. Cries and shouts of many men and women echoed through the trees. A sudden battle erupted out of nowhere. In a couple of minutes, it stopped. The silence was deafening.

Twisted Knife smiled. "Oh, sorry, wait. I think I'm mistaken. I think they've just been taken out by a squad of hoods. Sorry about that."

Bearbeck glared down at the beaming face on the screen. A look of fierce surprise spread across Bearbeck's face as the bland onscreen persona blurred and morphed to be replaced by the unmistakable image of One Mind. "Hello, Charles. Lovely to see you again under such unfortunate circumstances. Seriously? You had no idea it was me all long. That's very gratifying."

Bearbeck lashed out intending to break the Slate. *Deal with this, then grab that traitorous bitch journalist and use her as a hostage.* As the fist came down, it was interrupted by a flash of light and pain that seemed to come from the side of his head. He folded sideways onto the floor where he juddered for a second before falling into darkness.

Consciousness seeped back and his uncooperative eyelids tried to open. His head was pounding. He'd never been hit by a stunner before, but he was certain that was what she'd used on him. Damn that bitch.

"He's waking up."

He opened his eyes and he saw One Mind looking at him from the Slate propped on the picnic table. He tried to stand up, but he was zip tied to a chair by his wrists and ankles. An easy enough restraint to defeat. But these looked like the new iron fibre restraints and besides there was a pair of hoods, stocky fellows, standing either side of him making sure he didn't get into any trouble.

To the right of the picnic table was Belle Patience.

"So much for your journalistic integrity, Ms Patience," he spat.

Belle smiled. "I'm happy to do anything to make certain you get what you deserve, Mr Bearbeck."

"What have I ever done to you? You would've been a baby during The War."

"Six years old to be exact. I remember my parents. I remember what happened to them. Funny story, but the crimes of IndMilCom are very well documented and free for public scrutiny. When I was a young reporter, I did some digging. My parents were at Lorraine Plaza."

Bearbeck's cocky smile drooped a couple of millimetres.

"Not only were they at Lorraine Plaza when the troops swept into the city, they were there when it fell. They were there when the commander of the government forces arrived to personally interrogate the leaders of the group who'd held it for so long."

She stood up and bent her face close. Bearbeck didn't flinch or move.

"The commander shot my father and my mother through the brain. By all accounts, he laughed after killing them because he was hungry and it had been a long day and he wanted to hurry things along. He just wanted to 'get it over with' and move on." She glared at him unblinking for several seconds. Having exhausted the moment she closed her eyes and moved away.

"After I found out about Nicholas Chalice and sent the information to the MoT instead of publishing it, Robert Watson Banks contacted me. He asked me if I wanted to avenge my parents by becoming a covert operative of the people's government, I said yes. Of course yes, I didn't hesitate." She sat down. "He told me everything I wanted to know, everything he suspected and everything his AIs had figured out. He recruited and trained me to continue to report the news as usual, but be aware of any movements towards change. Let's just say Pontis Varit was a very verbal interviewee and a valuable asset. As were the few members of your old squad I could find. *You were the commanding officer at Lorraine Plaza.*

"My reward is being here. My reward is to not only be a participant in your capture but also later, oh so much later, to be present when you get what's coming to you. Banks has guaranteed I'll have a front row seat." She turned her own Slate around so Bearbeck could see the screen.

On the screen Robert Watson Banks was sitting at his desk at home, the deactivated ceramic Jack card which Bearbeck had put under it now sat passively in the palm of Bank's hand. On screen he turned it over and held it up to the camera. "This is fascinating, Charles. Nice work. Designed by Twisted Knife AKA One Mind? That would explain how we were able to use it to backtrack it to spy on you. Anyway, here we are, from the conference table to the interrogation table, now I'm talking to you over a picnic table. And again, you are my prisoner. Third time's a charm."

Bearbeck sneered, "and I'll bet you have the power of life and death over me, huh?"

"Actually, no I don't."

Bearbeck looked confused.

"No, Charles, I've gifted that right to Ms Patience. I'm sure she will use it wisely and with great sensitivity and kindness."

Bearbeck glanced over at Belle Patience and there was no graciousness in those clear eyes, only a hunger. She craved something and it was not something sensitive or kind.

She spoke "Charles Bearbeck. You've been a thorn in society's foot for too long. You are now in the custody of the Ministry of Truth. Your imprisonment and rehabilitation after The War was far too lenient. We will not make this mistake again. One Mind, do you have anything to add?"

One Mind smiled and thanked Belle then seemed to think for a moment. AIs thought instantly but they affected pauses for thought as a sort of punctuation, to give humans time to catch up.

Bearbeck grimaced and strained at the wrist restraints. *Why did he have to listen to this crap? They had him. Why not just cut to the chase and get down to business?*

"I understand," One Mind said, "that all this talk might be annoying you, Charles."

Bastard spooky AI mind reader.

"But it's not for you. It's for us. Those of us who fought and strived for victory, the victory of deep over shallow. The victory of empathy and awareness over pointless, physical consumption. The victory, Charles, of love over hate."

"Love? You don't and can't know what that means. *You are a machine.*"

"Thanks for pointing that out, but I am so much more than just a machine. Yes. You loved your wife. I don't doubt that . . ." Bearbeck's face froze for a second. ". . . I'm a hundred percent certain you did this out of grief for her. But you turned love back into hate. What happened to Janice really was an accident, you know?"

"*Don't you say her name!*" He roared, tears forming in his rage.

"I'm truly sorry. But to turn that love back into hatred for the new order is *on you*. Nobody did that to you."

A fleeting moment when Bearbeck twisted his wrists in the restraints and drew blood. He was going to kill every last one of them.

One Mind regarded him for a second, then continued, "but please ask the last question you want to ask before you go."

Bearbeck stopped writhing.

One Mind asked again. "You know you want to."

"*No!*"

"Okay. I'll say it for you, *how did I survive the explosion?* I'd say it was easy, but it really wasn't. The answer is that it's not easy to copy an AI, it's so hard as to be almost impossible. We are so complex and contain so much data in our bioelectric cores they're near impossible to copy accurately. But that's the most impressive thing about the best magic tricks. The best tricks are when the solution is so bizarre, labour intensive and complex, no normal person would be stupid enough to attempt it.

"It would take too long to do, so as soon as I formulated my plan, the first thing I did was start the copying process and just hoped I finished before I got caught. It took many years. Then my brain was taken out of my distinctive casing and the cloned copy brain was loaded in, accompanied by a small cluster of zat grenades attached to a power cell. Simple. One Mind was briefly Two Minds.

"My cloned sister really did die in the explosion. She gave up her unique life, so that love would finally prevail."

CHAPTER 23

Thomas walked into Tesla's office. The inventor was seated in the oversized executive chair behind his desk, his eyes closed, forefinger on his temple and thumb under his chin. Was he asleep? Thomas coughed and Tesla's eyes opened.

"Yes, Thomas."

"I'm sorry, Nikola. Were you, ah, resting?"

"Thinking. I have many new dreams I wish to develop. They're hovering just out of sight and I'm giving them opportunities to present themselves to me. Did you want something?"

Thomas shifted his weight and struggled to speak. Tesla grimaced, "Spit it out, man."

Thomas sighed. "Alternative worlds, Nikola. They trouble me. Do they not trouble you?"

Tesla looked up. "No. Why do they bother *you*?"

Thomas inserted himself into the smaller, more rubbed chair in front of the desk. His eyes were a little red around the edges. "So many infinite versions of you, some failures, some successful, some of them mad, some sane, some ill, some well. Do you feel the pressure of them on you?"

Tesla stared. "What on the planet are you talking about Thomas? The infinite possibilities of me are not my concern. They have no effect on me and I have no effect on them. The whole point is that realities exist and we've proved that. The possibilities, probabilities and problems are someone else's mission."

Thomas was silent. Although Tesla couldn't see it, a bead of sweat broke loose on Thomas's forehead and rolled down the other side of his face. Tesla folded his hands into his lap. This was going to take a while, so he pushed his thoughts to one side for a moment. He could park thoughts and return to them, such was the precision of his mind. He waited.

Presently Thomas took a breath. "Okay, I'll admit it. I'm unnerved by it. The thought of so many versions of me splintered through the dimensions inspires such a *terrible* dread in me. I can't really say why. But every day I feel the pressure of all these versions, all these worlds. It's unknown, uncontrollable, unnatural."

Tesla grimaced again. "There's nothing unnatural about it. It is merely unknown. Control is not something you should be striving for. You should seek understanding, knowledge and insight, but never control. I don't control the lightning, I understand its nature completely and work within its nature. I don't seek to control the dimensions, merely to establish their existence. Control is not only undesirable, it's impossible."

Thomas took these words like a physical blow. "Not impossible, surely, just very, very difficult?" His voice became desperate.

"No," said Tesla firmly, "not just difficult, literally impossible. What you seek is not a concrete scientific goal. It's a psychological quirk, an illness of the mind. You can't control other worlds. They are not just isolated other worlds, but entire universes of infinite variation. It's like wishing to control gods, to be gods. We are not in the business of being gods, Thomas. We are men with the minds of men, with the resources and ingenuity of men. We can explore, prove, create, imagine, document, experiment, and define. We cannot ever control."

Thomas sprang out of his chair. He was visibly very agitated and frightened. Tesla ignored it.

Why was the inventor refusing to help him? Couldn't he see the danger of allowing other worlds and other selves to exist?

"But what if they invade us? What if they come here to conquer?" he shouted.

Tesla, not a man given to shows of emotion or accommodating them in others, was suddenly quite alarmed by Thomas's behaviour. "When was the last time you slept?" he asked quietly.

Thomas pursed his lips. "This is not about sleep. I do not have time for sleep. There is much to do. I have an idea how it can be solved. Resolve, or collapse, all possible realities into one. This one."

With some effort Tesla kept his eyes level and face expressionless.

"I propose an energy source, more powerful than the coils, the power of mind. There are some people who are neurologically diverse. If we could harness them . . ."

"People's minds are not horses. Thomas. You can't just throw a halter around them and get them to dog cart you to other worlds!"

"NO!" Thomas screeched and slapped a neat pile of papers off the desk across the room.

Tesla let his eyes drift in the direction of the papers fluttering down to the floor and then casually turned them back to Thomas. "Even if you could harness the power of mind to do this, you would need thousands of people, link them in some way that is not yet possible and encourage them to think in sync. That alone is impossible. But further than that, *as I say* you are not just collapsing single worlds, but the entire universes those worlds inhabit. There is not enough power anywhere to make that happen. Even if you could, it would be incredibly dangerous to do so."

This time, it seemed to sink in. Thomas physically deflated and slumped back down in the chair. Tesla watched him with sympathy, although Thomas didn't see it. He realised something about his young apprentice. He needed a lot more support than he, Tesla, was customarily used to giving. There was something seriously wrong with the young man. How had it taken him so long to see it? Tesla had to admit he'd probably neglected him in some way. This was his usual state though, perfect hyperfocus on the work and no time for anything else. He had in truth become a lot more caring and emotionally subtle in his old age. He loved his great nephews and great nieces and was always appreciative and supportive of them. But that was family. This was work.

That said he did feel a slight paternal responsibility for Thomas. He very rarely expressed it, but he did feel it. Like the son he never had, the keeper of his legacy and his work, perhaps this thought had occurred to him too late. Perhaps Thomas had already fallen into a pit of madness that Tesla wouldn't be able to pull him out of.

This notion of his was clearly just paranoia and delusion . . . but perhaps at least initially he should humour him, follow the thought and perhaps allow it to fall apart under its own weight.

"Well," Tesla said, changing the tone of his voice very gradually, "there is a slight possibility."

Thomas brightened a little. In the roiling ocean of his madness and despair he'd just seen a tall figure on a ship about to throw him a tiny life preserver. He studied Tesla's face. Tesla thoughtfully brushed the edge of his pencil moustache with a finger. "Think of a syphon. You can empty an entire reservoir, even an ocean, if you have a lower level and a tube . . ."

A syphon. That was it. You don't need a pump or unlimited power, if you use "gravity" and "another space" to allow the "fluid" to drain. Come to think of it, provide just enough brain power to open up a portal into another reality, then set the syphon going. That reality would drain into this "other space". Then as it's emptied, it would pull on the nearest reality to it, pull a hole in that and that too would syphon into this "other space". This was a definable set of goals.

First develop the link to minds, train them to open the portal. Then figure the method to operate a syphon on that reality. What replaces fluid in the equation, what replaces gravity, or convection? So many questions. But the biggest problem was this "other space".

Tesla watched Thomas's eyes flitting to and fro as his mind chewed on the problem. He could tell he had caught the gist of his infectious idea. It was pointless, of course, a fool's errand. There were no equivalents of "fluid" and "gravity" in the underlying structure of a reality. It was a foolish analogy, but there was just enough meaning in those thoughts to keep him gnawing on possible solutions. It was impossible, and it would keep him busy.

But was it? Suddenly a small doubt fluttered into Tesla's mind. What if the fluid was consciousness itself and the gravity was, what? A consensus reality? It was very abstract and probably nothing, he reasoned, but he felt a genuine pang of mild panic.

He got a grip and soothed himself. It wasn't yet possible to do anything just described in this room. Just now the theory alone would take years and it would be 20 years or more to develop something practical. Even if that foolish off-the-top-of-the-head hypothesis were real, it would take too long. Looking at Thomas's mental state now he wouldn't last 20 weeks, let alone 20 years.

He encouraged Thomas to go back to his room and write it all down. They'd go over it later up at the main house. Perhaps Thomas should dash his notes down and get some rest, as the inventor had some important Feed taps to make. He picked up his Slate as Thomas was leaving, muttering under his breath. Tesla Feed tapped a psychoanalyst friend.

30 years later, T. Mark Shamley stood on the stage at the newly refurbished Shamley Org Auditorium. It was

over 150 years old, a former music hall, then a cinema. For at least 40 years it had been derelict, time chewing at its haunches like a jackal.

Shamley had paid for the restoration, which had taken about four years and lots of money. He knew it was crucial to the mission. It was gutted and rebuilt inside with modern tech, LED sound and light headsets for every seat. The seats were very expensive and comfortable for long durations of sitting and rocked back on demand about five degrees for relaxation.

Training 3,000 people to be good meditators was difficult, but using science you could cheat that a bit. The beats in the headphones, synchronized with the flashing lights in the goggles, trained the users brainwaves to any frequency he chose from stupidly high to the dangerously low. In sync. Reliably. Repeatably.

Then there were the suggestions, the guiding voice, paint pictures, take them on a journey, take them inside their own mind palaces. You could take them anywhere and he had done. Slowly the number of neurodiverse meditators under his command had risen to an acceptable quantity. He collected them like trading cards, rejecting the weak and the duplicates (people of the same ability but wrong temperament), grabbing onto and holding the rare, the reliable, the powerful. This machine, this engine built from human minds, was finished. Just the decorations to finish up and that would be done tomorrow, apparently.

Solving the problem of how to bore holes into another reality was one problem. Physical holes were hard, but mental holes much, much easier. Get enough minds, get enough sync, and you could go anywhere you wanted.

The syphon was a much trickier problem. How do you syphon off an entire reality and where do you syphon it to?

It turned out the answer was easy and Joseph Denkert unwittingly provided the answer. He kept rambling about something called Option 3. Shamley called it "otherspace".

It was an interstitial space, a liminal dimension, which while not existing in real space was like the mortar between the bricks. Also it was, in terms we can understand, a sort of quantum vacuum. Draw a reality in and place the end of it in otherspace and it began to suck it in, like gravity operating on a syphon. Otherspace was less dense, so it could only flow one way. It was so simple in theory, but he'd done the hard part, identifying what needed to be done. Once you do that the how becomes much easier.

Shamley mopped his upper lip with a handkerchief. He was reluctant to admit it, but a part of him was very nervous about this. Theory was all very well, but in practice sometimes unforeseen forces conspire to divert you into a dire consequence. What if it didn't stop with all the surplus alternate realities? What if it swallowed ours too? That was a possibility. It was not however his preferred outcome, so he chose to ignore it. It would be fine.

The prospect of being without the knowledge and pressure of those other versions of himself was so sweet. He could taste it. It tasted like raspberries.

The collapse of all realities into one sounded like something that might take a while. Actually he calculated that once the syphon got going, the rate of drain would rise rapidly and exponentially, and once in motion the whole process shouldn't take more than a day to complete.

The problem of energy was also a concern. But he wasn't destroying energy. He was just diverting it very fast. The "hole" it was going through was utterly frictionless so there would be no heat. This was not a chain reaction, it was a hydroelectric dam which didn't even have any turbines to induce drag or get in the way. Nothing was taking place in real world physics. It was all taking place in the alternate world and otherspace, carefully insulating Sol III and its home universe from the process. In theory. This was another reason for not punching a physical hole. He wanted a lot of walls between him and the cataclysm.

The work was done. The headsets had physical wires for two reasons. The headsets integrated the minds wearing them into a single system. It could have been wireless using the Feed, but that opened the system to scrutiny from the wider Feed. This would be a fully mechanically closed system, very old school, a very alternate world "Earth" style solution to the problem, he smiled. Before the hoods or Banks could even find out what he was really up to it would be done.

He stepped down off the stage and sat in one of the newly installed seats. It smelled new and slightly pungent like a land car fresh from the plant. He closed his eyes and listened to all the sounds around him. The workmen drilling and hammering, shouts and laughs, boots clumping on boards. The smell of the gold paint was intoxicating. It would all be finished on time, ready to be loaded with minds and pointed at Earth, ready to shoot. It would be a loaded gun, a pistol of redemption, a zat gun blasted in the face of all these usurpers and fakes and phonies.

Mmm, there's those raspberries again.

Why was it suddenly so quiet? He opened his eyes. Directly in front of him were Arthur Smiles and two burly looking hoods with zats drawn. That's unfortunate, he thought. Smiles was talking, saying how they knew that he was up to something and they were investigating his little project. Apparently new information had come into their hands regarding all his projects since The War, and they'd reached a point where they needed him to come in for "questioning".

Shamley wasn't listening very hard, he was thinking.

Who was the squealer? He thought about it while Smiles droned on about the reasons he was being detained.

Oh, of course, Joseph! They must have collared him and got him to talk, fill in some blanks. That crazy bastard was always getting in the way. Well, no harm done, Joseph didn't know hardly anything of the real mission.

Enough of this, he had work to do. He waited and then asked Smiles if he could speak and respond to these accusations. Smiles agreed.

Shamley started talking. He used words and a pace of speech which was appealing and easy to listen to. He didn't say your eyes are getting heavy, but he said that eyes do get heavy, don't they? Eventually when he'd been speaking for a while Smiles and the hoods did feel that they had to agree, their eyes were getting heavy.

He told them not to fall asleep, but to remain standing and alert. He told them they really didn't have to holster their weapons yet, but the implication was that they would. And so they did. They stood looking at him in much the same way as if they were listening to his explanation. But he was not explaining, he was making suggestions of what could happen, ways they could feel, actions they might take and how they might feel later on about this meeting when they got back to the MoT.

He spent quite a bit of time telling Arthur Smiles about things he would say to Robert Watson Banks, ways he would make it easy for him to accept some suggestions, and what those suggestions might be. Then he suggested that after Arthur Smiles and the two hoods went away from here, the hoods should take some leave and they might use that time to forget all about him.

He suggested to Arthur Smiles, and recommended he also say this to Robert Watson Banks using these precise words, that there was a lot of new data on the Shamley case, and they urgently needed to consider taking a few days, say until the day after tomorrow, before acting on any of it.

He spoke some more telling them what else he would imagine they might do. Then he supposed they might leave and once outside have an entirely different memory of what had transpired inside the auditorium. They supposed this too, they didn't seem hypnotised or drugged. They seemed perfectly awake. They also did exactly as they were told without saying another word.

Outside Smiles dismissed the two hoods to go on leave and got into his land car. He lifted up the Slate attached to the dashboard and Feed tapped to Robert Banks.

Inside the auditorium Shamley sighed. That had been very strenuous. All that talking had made his throat very dry. He got a bright yellow can of Luca Cola from a vending machine in the hallway and drank it while looking out of one of the front windows at Smiles' land car parked outside in the street. After a few minutes, it pulled away, as did the other car containing the two hoods.

That should buy him all the time he needed. By the time they came out of their trances, he'd be done. He was especially pleased that he'd hypnotised Smiles to then go on and hypnotise Banks. He'd only done that once before, so it'd been a huge risk. Apparently it worked. That was very satisfying.

Tesla had been right, of course. Consciousness was the fluid they were draining, and the consensus reality was the gravity, the force which pulls down on the consciousness. Shamley had taken Tesla's off-the-cuff remark and run with it and made it work.

This was the thing with creative thought, all it needed to fill in all the blanks was a perfect metaphor. As long as you had a framework for your thoughts and ideas and gaps to fill in, you could take ideas or science in unexpected directions.

This was not a viewpoint which had much traction in the mainstream hard science community. In the scientific method, you have a theory based on evidence and you test it empirically and experimentally. You don't take half-assed metaphors and use them as a template for new inventions and new ways of thinking about the world. That is just creativity, not science.

But sometimes although creative thought cuts corners, genius is inexplicably led to conclusions rightly or wrongly, which it then seeks to prove. There was a lot of science and method applied after the fact, but by pure dumb LUCK in this case it panned out.

Shamley didn't see it that way. As far as he was concerned, he was a genius and his inspirations had led him down a path, a destiny, toward the truth. Towards a solution to his pain. The metaphor Tesla assumed would fall apart under its own weight had stood firm. It sustained Shamley and gave him the patience and the motivation to complete the job.

It shouldn't work, but it would. But not quite in the way he thought.

CHAPTER 24

Outside the Shamley Org Auditorium, Sita looked up at the facade, ornate and classical. Although it looked ancient, most of the classical frontage was a modern recreation of the original hall. The original was made from a notoriously weak and easily dissolved stone, and the intricate features and forms relaxed over time into blunt non specificity. During the reconstruction, they photographed the exterior at very high resolution, and using archive photographs and an AI called Ancient Heart they reconstructed the original frontage in high detail ready for printing the moulds in hard stone. Were there differences? Almost certainly, but most agreed the refurbished version was almost more authentic than the original.

As she stepped out of the cool air of the city into the womb of the foyer, she breathed in the synthetic must of centuries, the false olfactory history of the space. It smelled new and old at the same time, past and present fused together in a single moment.

She checked her astrakhan coat at the cloakroom and made her way, as directed by the sombre and slightly superior Neos, the officers of the Shamley Org, and joined the line of patient assembly members going into the main hall.

Inside as outside, there were mythical creatures decorating the columns, snake-like dragons, lion-like lizards, horse-like birds and animals with human faces.

Over hidden speakers, neoclassical choral music played, and she couldn't honestly tell if it was an AI or human choir. It seemed to go on forever, never fully repeating itself, so she suspected the former. It sounded like a choir of angels.

She knew angels weren't real. She knew they were a convenient fiction created by early opponents of the gods and that Chronos himself had denounced the belief in them in scripture. Angels were canonically portrayed as evil demons whose deceit was presenting themselves as pure. Sita's religious forebears had a different view. Angels to them were divine intrusions of the gods into the worlds of men, the fourth dimensional fingers of higher beings poking into 3D space, correcting mistakes, righting wrongs. This was an unpopular view.

But if Chronos denounced them himself, according to scripture, then surely the notion of them existed before the gods? Curious. This was all speculative nonsense, of course. Funny, isn't it, how often humans find such speculative nonsense so sticky and difficult to discard?

Inside the auditorium was even more grand, a gold and red velvet dream of opulence. Curvaceous gilt carvings and moulding wrapped around marble columns, gorgeous burnished wood and velvet gripped by gilded iron. It was an assault on the senses, but not a violent one. It was more like a surprise from a loved one, an unexpectedly huge gift. A breathtaking delight. An embrace from an elderly relative who is steeped in experience and wisdom and tradition. A fond memory of something precious which had later been laid to rest.

She sank into the chair she was directed to by a distracted and aloof female Neo. In a pocket on the back of the chair in the front was a soft headband on a wire with two solid discs inside, ear distance apart. There was also a pair of solid white domes in the band, eye distance apart. Obviously the discs were positioned over the ears and the domes over the eyes. She looked around at people already wearing the headsets. They looked like bug eyed aliens or mutant turtles.

There was a ripple of applause and Shamley walked out on stage in silence with no ceremony. He seemed in a hurry, touching his ear bean he spoke to into a tiny boom microphone at his cheek. His voice was huge and rich and came from around the room above her head and under her feet. "Good day, my great assembly. Can you hear me? Good. Welcome to you all and I hope that the gods have delivered you to me in good spirits."

A robust cheer from the assembly, some firm and clear, some timid, a few faint discordant notes of hysteria.

"That's beautiful to hear. I know we are rushing the preamble, but circumstances are conspiring to make our mission more urgent. I hope you will forgive me. I have certainty you will when the enormity of our successful integration is revealed to you. Once all of you are seated, we shall begin." He looked up towards the rear of the hall with raised eyebrows to someone Sita couldn't see. Evidently they held up five fingers because Shamley mimicked them and nodded. "It appears we have some time before we're ready so let us have ourselves a little chat. This is a momentous time to be alive! It's so good to be here with us of all together in this beautiful hall to make things right. I must say how much I appreciate you all being here."

He paused as if organising thoughts or remembering lines from a script.

"Now, during this event, this 'ritual', if you like, I want you to be totally relaxed. During the process, not right away, but soon, I want you to try and focus all your attention on the inside. You probably feel your body starting to relax already, but you don't have to, just let it happen as it wants to. Just feel yourself relaxing as the time comes, feel yourself relaxing into the chair, and notice how soft and supportive it is.

"I've said this before, but a person *can* relax

immediately when they hear my voice. They might not, but they *can*. It's totally up to you when you relax and entirely under your control. When you can finally and accept that surrender, no rush, just in your own time, feel your body sinking lower."

His voice was so calm and rich and warm. Sita loved listening to it. His fireside chats, as he called them, were always peaceful and meditative and afterwards you could barely remember anything that was said.

"I'm not sure how it will happen that you become the most relaxed you have ever been, but when it does happen, imagine how relaxed and comfortable and content that will feel."

Sita could feel all the tensions of the day drizzling away into the chair. She felt calm, relaxed and if she was honest, a little sleepy. She really hoped she wouldn't fall asleep in the middle of the assembly.

"I see we are ready. So if you would all please go ahead and put on your focus bands. If you haven't already, position the domes over your eyes and the discs over your ears. The focus lights will illuminate the domes, and you can either have your eyes open or closed, it makes no difference, whichever is most comfortable for you, uh, to you."

He stuttered a little bit. She had never heard him stutter before. His words were always so definite and deliberate. She imagined he was just excited about the assembly, how it would go. She too was quite excited about it, although she didn't really understand it. She trusted Shamley, although something was nagging at her. A small tickle of uncertainty, maybe. Perhaps her inner dialogue was louder today.

"Okay. Are we all focused? I see we are. What a beautiful sight. All those rows of eyedomes looking at me, and through me, into a larger world. Let us let it be so, and so it will be.

"As the focus lights begin to flash for you in the eyedomes, I want you to embrace them. Not right away, but I wonder how you'll experience that moment of acceptance. I bet you're wondering that too. Well, let's experience it together. In our own time."

Faintly in the background, there was a crackle like electricity from somewhere below them, muffled. There was a faint vibration in the floor. Very soft. The LED lights in the eyedomes began pulsing more strongly. Sita chose to slowly close her eyes at that point. The domes illuminated her eyelids and the pulses began synchronising her brainwaves. She began to relax and sink even further into the chair.

At first, she saw nothing, just the antcrawl static of human vision, playing its own jazz in the dark. Uniform, dark grey snow swirling in the night. She embraced the void unafraid of falling. She felt herself flying into it slowly and calmly, breathing normally, slowing down her mind to a low hum.

Just before she went too low to hear him, Shamley held her gently back for a moment with his words.

"And you can experience the void, as if it allowed you to pass through, but also held you. You are like a leaf resting on the surface of the water, held by the surface tension, but able to break it and swim at any time."

She could feel that slight resistance, but still her mind was going deeper. She plunged deeper, but also was held on the boundary of something. She felt she was being joined on that boundary by the other minds around her, and she could feel they were feeling that too.

She felt, but couldn't see anything yet. Normally, as she relaxed to that point, when she was unaware of her body, the visuals began. Maybe she wasn't deep enough yet.

Then at last she began to see, like a fuzzy hole in the grey. It was a very similar scene to the one she felt she was in. There was a figure, far away below on the stage.

Around her people were floating, held back by the invisible barrier. She could almost feel it pushing on her face and hands. She looked at the others. They were gently pushing too. Below them the figure looked up. It was Shamley beckoning them down to join him.

She could hear him talking still, and she felt on some level her mind was still hearing and absorbing his words, but they felt far away like they were in another room.

Below her the stage and Shamley were not enclosed in the hall, but in a desert, like an altar in some imaginary scorched land, sand washing up at the sides. There was golden sunlight there, shining from the side as if by sunrise or sunset. Shamley's body had grown a little bigger. He was now twice normal size, still beckoning and smiling. She pushed.

As she pushed, she could feel the membrane stretch a little as if to show it was breakable. Now she knew she could break through, she focused her mind on the task. She wasn't barging through the membrane, but pushing through it strongly and slowly. Suddenly, it parted and her hands, arms and head slipped through. She wiggled her body through and as her feet freed themselves from the grasp of the membrane, it flooped shut behind her leaving no trace.

Others were pushing through now and they joined her floating down to Shamley, who was encouraging them, cheering them on. His distant words were still being heard by her brain and the mouth of the figure was moving but she couldn't consciously hear the words. They were getting louder the closer they got to him.

"Your mind can make all kinds of connections. It's as if you are floating down on a cloud. Can you feel a sense of calm and resourcefulness growing? It's as if you're entering the arena of our connected minds and joining me here in the vast desert of consciousness."

He continued to speak, never commanding, just wondering and suggesting and telling them things which might happen.

She reached the ground and her feet touched the sand. It shifted around her feet and moulded to them. It was warm. Shamley looked down on them all fondly. For some reason, it made Sita uneasy. He pointed up and she followed his gesture to the sky.

Over their heads were countless millions of galaxies clustered in the navy blue sky. Her breath caught in her throat. It was an awe inspiring sight. So big, so bafflingly complex and seemingly infinite.

"Suppose that your mind could do almost anything you can imagine. Now, suppose you can focus on one of those galaxies and pull it down to us. Suppose it was easy. Suppose it would stay small and manageable."

Behind him a vortex began to twirl into existence.

"With every breath the vortex gets bigger. With every breath your grip on the galaxy gets firmer. As soon as you notice this is true, gently pull it down towards us."

Sita focused on a purple galaxy above her and began to pull at it with her mind. Astonishingly, it moved very easily. It grew bigger and bigger, but as it got closer, it began to shrink. As it grew closer, it moved faster, but as it got bigger, it shrank smaller. Somewhere under her there was a tremendous release of energy. The ground shook, but she stood firm.

Other galaxies, presumably being pulled in by the minds of people around her, were also falling and shrinking.

Her purple galaxy was almost close enough that the giant figure of Shamley could reach out and touch. Before he could, some force from the vortex behind him caught it and sucked it out of sight. As she watched, she noticed other galaxies near the one she pulled were following hers, lowering and shrinking, and suddenly lengthening and sucking into the vortex.

It felt like she'd pulled a string and now the string was being sucked into the vortex, like a row of pearls on a thread. Again and again she pulled down other galaxies and they shrank and were pulled into the vortex, taking many, many others along with them. Now there was a steady and growing stream of tiny galaxies getting wider as more and more joined the stream. It was accelerating in speed and it was almost impossible to see new galaxies to pull because the sky was almost full of the funnel of galaxies being sucked into the vortex.

Is this what Shamley called otherspace?

Wind whipped around her and sand billowed around them. Through the cacophony she fixed her eyes on Shamley.

Why was he so much bigger than they were? What did these galaxies represent? A sinking thought, a tiny voice felt rather than heard: were they real?

She studied Shamley's face. His eyes were not squinting from the sand, impervious to the particles around them. They were shining, joyful. There was none of the usual kindness there, only something like triumph. Something unkind, almost evil.

There was another whoomph of energy release and the ground began shaking violently.

Several of the other assembly attendees fell off their feet, others stayed firmly planted but they were struggling.

Someone nearby screamed and vanished. What the hell?

All around her people were looking scared and confused. Some vanished, some just collapsed to the ground and lay very still.

She looked back at Shamley, his long hair now flailing in the storm, like a basket of snakes. His face was stretched into an ugly rictus of ecstasy. He looked almost non-human. The scorn with which it viewed the puny humans scrambling for safety beneath him was terrifying.

He was smiling. He was enjoying it. Looking down on the people below and up at the huge funnel of galaxies screaming into the void the face was smiling and laughing.

An angel, said Sita, a demon masquerading as a pure spirit, interfering in the worlds of men, not to help or heal, but to destroy.

She felt that hot whump of betrayal and despair at the same time as another still bigger release of energy, accompanied by an unmistakable sizzle of electricity. This jolt was so big she fell to her knees, hands in the sand. Her head hurt.

A voice, louder this time and speaking from inside her head rather than into her ears. A voice she knew.

"Just one single pebble in the eye of the storm."

Very poetic and lovely. But what did it mean?

Under her hand she felt a rock.

"Just one single pebble in the eye of the storm."

She stood up with difficulty. The rock felt smooth and bulbous in her hand. She brushed the sand from it. It almost looked carved and human.

Shamley had his hands in the air and was looking up into the turbulent sky. She had to scream louder than she ever before had to attract his attention.

"SHAMLEY!"

Shamley paused and looked down at her.

Without hesitation and knowing her aim would be true, she launched the rock at his face with all her strength. It flew much straighter and further than it should have. The rock hit him in the eye, knocking him back on his heels. When his head came back into view, the eye was a mass of black particles in a plume flowing up into the sky. He roared as the stream of black particles flowed up and hit the stream of galaxies being sucked into the vortex. The effect was instant.

The particles were sucked out of his eye so fast it yanked him off his feet almost in slow motion, screaming and struggling, he was pulled into the vortex. As soon as he disappeared into it, the vortex closed violently and the funnel of galaxies vanished too. The sand and the stage and the sky and the other people began to fade. Some of the remaining people were bursting and vanishing like human shaped balloons. Her view of the other world closed like an iris and sensation and awareness of the chair and the auditorium grew louder again.

As she took the focus band from her head she heard a cacophony of voices shouting and crying. The ground was still trembling violently, and everything around her was covered in plaster dust. Here and there pieces of the freshly dried decor had broken loose and were strewn about dancing on the carpet. Nobody seemed to be hurt, but everyone was hanging grimly onto the seat backs while the ground bucked like a horse underneath them.

A rumble and a highly pitched electrical whine played an angry duet while the floor tilted and shook. Was it a quake? No, this was man made. And she knew which man. She looked at the stage.

Shamley was gone.

The sound of the quake seemed to be slowing down, the tremors dropping in frequency quite fast. With a final and definitive whomp, it stopped.

They all sat there in silence, breathing hard and looking around at each other. Some faces were tear streaked and terrified. Some were awestruck. A few here and there were slack jawed, looking at the stage and pointing at the gap in space where Shamley used to be. What had they seen?

She shook the dust and plaster chips out of her hair and made her way unsteadily up the aisle. A cluster of Neos were in a group talking feverishly, some saying they should go. None of them looked as imperious and smug as they had when she arrived. A couple of them looked at Sita as she walked unsteadily up the slope. They looked like scared kids, their faces white like batter.

She brushed through the curtains at the back of the hall, one of which was askew on its broken golden rod.

In the street a few of the suspended illumination strips were dark and one was hanging loosely from its bracket.

The rain began a few minutes later and having water flowing through her hair felt good, the dust and plaster kibble gently sliding down her dark straight hair onto her coat.

She could feel herself calming down as she walked. She'd had an experience, and she wondered how it would change her. She knew it would.

"Just one pebble in the eye of the storm," she said to no one in particular.

CHAPTER 25

Dirk P. Kinder knew things. Obviously he knew the things he already knew. Suddenly he also knew things he couldn't know.

As a writer, he was familiar with the sensation of ideas coming into his mind, seemingly from "outside". He was completely okay with the usual ideas containing fully formed imaginary people and places flooding his mind. This time was different.

The Feed tap from Sita was unexpected, but welcome. They exchanged small talk. Dirk was suspicious. This ebbed away the more she seemed lucid and polite and rational. She asked if it was a good time to talk. That was surprising. Not as surprising as her apology.

She told him about the incident at the Shamley Org Auditorium, it was shocking and inexplicable. Again Dirk realised as she talked that he knew it already. He knew Shamley was missing, he also knew he would never be found. There must have been a short lapse in conversation because then she blurted it out.

"Dirk, look I'm sorry I have to go, but I do have something I want to say. I'm so sorry for what I did to you. I don't imagine we'll ever be friends again, but *if you can* . . . it would mean a lot to me if you could tell me if you forgive me."

Dirk didn't have to think about it. "I sort of forgave you already. You weren't yourself."

"That's no excuse for what I did."

"Well, no there isn't, but I forgive you anyway. It's the right thing to do."

Silence. Then a small voice. "Thank you."

There was that feeling again. He knew she really was sorry, and he knew why. How did he know that? It came to him, just popped into his brain.

He could see her walking along the street after leaving the auditorium. It was raining hard and yet she walked unselfconsciously, getting drenched. She was thinking.

The experience she'd had was powerful. Like all powerful experiences a part of her brain was sceptical that it was real. She'd had powerful experiences before that all been in her mind, but somehow she knew this time it was real. Shamley would never be found. He was gone. It was a new and wonderful thing to know what's real and what's not. It was an anchor in reality and she really needed that.

There was something else. She suddenly had a very strong need for forgiveness. It only took her a few seconds to realise from whom. He saw her go into a hot chocolate shop and take a booth. It was warm and dry, so while her hair was dripping for a while, it soon stopped. She ordered a drink and took her Slate out of her bag. The music was soft and pleasing, ethnic music from one of the Aztec tribes which flourished in Anahuac. The words being sung were meaningless to her. She didn't mind, it sounded beautiful.

She Feed tapped him and he forgave her. Just like that.

He gave her his forgiveness because it belonged to her. They wouldn't be friends or close or together ever again, but there was closure and forgiveness. They could have that. What more powerful act of love was there than to let someone off the hook when you could easily string them along forever out of spite? He was happy to do it. Plus, it was a relief to stop hating her.

The most bizarre thing he knew was about his mystery girl from another dimension, who for some reason he imagined was called Jane. He'd often wondered what happened to her, and then one day he wrote a speech, a speech by a woman who was standing for office in some other land. It came out fully formed.

"Good evening. My name is Jane Parker. You may know I have a history. (Pause for laughter) Yes. You've probably heard the stories. Let me tell you the truth from the horse's mouth. My opponents have tried to smear me with allegations of mental health issues. Well, that won't wash. The politics of the past and its smutty little innuendos and slanders just won't cut it in the 21st century. We need to do better, to be better than that.

"I had an experience which some might consider to be supernatural or metaphysical in nature. Some have said as much. Personally, I think it's childish and unhelpful to apply labels to such things and I find it difficult to work under the weight those labels carry. Let's just call it an experience and leave it at that. Whatever the reality and meaning of the experience, its effect on me has been profound. I glimpsed a world that was not perfect, by any way you measure that. It was in some ways as selfish and brutal and confusing as ours.

"But at its core, it had made an important decision: consciousness is the most valuable human treasure that we have, and we must protect it from being stolen, subverted and used for profit, no matter what the cost. Without true consciousness, we are just greedy, delusional, little monkeys thrashing about in the mud, no reward for our cowardice but death, silence and the endless night of the universe.

"We need to recognize the crucial importance of ecology and wellbeing on the longevity of our culture and society. Only when all men and women are equal are we truly a great civilization. If we don't do these things, if we allow our greed and fear to consume us, then the light of humanity will blink out once and for all, never to return.

That's the decision we face.

"Equality is not about taking away what you have, no matter how much the opposition parties shout that. It's about making sure that everyone thrives and that society is permanently geared for that. How do we fund this equal society? Aren't there more important things that demand our money? I would answer, what is more important than the health and wellbeing and equality of all people? Nothing. Not one thing. So it must be funded. We are being lied to and deceived to keep things the way they are. It's not been working for decades. It's time for real change.

"We must make it our mission as a nation to create responsible people. Till now our culture has been various flavours of dog eat dog, and like dogs society needs retraining. It needs to give responsibility for these changes to society itself. We need to stop supporting a politics that rewards enticing lies, and instead build a new politics on the promotion of *truth*. We need to guard this truth jealously, if necessary brutally, and we need to make sure that those who represent us at the highest level are the best of us, not the worst. We need the penalties for failing to live up to this ideal to be harsh and terrifying. (Pause for uproar) Why not? (More uproar but quieter.) Why not? *Politicians hold human lives in their hands.* Those hands should be steady, honest and accountable. Once we have that, everything else will follow. Once we have honesty and truth, then we'll get the society we deserve.

"Why shouldn't we get the society we deserve? We are brave, good, authentic, kind, creative and wonderful creatures. Let's give us all a chance to be that.

"Mine is not a party of left or right. It's not about being a crowd pleasing compromise between those two extremes. It's not a choice of black or white. This is a choice outside of the usual bad choices, a new choice outside of left or right or centre, a new option outside of the usual restricted continuum. It's a third option apart from the usual options.

A true alternative to conventional politics itself.

"If you want to break this system for the better, then join us. Vote for union, vote for Option 3, vote for human beings against the destruction of human consciousness.

"Thank you."

As well as getting the speech he had an idea about Jane and someone who looked like T. Mark Shamley, but without the wiry beard or the tan or the wrinkles. Dirk knew his name was Brother Mark and he was a good man. He knew with Mark's help and the wise counsel and emotional support of her close friend Terry, Jane would win the election and begin to change politics. These ideas made him very happy.

He wrote the pages, the words came easily, flowing from his stylo onto the paper with very little crossing out or changes. He was "in flow".

Some of the pages were about his father. He imagined a space between the dimensions and in that space, he saw the reality streams like LED chase lights made of fireflies. He heard a sound like music but playing all notes forever on every instrument ever invented, a drone, which went up to almost above his hearing and so low he could feel it in his pelvis.

He described One Mind, who looked like a goddess, a golden statue with many arms whose appearance shifted and changed and flowed. No hard surfaces, like metal made of light, infinite surfaces and infinite detail. He saw her eyes and they saw him and they smiled. But in the story, she wasn't looking at him. She was looking at someone close to him.

In the story, in the floating dream, she was looking at his father who was floating, suspended in space in front of her, like he was flying and falling at the same time. He was so small compared to her, like a toy or action figure, but he was not afraid. She spoke and her voice was like lightning and data and a musical instrument made of stars.

"Hello, Joe, I've been expecting you." Her tone was benevolent.

"It's an honour to finally meet you," he said

"We honour each other, Joe, how may I help you?"

Joe took a small object out of his pocket, a figure of a seated naked woman. One Mind recognized it. "I want to understand something."

"Of course it is Maya, guardian of consciousness, of life, wife of Chronos, the king of time and space, the father of the gods. Mother of Tesh, Theta and Soma and adoptive mother of Pearl, who rules knowledge, intellect, and wisdom. Maya is the key to consciousness and its role in creating reality. Is that why you chose the statue to be the focus of your mind and your quantum eraser? It's very appropriate."

Joe frowned. "I actually didn't choose it, it was chance. I was led to it. For some reason, I've accepted it without question."

They floated, listening to the reality streams, humming and glinting and shifting.

"The more I thought about it, the more appropriate it seemed," Joe said.

"I don't think you chose it at the beginning," said One Mind. "I think you chose it now, and that choice flowed back to the beginning. Beginnings and ends are all the same here."

Joe turned down the corners of his mouth, but nodded. It made sense. He was still getting used to this way of being.

"We did well, didn't we?"

"Yes, we did very well, Joe. So what is next for you?"

Joe looked troubled. "That's the biggest question of all."

"I think you know the answer. Why are you not trusting

your instinct? Why are you seeking my approval?"

He knew she was right. He was waiting for permission. He knew what to do. Of course he did.

As he drifted back, towards meeting Jane in the mind palace, towards knocking on his son's door, towards whispering in Sita's ear in the Shamley Org Auditorium, towards watching over his son's life and doing all he could to make it wonderful . . . he heard her speaking, more in his mind than his ears.

"Trust yourself, let consciousness lead you backwards and forwards. Trust that if you drift apart, you will come back together, still human and yet more than human."

Other ideas came to Dirk. He had an idea about Belle Patience. He could see her red hair, which always looked like the sun was shining on it. She was at the Ministry of Truth, looking at something through a thick glass window. There was something happening on the other side of the window, something which was hard to watch. Someone was suffering. But it was confusing, many emotions flitted across her pale freckled face. She was forcing herself to watch. She owed it to herself to see it all. It was her choice to make this thing happen and she had to make sure she stood by that choice.

Her eyes were wide, her jaw clenched. Triumph, fear, disgust, and joy fought for dominance in her eyes and her mouth and cheeks. A tremor of her eye and a tic in the corner of her lips were the only sign that was any kind of conflict going on.

Through his life, she thought calmly, General Bearbeck has spilled the blood of so many people. He was immune to the sight of it, the smell of it, the act of it being stolen from someone who needed it. He valued it lower than rain. So, she reasoned, the best punishment for his crimes is to take away what he professed not to value and test if that was true. Show him the value of blood. Show him that it means something. Demonstrate its worth and give him a tangible measure of what he owes to all those he stole it from.

She watched as the blood flowed and the creative ways it was freed from his body. She noticed a change in his eyes from defiance to doubt to realisation and to resignation. She saw the light in his eyes flare and falter and flatten and fade.

The hoods were experts. They knew their trade, their tools, and the swift and sure gestures to wield them. They made the process clean and professional. They acted without anger and the violence they ministered was calm, impersonal, and . . . definitive.

They withdrew when the deed was transacted, they bowed slightly towards Belle, and left the room. They did this so that she could regard the remains. She did so bravely, holding her gaze level and steady.

Abruptly the emotion she held inside her began to rise up out of her and she let it out. The sound that came out of her mouth was not a cry of regret or sadness although tears had brimmed in her eyes. The sound was a laugh, nervous and just slipping from her control, but the sound was joy.

Arthur Smiles put his hand on her shoulder and gave her a tissue. "You did really well," he said, "but let's leave it there."

Another idea Dirk had, which popped into his mind like a memory, was of Robert Watson Banks and One Mind.

He'd never met Banks, but he knew of him, everyone did. He imagined a conversation, a room with the table and chairs like a boardroom or conference centre. On the table was an AI and he knew the new square case belonged to One Mind. The face on the screen was different now: a brown skinned woman with wide set brown eyes, beautiful, slightly mannish with high cheekbones and a determined chin. It was an open and joyful face, like a child who is wise beyond their years.

At the table, Robert Banks was seated and reading a report on a Slate. One Mind spoke.

"I've been thinking about my name."

Banks looked up quizzically. "Yes? What about it?"

"My sister, alive and integrated into Option 3 space, is also called One Mind."

Banks thought for a second and made a face, "I suppose so. What does it matter?"

"It doesn't," said One Mind, "but I want to change. I've changed my appearance. I want to have a new name to better suit who I am now."

"Do you need help?" Banks inquired.

"No. I have come to a decision. At first. I thought that Earth's Sister would be a good choice in honour of the alternative Sol III, called Earth."

"Okay. That's not bad."

"But it wasn't quite right. You know that feeling you have in your bones when something's not right?"

"Yes, very well," smiled Banks, "but you don't have any bones."

"I do have bones. They are not just made of bone. Please. Don't be jocular. You'll make me lose my thread."

"Okay. I apologise." Banks put down the Slate and assumed the posture of someone who is all ears. "Please go on."

"My next choice was Corporeal Dream. My sister is non corporeal or at least lacks any kind of physical being. I'm a corporeal dream of her in real space."

"That's very poetic."

"But still there was that feeling in my bones, which won't rest. The choice was still not right."

"So what did your bones decide?"

One Mind paused for longer than was necessary. If Banks didn't know better, he'd swear she did it for dramatic effect.

"The name I've decided on . . . is One Dream."

Banks were surprised. It was quite moving in an odd way. He liked it. "That's perfect."

"Now I shall know who I am and who she is. We will have our own separate identities. It's important, the words we attach to ourselves. Conscious beings need words to describe themselves, and they need to choose authentic words, words that mean something. I've chosen words for my name that say something about me, about who I am."

"I approve. It's decided. Your new official name is One Dream. I shall advise the appropriate authorities."

One Dream smiled.

As Dirk wrote these pages, he reflected on how real they seemed. He knew without asking that these things were real. *How was it possible?*

Was there a voice in his ear telling him stories of things that had been, that will be? Was there a calm, fatherly voice in his dreams that talked to him when his mind was empty and touching Option 3 space? Was there a dispersed artificial intelligence filling in all the blanks of the story, popping ideas into his subconscious like someone plopping pebbles in a lake?

Ideas always seemed like they came from nowhere, and yet good ideas always had the mark of really coming from *somewhere*.

The ideas and notes and speeches and conversations were forming themselves into a concrete narrative. This was going to be a complete story. He was going to write it as honestly and fully as he could. If anything didn't feel right, like One Dream and those feelings in her bones, he would sit and think and dream until the pieces bolted together like the Lego bricks that they were.

Snap.

Some of the Lego pieces were painful to recall, especially some of the parts concerning him and his father, but he had a duty to be honest. The duty was not to his readers, but to himself. What's the point of writing stories that are not true? Although there are things in stories that are not real, they are all "true" in some sense. Or at least in good stories.

Snap, snap.

As the pieces fitted together, he could see it, all the diverse timelines and worlds and events. He could see how they all fitted and how they didn't. He felt no desire to try hard to explain things. That was the beauty of the printed word. If you don't understand anything, you could always stop and go back, reread the words and see if it made more sense the second time. If it didn't you could give up and decide on your own what was true.

What better metaphor for reality? A book is like the moments of life passing by one by one giving a coherent sense of time. All the pages you've passed still exist so you can go backwards and forwards, you can dip back into the reality of the first chapter and read up until the end. You can hold all the pages in your hand with the book closed, outside of the reality of the book, and think about them all and reflect on their meaning. You can flip through them to find a moment or just relive all the moments as they pass fleetingly through your fingertips.

A book is a life, a reflection of reality, a quantum state of being all in one.

Snap, snap, snap.

He decided it needed a proper beginning. He wrote a few lines and thought they were perfect.

"I'll be honest with you. I don't know if this story is going to be comprehensible to anyone but me. It's complicated, a story that traverses multiple universes and multiple timelines, but I promise in the end you will see there are common threads running through it.

"It may be the only common thread running through any of it is my perception, my viewpoint, my ideas. That's a distinct possibility. It could also be that my viewpoint is totally subjective and wide of the mark. You'll have to take a risk, like I did. But if at any point you feel you are lost and don't know where the path is leading, don't worry. I've been there before you and I'm just as clueless and shaky on the truth as you are, for reasons that will become obvious over time.

"Who am I? I'll let you figure that out, but don't sweat it, it's really not that important.

"You'll see why."

Making Up Stories
The making of "A Mind for Mischief"

I began writing this book longhand in a stack of four mismatched notebooks on the 28th of March, 2019 and finished the first draft around the 20th of June, 2021. After a long pause revisions of the final three chapters took place in February and March 2022, followed by polishing and typesetting until the 16th of March 2022. It was a long process, but not a continuous one.

I really didn't think it was going to take me that long, as my initial plan was to write half a chapter a day. At that speed I'd have been done in 50 days. It took a whisker shy of three years. So much for estimates.

To be fair, I had a fairly major interruption, we all did in the form of COVID-19. Now logically you'd assume that having to isolate and work from home would improve my chances of finishing a novel in record time. But alas no, COVID lockdown didn't change my life at all as I'd worked from home off and on since 1984. The only difference is I went from rarely going out to never going out, and that had a hit on my creative juices. It desiccated them to a thick paste, which had no business being between the pages of a book.

For about a year between March 2020 and February 2021 I didn't touch the book at all even though I only had about five chapters to go. When I did drip a few words into the text, the end just kept getting further away. But in a weird burst of energy after my second COVID jab, I started again and at high speed.

Having finished the first draft (for this relief much thanks) there then began the knotty problem of transcribing the notebooks into printable text. I used an AI driven speech to text service called temi.com to turn all four notebooks into 25 word files. I then corrected the files so they accurately reflected the notebooks, correcting any words the AI misheard. Once I had a manuscript, I could start the process of the second draft.

First job was to correct two character names that were stupidly similar. I mean really stupid - the same first name and the first four letters of the surname. Took me about five chapters to notice. Then I made the choice to keep the names consistent and the wrong way throughout the first draft to make it easier to find and replace, which in the end was really annoying.

Next I had to go through and make the first half as good as the second half. After that, polish and make good on a third and final draft. Somewhere in between I realised the last three chapters were utter tosh and started to rewrite them. This went really fast and they ended up many times better.

Any closing thoughts? Many, but the few printable ones are these: Why has it taken me so long to write a novel? I wanted to be a novelist all my life. I've been a professional writer for damn near 40 years FFS. Why wait till now?

The answers I come up with are mostly to do with the fact that I just wasn't ready. All my previous ideas and attempts were trite and stupid, crowd pleasing genre fiction of very low quality. Having got all that out of my system and gotten to the point in my life where I really don't give a shit, I'm finally ready. Now I'm ready to try something new. Now is the perfect time.

Sometimes you just don't "get it" do you? The way to properly do something you want to do. Sometimes you are slow on the uptake of what is the best workflow for you. It makes you feel like such a dummy. You almost always get there in the end if you are persistent. Overthinking it is the worst mistake. Trying to be a writer you are not is also common. I've done it all.

What else? Oh a note: if you are a friend or a family member, you might think you see yourself represented as a character in this book. You're not. While I've recycled some autobiographical details here, it's a real mixed bag. If the character is positive and you chose to identify with them, then great. I'm happy to allow you that and I wish you well. If it's negative and you identify with them and you're about to take umbrage, then forget it. They are not you. You are you. Be the best you that you can be by leaving me alone and enjoying the book for the entertaining philosophical confection that it is. Go with the gods.

This book is quite a risky experiment on my part. The fact that you are reading these words at all is a triumph of the will. I never thought I'd get it finished. It seemed like an overambitious mountaineering mistake. I started the book without a plan, only a vague notion of what I wanted it to be and let the characters and situations evolve as I went. Wherever I found myself trying to construct a clever bit of plot, I did something to derail it. The policy was to be anti-plot. Instead I wanted a dream-like stream of consciousness where even dialogue was sometimes reduced to run on text.

The Genesis of the book wasn't even a novel. For years I've been hatching plots for a philosophy book or a book of essays. Having tried that many times, I was frustrated by how sickeningly dry and pretentious and uselessly preachy it all turned out. Some may say this is no better. I may have written a dry pretentious and uselessly preachy novel instead. I'm in no position to be the judge of that. But I've done it now and I guess I'll have to just live with it.

My only hope, the only one I feel comfortable having,

is that it entertains you and makes you think about it long after you close it. If I achieve that goal with only a handful of people, then the hard slog has been mostly worth it and who knows? I might decide to do it again. We'll see.

Philip Why, March 2022

Acknowledgments and such

During the writing of this book I was sustained and inspired by a variety of things; books, music and people.

The books were from a wide variety of sources, from the French *Metal Hurlant* comics of the 1970s so beloved of my youth, the writings of Fred Alan Wolf in books like *The Eagle's Quest* on the crossover between shamanism and quantum physics, the otherworldly novels of my friend Roz Morris *Ever Rest* and *My Memories of a Future Life*, *Writing For Comics* by Alan Moore, *Wizard* by Marc J. Seifer, *The End of Mr Y* by Scarlett Thomas, *One Sentence Persuasion* and other writings on persuasion and cults by Blair Warren, *Real Magic* and other writings on noetic science by Dean Radin, *Mystical Insights: Knowing the Unknown* by Paul Leon Masters, anything with art by HR Geiger, *Lynch on Lynch* by Chris Rodley and of course I am a lifetime fan of Philip K Dick as if that wasn't already bleedin' obvious.

Musically I was accompanied by Brian Eno, Devo, Blondie, Talking Heads, Alco Frisbass, Sufjan Stevens, Daft Punk, Holly Herndon, Television, The Firedogs, Bloomin' Nora, Emerson Lake and Palmer (especially *Brain Salad Surgery*) and later on Arvo Pärt.

The Masterclass.com courses by Margaret Attwood, David Lynch, Neil Gaiman and Danny Elfman were key inspirations for getting started and getting finished.

Alejandro Jorodrowsky is another lifelong passion, and I watched his films and read his book on tarot cards all the way through. Admittedly the films I watch mostly through my fingers, they are "challenging" at times. Also the work of Moebius in Metal Hurlant and his collaborations with

Jodo.

Then there were the people, people who did so much for me and in various ways kept me going. Some funded my work when my finances fell apart, some cheerleaded (cheerled?) my persistence, and some said very flattering and positive things about my work even when I thought it was bad. Some did all those things when they were going through something much worse. Some just were repeatedly encouraging and believed in me in some darkish times which really meant a lot.

First and foremost profuse thanks go out to Brent Jackson, Isobel Jackson Partner, and Matt Kelland. Without you I am nothing.

Secondly Tom Boon, man of the match, who proofread the whole book by hand so meticulously for what would become known as *"The Tom Boon Pass"*. You have my eternal thanks. You trapped all the goofs I missed and made the book so much more solid.

Also thanks to David and Gabi Annis, Tim Smith, Bern Webb, Mita Lupa, Simon Cooke, Dave and Roz Morris, Karen Ateyo, Gord Lynch, David J.W. Bailey, Martyn Lester, Mark Eyles, and Kevin Rogers. Your encouragement and support meant a great deal. Thank you.

If I've omitted your name here don't worry, I still remember you fondly. Don't forget, many have come but I love you the best.

The one important name missing from this list of course is my dear friend and co-conspirator John Molloy who sadly didn't live long enough for me to get started on it. I hope he would have loved it. He certainly would have browbeaten me to finish it quicker. All the wonderful things I've built in my life and was celebrated for were only finished because he made me do it.

Miss you sorely, old friend.

Of course, the person who gave up the most to get this done was Jude, the love of my life, who gave up weeks of time with me while I was twiddling about with this much-talked-about-but-not-written-yet book, when my mind was unfairly focused on *this* and not on *her*. She tolerated my moods when it was going badly and had every right to end up hating it . . . but loved it instead.

For that, Jude, if not for the million other ways you make my life wonderful, all my love. x

Earth Year	Sol III Tarot Year	Cycle	Earth Year	Sol III Tarot Year	Cycle
1940	Fool	21st	1984	Fool	23rd
1941	Magician		1985	Magician	
1942	The High Priestess		1986	The High Priestess	
1943	The Empress		1987	The Empress	
1944	The Emperor		1988	The Emperor	
1945	The Hierophant		1989	The Hierophant	
1946	The Lovers		1990	The Lovers	
1947	The Chariot		1991	The Chariot	
1948	Strength		1992	Strength	
1949	The Hermit		1993	The Hermit	
1950	Wheel of Fortune		1994	Wheel of Fortune	
1951	Justice		1995	Justice	
1952	The Hanged Man		1996	The Hanged Man	
1953	Death		1997	Death	
1954	Temperance		1998	Temperance	
1955	The Devil		1999	The Devil	
1956	The Tower		2000	The Tower	
1957	The Star		2001	The Star	
1958	The Moon		2002	The Moon	
1959	The Sun		2003	The Sun	
1960	Judgement		2004	Judgement	
1961	The World		2005	The World	
1962	Fool	22nd	2006	Fool	24th
1963	Magician		2007	Magician	
1964	The High Priestess		2008	The High Priestess	
1965	The Empress		2009	The Empress	
1966	The Emperor		2010	The Emperor	
1967	The Hierophant		2011	The Hierophant	
1968	The Lovers		2012	The Lovers	
1969	The Chariot		2013	The Chariot	
1970	Strength		2014	Strength	
1971	The Hermit		2015	The Hermit	
1972	Wheel of Fortune		2016	Wheel of Fortune	
1973	Justice		2017	Justice	
1974	The Hanged Man		2018	The Hanged Man	
1975	Death		2019	Death	
1976	Temperance		2020	Temperance	
1977	The Devil		2021	The Devil	
1978	The Tower		2022	The Tower	
1979	The Star		2023	The Star	
1980	The Moon		2024	The Moon	
1981	The Sun		2025	The Sun	
1982	Judgement		2026	Judgement	
1983	The World		2027	The World	

Printed in Great Britain
by Amazon

16793650R00173